THE SILVER TOWER OF OZ

by Margaret Baum

Copyright © 2011

All rights reserved. No part of this work may be reproduced or transmitted in any form or by any means, mechanical, electronic, recording, photocopying, photographing, handwritten, magical, or otherwise without prior permission from the holder of the copyright.

Based on the books written by L. Frank Baum.

Only the wicked would steal.

List of Chapters

The Silverglade Family Farm
The Village of Illume
Botania
A Blue Tempest
The Artificer of the Cypress Savannah
Mr. Hairold Bunnymunch
The Tree Guard
The "Good Witch" of the Majestic Moonlit Mountains
Weathered
The Black and White Lotus Bog
Lady Thorn and Lady Thistle
The Silver Tower
The Room of Magic Rings
Glinda of Oz
The Return to Lilibeth
An Army of Friends
The Good Warlock
The Road to Lilibeth
Lapis Lazuli
The Castle of the Wicked Witch
The Unbinding of Lapis Lazuli
The Village of Poofle
The Return to the Castle of the Wicked Witch
The Silver Goblet
The Ladies
Theresa's Plan
The Good Witch Lilibeth
The Next Adventure

Chapter One
The Silverglade Family Farm

Long before Dorothy Gale had visited the Land of Oz and before the Great Change had occurred …

At the precise moment of the sunrise on the first Monday of the month of May, a very special event occurs on the farm of Mr. and Mrs. Silverglade. Each year at this time the Silver Lilies are ready to harvest. Sunrise was just moments away.

On this particular morning, the three Silverglade children were each positioned at the start of one of three rows of Silver Lilies on the farm. Now this may seem like a small field – each row of Silver Lilies is only four inches wide with four feet between each row – but anyone who has paid a visit to the Silverglade Family Farm knows that this arrangement was merely due to the interesting path of the stream that flowed through the fields of the farm. The field really wasn't as much a field as it was a smooth slope of a mountain, which was more of a very tall hill than it was a true mountain.

The Silverglade Mountain, as the family's large hill was called, was a piece of natural beauty that was especially magnificent, even for the Land of Oz. At the top of the mountain was a small rock formation composed of seven small boulders. These rocks were made of sterling silver. At the center of these rocks was a spring that could have been natural or magical – no one knew for sure because everyone was afraid to do any exploratory digging out of fear that the spring could be damaged or any enchantment on the land be made undone. The spring was very unique, as instead of water bubbling forth from it there was a very consistent supply of Silver Water. The water was cool to the touch and could be consumed by humans and animals just like water, but it was made entirely of liquid silver. How this magical liquid had become cool to the touch and did not burn those curious people who touched it

The Silverglade Family Farm

was beyond anyone's understanding, which was why many believed the rock formation to be enchanted.

The Silver Water from the spring formed a small pool around the silver boulders. On the south side of this pool began a stream that flowed down the mountain. Four feet from the edge of the pool the stream made a sharp turn, due east, and spiraled all the way down the mountain in a perfectly even pattern that allowed for exactly sixteen-feet-twelve-inches of space between each ring of the stream of Silver Water. This space gave the Silverglade family exactly enough room for three, spiraling rows of Silver Lilies with exactly four feet of space in-between each row and exactly four feet of space from each waterfront. This was important because Silver Lilies required Silver Water in order to grow. If you want to grow a Silver Lily and you don't have any Silver Water, then you're going to have one unhappy seed that refuses to wake up and take root. The Silver Water on the Silverglade Family Farm was the purest Silver Water ever discovered, although it is said that the great sorceress Glinda had an equally pure source in her Great Garden.

In the middle of the stream were minute, little islands that were each just large enough to provide sufficient support for a single Lantern Tree. The islands appeared every twenty feet. The Lantern Trees had a special beauty of their own. In other parts of Oz, the bark of a Lantern Tree resembled that of a palm tree and was normally dark green with the green color becoming lighter along the base of the branches. The branches were arranged similarly to those on a palm tree and were curved with a hook located at the tip. The leaves were normally emerald green and were found in clusters of seven at the tip of each branch, at the base of the hook. From each hook would dangle a lantern flower that was normally emerald green with a glowing, emerald-green gem situated where a wick would be found in a common lantern. The Silverglade's Lantern Trees had a special location that made them quite unique. You see, Lantern Trees thrived in Silver Water, although they were quite hardy and could survive in nearly any environment. In fact, one Lantern Tree was said to have grown in the Deadly Desert without

Chapter One

being turned to sand, but no one had been able to venture out far enough into the Deadly Desert to verify this claim. Since the Silverglade's Lantern Trees were watered by the Silver Water stream, they were pure alabaster in color, except for the gems at the heart of each lantern. These gems had the most brilliant emerald-green glow anyone in Oz had ever witnessed.

The few inches of land remaining at the base of each Lantern Tree were filled with Lightning Grass, which also filled every inch of the mountain that was not home to a Silver Lily. The Lightning Grass was made of the finest silver and was well-illuminated by its static electricity. This field of little bolts of lightning was very weak and was just enough to tickle your feet and make your hair stand on end. The Silverglade family considered themselves blessed to have had the good fortune to come across land with Lightning Grass for their Silver Lily crops, because the Lightning Grass kept away all insects, other than the Lightning Bugs, of course. Lightning Bugs pollinated the Silver Lilies, so they were most welcome on the farm.

The Silver Lilies were the most impressive plant life on the mountain. Each Silver Lily was composed of pure silver. The flower of the Silver Lily just also happened to be the fruit, meaning that the Silver Lilies were quite edible, but only if you were one of those people who had an appreciation for the taste of silver. The seven petals of the lilies gave off a medium-soft, glowing, silvery light. Even the silver leaves and silver roots of the plants had a very soft glow to them, although the lilies themselves were noticeably brighter. Around each lily slowly floated seven small orbs of silvery light. You could try to catch the orbs, but you would have no success. The orbs would just pass right through your hand, leaving a cool-yet-warm sensation that most people found to be quite pleasant and even relaxing.

As the sun just started to peak over the tops of the surrounding mountain range the three children began their work. The children were each carrying a bamboo-and-Lantern-Tree-wood basket, bamboo being a favorite material of Mrs. Silverglade. These baskets were bottomless on the inside so that only one basket was needed

The Silverglade Family Farm

to carry each row of harvested Silver Lilies. The weight of the baskets never increased no matter how much was carried in them.

Aiden was the eldest child, at eighteen years of age. He was of above average intelligence, just like all of the Silverglade family members, and he had a strong fondness of the land. He had always planned to take over the farm once his parents were ready to retire. This was his first year being the leader of the harvest, as his parents had become lost shortly after the last harvesting of the Silver Lily crop. They ventured out one evening to take a walk in the Silver Lily field and they never came back. Aiden last saw them taking a drink from the spring atop the mountain. He looked away for a moment and when he looked back they were gone. That was the last he had seen his parents or heard from them in a year. No one in the nearby Village of Illume had ever discovered any information on the Silverglade parents, but they promised to let the children know if their parents ever showed up in the village's lost-and-found box at the post office. In the absence of Mr. and Mrs. Silverglade, Aiden had taken it upon himself to raise his little brother and little sister, who were never any trouble to him. He enjoyed his role as surrogate parent to them, because the three had always gotten along so very amicably.

Theresa and Terrance were twins. They had just celebrated their eighth birthday the previous week. Theresa made her appearance only thirty seconds before Terrance made his, but during the same minute. She never held her "older age" over his head. Her forte in life happened to be books. She most especially loved reading about the life of Glinda of Oz. It was unfortunate that she only had one-and-a-half pages of material on Glinda from her parents' Encyclopedia of Oz. She had managed to pick up a few tidbits of information on Glinda from several villagers who liked to pass along to her any information that they picked up from the occasional traveler. With this collection of information, she was working on compiling her own book about Glinda the Good Sorceress. So far, Theresa had accumulated fifty pages of text, most

Chapter One

of which consisted of her personal comments on Glinda. For a child of eight years of age that was a great accomplishment indeed!

Terrance had a strong interest in bugs. There was just one problem with his interest: there was only one type of bug that he had ever seen in his entire life. He had studied the Lightning Bugs as best he could, as he too shared Theresa's enjoyment of books; however, there was one major dilemma. Lightning Bugs had much stronger lightning than did the Lightning Grass. Terrance learned at the age of three that if you tried to catch a Lightning Bug then you would quickly come to have a tiny burn mark on your hand that hurt for several days. Fortunately for his studies, Terrance had learned that he could view the Lightning Bugs up close by allowing the bugs to land on him or in his hand. The lightning was tolerable when you weren't trying to catch them.

All three children shared as their greatest joy in harvesting the Silver Lilies the tickling effects of the Lightning Grass. For this reason, the children always went harvesting in bare feet. They needn't worry about stepping on any bugs because only the Lightning Bugs lived in the area and they were all asleep by that time of the morning. There was always an abundance of laughter on the Silverglade Farm on Silver Lily harvesting day. Even though the children missed their parents, they still were able to have fun together, especially when tickling Lightning Grass was involved.

"Do you remember when we were young, Terrance, and mother and father would help us with the harvest?" asked Theresa. Her question was meant to be somber and indicative of her longing to be with her parents again, but the Lightning Grass made it impossible to sound anything but joyous while harvesting the Silver Lilies.

"Oh yes, Theresa, I do. Father would always help me and mother would always help you. Father was very good at learning from watching me how to correctly remove the lilies at the base of the stems," said Terrance, who was having difficulty not bursting into laughter while he spoke.

The Silverglade Family Farm

"You two are so funny! Mother and father were not the assistants. You were. They just knew how to keep you two feeling like you were in control," added Aiden, just to tease his brother and sister a little. "I remember the day when Theresa discovered the Silver Lilies were not quite as delicate as mother and father had led you to believe. You two took off and ran right up the center of your lily rows all the way to the top of the mountain, stepping on every lily along the way. You were so delighted when you reached the upper pond and there was no evidence at all to prove you had trampled all the lilies."

"That was the first time we managed to climb the mountain and laugh without there being Lightning Grass involved in the humor," said Theresa proudly.

"Aiden, how long do you suppose mother and father will remain lost?" asked Terrance. "I hope they find their way back soon."

"Yes, Aiden, when do you suppose they'll return? I miss them so much and want them to be excited for my latest page in my book," added Theresa.

"I miss them too, my sweet, but I don't know when they'll return. I suppose they'll return whenever they find their way back," said Aiden, just as he stepped upon a particularly ticklish patch of Lightning Grass that caused him to release a loud guffaw.

"I wish they'd return right now. They'd be the proudest parents in the world if they could see how well we've done harvesting this year's crop!" Terrance exclaimed as he picked the last Silver Lily in his row and placed it into his bamboo-and-Lantern-Tree-wood basket.

"They already were the proudest parents in the world before they became lost," responded Aiden. "I'm also very proud of the two of you. You are both very talented children and I'm glad to be your big brother."

"Let's see if we can make you even more proud of us, Aiden, by breaking father's selling record. If we go into the village

Chapter One

tomorrow I'm sure we can find someone to buy the whole crop!" said Theresa with great excitement.

"That's a good idea Theresa, but I think father usually had to go outside of the village quite some ways in order to find enough buyers to sell a whole crop. His record was two weeks, and that required him to go to the City of Rootworth. It was only due to finding a wealthy lord traveling through the city that he was able to sell the whole crop so quickly ... but maybe we'll have such luck this week in the village. You never know who will show up in Illume," Aiden said trying not to let Theresa and Terrance get their hopes up too much while also trying to give them some brotherly encouragement.

The three siblings finished their walk down the mountain, following the Silver Water stream, which ended in the middle of their mother's garden, next to their house. The stream emptied into a small pond that never overflowed. Mr. and Mrs. Silverglade always wondered where the water went. They taught their children that the land naturally recycled the Silver Water, but this was just a guess. Soon after their parents had become lost, Theresa and Terrance came up with the suggestion that maybe their parents had become lost while trying to find where the Silver Water goes when it empties from the lower pond. They had a theory that one day their parents would reappear at the top of the mountain, because they would be recycled with the Silver Water.

The Silverglade's house was a seemingly-small cabin made from Lantern Trees. This caused the house to have a very soft glow to it. Since no paint was used, nearly the entire house was alabaster in color. The cabin was two-stories tall, plus an attic. The front porch was as long as the house was wide. At either side of the front stairs were two Lantern Trees. All of the lighting in and around the farm was provided for free by the Lantern Trees, which gave a pleasant emerald-green hue to everything. The Silverglades never had to spend money on lights or water. The farm was very self-sufficient. Within the garden were several lunch pail trees, some waffle bushes, and two cake-and-pie trees. The few things that they weren't able to produce for themselves on the farm, such as certain metal tools, they were able to purchase in the village. The children were raised to always be self-sufficient and independent, although helping to provide for the needs of family members was always highly-encouraged.

The interior of the Silverglade's house was decorated with a variety of plants from Mrs. Silverglade's garden, artwork done by both Mr. and Mrs. Silverglade, and several antiques that the family had collected through the generations. There was quite a lot of room for their decorations within the house because of a little-known magical characteristic of Lantern Trees. Any building made out of Lantern Trees is larger and has a lot more space on the inside than it does on the outside. This allowed Mr. Silverglade to build a home for his family that contained twenty-one rooms. He could have easily constructed more rooms than this, but he didn't want his family to learn the nasty habit of hording unnecessary items. He and the children's mother never wanted to impart upon the children any sense of greed or an overzealous fondness of possessions.

All of the rooms in the cabin were quite spacious, with the family room of course being the largest. Each child had a large, private bedroom, although the children almost always kept their doors open because they had no greater joy in the world then spending time with one another.

Theresa's bedroom was a library with a bed and amply-sized desk in the center. Every shelf was filled with books. She had every type of book imaginable, from children's tales to the history of Oz to the art of bumblesheep yarn weaving.

Terrance's bedroom was just like his sister's room, only he also had a small laboratory area reserved for the study of Lightning Bugs.

Aiden's bedroom walls were full of nature paintings done by his parents. These paintings perfectly fit his indoor garden that took up three-quarters of his living space. He grew such plants as the Emerald Sparkler, the Emerald Fern, and the Emerald Jack-in-the-

Chapter One

Pulpit because they all grew extraordinarily well in the emerald-green light of the Lantern Tree lanterns.

Since the harvest was completed, the trio went straight down the main hall of the cabin to the Silver Lily storage room. They didn't have to turn on the lights as they entered because their lights are always on. Even when a Lantern Tree lantern is removed from the tree it retains its full glowing power until damaged. The children also never had to remember to turn off the lights. When they entered the room, Aiden immediately went to a shelf to retrieve a silver bag. This was an enchanted bag that Mrs. Silverglade had purchased many years back at the same shoppe where she found the bamboo baskets – she had added the Lantern Tree wood herself. Like the baskets, the silver bag could hold an unlimited number of items. Aiden held open the bag for Theresa and Terrance so that they could empty their Silver Lily harvestings into it.

"Theresa, would you be kind enough to help me pour my harvesting in here?" asked Aiden as he continued to hold open the enchanted silver bag.

"With pleasure, my sweet Aiden," joyfully responded Theresa, who then picked up Aiden's basket and poured out the contents to join the rest of the Silver Lilies.

"Thank you, sister," said Aiden with a big smile on his face. He had always been very proud of the twins for their genuine politeness and willingness to help everyone. He thought that the only people on earth who could possibly be any nicer than his parents were his brother and sister.

"I can't wait for tomorrow! We're going to have so much fun!" exclaimed Terrance.

All three of them were excited about their coming journey. Only Aiden was old enough to have accompanied their father on his travels to sell the Silver Lilies. They were all looking forward to spending some time out in the world and traveling like their father did every summer.

Chapter Two
The Village of Illume

"**I**'m so excited!" exclaimed Theresa and Terrance in unison. The twins were anxiously waiting just inside the front door of their home for Aiden to bring the silver bag carrying their entire crop of Silver Lilies, save the five that remained in Ozmite Crystal vases for each member of the family. It had always been a tradition to save one lily for each of them. They had no need to save any flower-fruits for seeds because the plants never died, although Mr. Silverglade had saved a stash of Silver Lily seeds just in case an emergency should ever arise.

"Aiden!" shouted the twins with great joy as Aiden appeared down the main hall, exiting from the Silver Lily storage room.

"Are we anxious to go?!" Aiden asked in a playful manner so as to encourage the excitement of the twins. He always enjoyed putting smiles on their faces. "Now, let's make sure we have everything packed properly. Do we have our suitcases packed and in the carriage? What about Father's Travel Kit?"

Terrance was quick to respond. "The suitcases are all packed and I placed them in the carriage an hour ago." He was proud of having been completely ready for an hour.

"That's when I retrieved father's Travel Kit from his workroom and took it to the carriage. We are all prepared, Aiden," said Theresa with a huge grin on her face.

The twins could barely handle the anticipation any longer, and Aiden could see this. The twins were about to head out on their very first Silver Lily sales journey. They had grown up hearing about all of the wonderful stories of their father's exciting adventures throughout the country. The two were especially fond of the stories of Aiden's trips with their father. The more family involved in a story the happier the twins were.

Chapter Two

"We'd better head on out then, before the two of you burst from excitement," said Aiden. He too was very excited, although he did feel a little sad that his father was not there to lead them. When Aiden stepped off of the porch he looked back at the front door for a moment. This was when his mother would always come and give him a big send-off hug. As he thought about this for a moment, he realized that this being the twins' first sales adventure there needed to be some sort of tradition for them to enjoy.

"Get back here, you two! We're forgetting the most important part of traveling preparation," said Aiden with an expression of fake seriousness on his face.

"Oh no! What are we forgetting?" the twins said in unison as they ran back from the carriage to Aiden.

"We forgot this!" said Aiden as he embraced the twins. "This is going to be the best adventure we've ever had, little ones."

After spending a few moments hugging, the three looked at each other in an almost daring way ... and suddenly they all took off as fast as they could towards the carriage.

"You two are no match for me!" shouted Aiden as he jumped into the carriage before the twins arrived.

"One day I'll be as fast as my big brother. I know it!" said Terrance.

The Silverglade's open carriage was a magnificent piece of craftsmanship. The carriage was composed of Lantern Tree wood, as were most objects that the Silverglades made, except of course for the bamboo artwork that was done by Mrs. Silverglade. The elegant design of the carriage was very intentional. Although the elegance was very good for sales – since, according to Mr. Silverglade, people are more likely to be willing to make a purchase from someone who has an air of sophistication and doesn't look the crooked type – Mr. Silverglade had made his decision to craft the most elegant carriage that he could in order to provide his love, Mrs. Silverglade, with a vehicle worthy of her beauty. At each corner of the carriage was a post with a Lantern Tree lantern sitting atop it. There were intricate carvings all over the carriage that depicted various relatives of the Silverglades harvesting Silver Lilies. The cushion seats were covered with a cloth made from Mrs. Silverglade's Sapphire Silk Salvia plants. The cloth looked very regal and was very soft. The stuffing for the cushions was also from the Saphire Silk Salvia plants. The salvias were hard to miss in Mrs. Silverglade's garden when they were in bloom, because each of the flowers was a two-foot-large puffball of silk thread. This was the same material used in the hair ribbon that Theresa was wearing that day.

Theresa and Terrance sat in their seats patiently, yet also a bit anxiously, as they waited for Aiden to put away the silver bag.

"I'll be back in a flash!" said Aiden as he opened a hatch in the floor of the carriage. From the outside it looked as though the only place the hatch could lead was to the ground, because there were very few inches between the top of the hatch and the underside of the carriage. Aiden stepped down into the hatch and descended what seemed to be a staircase that did not lead out of the carriage, thanks to the magical properties of the Lantern Tree wood.

"I hope we meet a good witch in the village. I want it to be Glinda, but I know she would almost never come to a village like Illume," said Theresa.

"As do I, Theresa. I think a good witch would be able to help us find our lost parents. A good witch would have to know a spell for finding lost things, right?" said Terrance.

"I would imagine so. Now Glinda, she would surely know such a spell for us. My research shows that she once enchanted a gentleman's map to help him find his lost pair of glasses. The sorceress is also very smart because she gave the map the ability to speak so the gentleman wouldn't run into anything while he searched and so he wouldn't have to strain to read the map," responded Theresa. She sounded very academic whenever she spoke of Glinda, because she was very passionate in her research.

"Well, if we don't find anyone in the village to buy our Silver Lilies then I hope Aiden lets us go to Rootworth. That's where Botania the Good Witch lives. She's the one who enchanted our

Chapter Two

carriage for father in exchange for a half-dozen Silver Lilies," said Terrance.

"Oh yes, she would be a wonderful person to meet. Father spoke so well of her. Those enchantments were expertly performed. Water has never dripped inside the carriage through the hatch and the travel spell has always followed our commands perfectly. Maybe we can trade her some more Silver Lilies for some seeds from her budgeberry tree. I think one of those would be lovely in mother's garden. It would be a nice surprise for her when she and father become unlost," said Theresa.

Suddenly Aiden's head appeared from the floor of the carriage. "Let's be off!" he said with a very cheerful tone to his voice.

"Aiden, we've decided that we want to find a good witch while were traveling," stated Terrance. He wanted to make sure that his sister's desire to meet a good witch was met. Neither one of the twins had ever met a witch, and Theresa was particularly anxious to meet one, as long as she was a good witch.

"We think one could help mother and father become unlost. Botania the Good Witch of Rootworth would be an intelligent choice for us, because she knows father and that might help her magic work even more effectively," added Theresa.

"That's very clever of you, Theresa, and I think that finding a good witch is just what we will do after we sell these Silver Lilies" said Aiden. His pride for the twins was very evident in his face. Aiden quickly jumped up into the box of the carriage and took the reins into his hands.

"Could we please come up and sit with you, even if it's just for a few minutes, Aiden?" asked Terrance.

"It's always more fun sitting in the box," said Theresa.

"Of course you can," said Aiden. "I would love to have a couple of driving assistants for when I become tired."

Aiden knew that he wouldn't really become tired during the trip into the village, since it was about one-and-a-half hours away at a casual-yet-steady pace. He was planning to give each twin ten minutes to be driver so that they could know they too were important parts of the family team.

During the journey to the Village of Illume, the family played many games that their father had taught them. Aiden's favorite game on his journeys with his father was counting the lunch pail trees. This game was not just for fun, because Mr. Silverglade knew that if anything happened to their food supply the location of the trees would be very important for eating needs. Aiden was able to identify any of the one-hundred-seventeen species of lunch pail tree from a mile away. He thought that this would be an excellent time to pass along this family game to the twins.

***

The family arrived in the Village of Illume during the mid-morning. The roads of the village were adorned with Lantern Trees on both sides; however, they were of the normal green variety since they were too far from the Silver Water to have experienced any color change. The twins were particularly attracted to these trees because they only saw green Lantern Trees a few times a year when the family would all go into the village together for special outings, for such events as the Lightning Bug Festival and All Families Radiance Day. With all of the green hues in town caused by the abundant usage of common Lantern Trees, the Silverglade's carriage stood out with its alabaster and sapphire colors. The elegance of the carriage furthered this grandiosity. The villagers always appreciated visits from the Silverglade family, because the Silverglades were never haughty with their elegant transport. In fact, the family was always quite humble and very kind to everyone, regardless of one's position in life. The villagers also knew that the family didn't care for wealth, other than the riches of family love. The family just had a great appreciation for artwork that showed in everything that the Silverglades crafted, such as the carriage. Indeed, much of the artwork that was visible around town was crafted, painted, or designed by the Silverglades – and this was done mostly free-of-charge as gifts from the Silverglades for various

Chapter Two

birthdays, anniversary celebrations, holidays, and other momentous occasions.

Coming from the west on Illume Road, the carriage, being guided again by Aiden, approached the village square at the center of Illume. This is where the two main roads, Illume Road and Luster Avenue, crossed. Luster Avenue was particularly beautiful because common Lantern Trees and Emerald Halo Bushes were planted along the center of the road. The Emerald Halo Bushes were in full bloom with Bird of Paradise flowers that sang a beautiful song to anyone that passed by them. At the apex of the two roads was a small park area with a clockwork traffic officer for directing the traffic. The officer was rarely busy, since this was just a village; however, she was worked rather well every Lightning Bug Festival, since many travelers from out of town visited the village to witness firsthand the beauty of the Lightning Bugs. This festival was about to start the next day. This was very beneficial timing for the Silverglade family because the festival always coincided with the harvesting of the Silver Lily crops.

"There are so many people here! This is going to be the best Lightning Bug Festival ever!" exclaimed Theresa.

The village square was where the villagers had all of their various shoppes and businesses. There was Mr. Pea's Garden Supply Shoppe, Ms. Goo's Potions Aplenty, Illume Grocery & Slime, and several other businesses that were rather unique to the region.

At the south-east corner of the square was Madame Lumen's Kitchen. Aiden was excited to take Theresa and Terrance to Madame Lumen's Kitchen because it was the restaurant where the children's father had always taken Aiden as soon as they arrived in the village each summer.

Just before the family arrived at the restaurant, the three Silverglades were startled by a man running by them screaming in horror.

"Oh no! What's happening!? Is he ok!?" cried out Theresa as she quickly grabbed hold of Aiden and buried her head in his chest.

"I don't know ... but ... oh, wait. I see. It seems that he has committed an act that the three of us are far too wise to commit," said Aiden.

"What's that? What wouldn't we have done?" asked Terrance.

"Do you see the small ball of lightning following him?" replied Aiden.

"It's a Lightning Bug!" said Terrance and Theresa in unison.

"You've got it. That man probably was messing with a sleeping Lightning Bug and has now found out the hard way why you should never disturb one of our little friends when it's fast asleep," said Aiden.

"Is he going to be ok?" asked Theresa, who released her tight grip on her brother somewhat.

"He's going to be just fine ... although he might have to deal with a few, small burn marks when he gets to wherever he's going," noted Aiden. "Now let's get ourselves over to Madame Lumen's Kitchen so we can enjoy one of her astounding meals."

Aiden parked the carriage alongside the road in the parking area for the Madame Lumen's Kitchen. The three Silverglades descended from the carriage and entered the restaurant.

Madame Lumen herself greeted the children almost immediately as they entered her Kitchen. Everyone in the village knew everyone else, so joyous greetings were a very commonplace occurrence for the children when they visited. Kindness was always found in abundance in the Village of Illume.

"Hello, my little ones! How are my young Silverglades doing on this fine day? Is everyone excited about the festival?" said Madame Lumen. She had a very energetic personality with a strong sensation of being everyone's aunt.

"Yes, Madame Lumen, we are" said the twins in unison.

"How wonderful to finally have all of you little ones here at the beginning of the festival. I had always told your father he should have the whole family come for the entire week of the festival rather than just the final day," said Madame Lumen.

Chapter Two

"Well, Madame Lumen, with having only the one carriage and father needing to make some sales, it just wasn't easy to have the whole family stay for the week," noted Aiden.

"True, true, my little Aiden who's all grown up. But still, it would have been nice to spend more time with you little ones," Madame Lumen said with a great smile on her face. "Now let's get you to your usual table."

Madame Lumen escorted the family to their usual window seat facing west and providing a beautiful view of Luster Avenue. "Who wants some of my special recipe whiffle waffles and some bubbleberry juice?" asked Madame Lumen, knowing that all three would respond in the affirmative.

"I do!" said all three Silverglades in unison.

With that, Madame Lumen cheerfully went off to prepare their order herself.

"We should give Madame Lumen some of our lanterns," stated Terrance as he looked around the restaurant. "Ours are prettier than these common Lantern Tree lanterns."

"What a wonderful idea, Terrance," said Theresa. "I think that would make an excellent All Families Radiance Day gift."

"Oh look!" exclaimed Theresa as she pointed out the window.

The other two Silverglade children looked out onto Luster Avenue to see that a large ruby warbler had just landed on an Emerald Halo Bush and was having a pleasant conversation with the Bird of Paradise flowers.

"I wonder what they're saying to each other," said Theresa.

"I know what they're saying," responded Aiden. "You see that red bird? Well, she's what you call a ruby warbler. They are known for their appetite for rubies. They only need one, small ruby a year – that helps when you're such a picky eater. She's asking the Bird of Paradise flowers if they have seen any rubies lately. They see a lot of people pass by since they live in the middle of Luster Avenue, so the ruby warbler can find information on any passersby who may have a ruby or, with any luck, a passerby who has dropped a ruby that the warbler could easily retrieve."

Most children would have thought Aiden to be joking, but Terrance and Theresa knew better. Just a moment later the ruby warbler flew over a few feet to the base of one of the common Lantern Trees and picked up a small, red stone with its beak. The color was very easy to discern due to the abundance of green in the village.

"She found one!" said Terrance excitedly. "I wonder if she's taking it home for her babies."

"Oh, I'm certain she is," added Theresa. "Any good mother would think of her babies first when she found a good meal like that."

"Theresa, Terrance, it seems to me that our meal is making its way towards us now," said Aiden.

The twins looked over towards the actual kitchen area of the Kitchen and saw three plates accompanied by three glasses gently floating in the direction of the family's table. Sounds of whiffling came from the whiffle waffles and sounds of bubbling came from the bubbleberry juice.

"Enchanted dishes do make life a bit easier, don't you think, Aiden?" asked Theresa.

"That is very true, my sweet sister, but these dishes are not enchanted. These are just quick spells cast on the dishes by Madame Lumen, who just happens to be one of several basic conjurers in the Village of Illume," noted Aiden.

"She's a witch? Maybe she's just the good witch we could use to help make mother and father become unlost!" said Terrance with a glimmer of hope in his eyes.

"She's not a witch," said Theresa, in a very matter-of-fact yet polite way, as they all began to eat their food. "She is a basic conjurer. That means she has very basic magic abilities and is quite limited in what spells she can cast. It may be that her entire repertoire of spells is restricted to levitation magic and whiffle spells."

"So what makes a person a witch rather than a basic conjurer?" asked Terrance of his sister.

Chapter Two

"A witch or a warlock, as male witches are called, is a much more powerful spellcaster than is a basic conjurer. Witches are more powerful than magicians, like Mr. Illume, after whose family this village is named, and more powerful than wizards. Witches are not, however, as powerful as sorcerers or sorceresses. Glinda is the most powerful of all the sorceresses, and is almost unlimited in her magical aptitude. For us to use a basic conjurer, magician, or even a wizard to help our parents become unlost would require us to find someone who specializes in magic of becoming unlost. A person who practices the magical arts must be at least a witch, or warlock, to have sufficient skill to know a broad range of magics. It would be much easier to locate a good witch than to find a basic conjurer, magician, or wizard with adequate skill in unlost magics. Even with a witch, though, there's no guarantee."

"It's nice to have an expert on witches in the family," commented Aiden. He always appreciated how intelligent his sister sounded when she discussed witches.

"It certainly is. Thank you, Theresa. Who would have known there was so much to learn about witches!" said Terrance.

"How's the Silverglade family enjoying their breakfast?" asked Madame Lumen. "And what's this I hear about witches? I do hope she's a good witch. They make much better friends."

"The breakfast is fantastic as always, Madame Lumen," responded Aiden. "The witch in our conversation just happens to be you."

"Oh my stars! I'm no witch," Madame Lumen said with great laughter. "I'm just your basic conjurer. I can just do a few little things here and there to keep the restaurant running."

"Theresa pointed that fact out to us just before you arrived, Madame Lumen. She was telling us the differences among the types of magic users," said Terrance.

"How nice, my little ones. Theresa, how goes your study on Glinda? I know how fond you are of her," said Madame Lumen.

"I haven't been able to find much information on her at all this last year, ever since mother and father became lost ... but since you're acquainted with magic, might you have any friends who are witches? We're looking for one to help our parents become unlost," said Theresa.

"Or maybe you know a wizard or … magician … who is good with unlost spells?" asked Terrance, who paused to look at his sister to make sure he was remembering his terms correctly.

"There's no witches in this village. There's no one in this area who's good at those unlost spells … at least no one I know of. I do write regularly to my cousin, Botania. She's a good witch over in Rootworth. She's also a friend of your father's, if my memory serves. I'm sure she could help you," said Madame Lumen.

"That's the good witch we plan on visiting, once we have sold our crop of Silver Lilies, that is," said Aiden. "Our father has told us so many good things about her, but we've never met her. She seems like an especially good witch."

"The especially good witch she is! She's always been very kind to me with suggestions for adjusting my spells. And wouldn't you just know it," Madame Lumen said in a softer voice so only the Silverglades could here, "my cousin, Botania, is coming into town for the final day of the Lightning Bug Festival. You won't have to travel far at all to find her. You come here that morning and the five of us will have whiffle waffles and bubbleberry juice together, on the house!"

"How wonderful! Thank you so much, Madame Lumen!" exclaimed Theresa.

"Our parents are going to become unlost!" exclaimed Terrance.

"Yes, thank you, Madame Lumen, but please, we have some money left from last year's sales, so we can pay for the breakfast," said Aiden.

"Oh nonsense! It's my treat to you children. I know it's been difficult having your parents be lost and all that, so I want to treat you to nice breakfast to let you know that people care," said Madame Lumen. "Now, why don't you all get back to your breakfasts before the last few bites get cold and stop whiffling. I'll

Chapter Two

see you all back here on Sunday morning for the best whiffle waffles and bubbleberry juice you'll ever taste."

"Good-bye, Madame Lumen!" the Silverglades all said in unison.

"We hope to see you again during the festivities this week," said Aiden.

"I'm sure you'll see me every evening. I have a stand over in the North Illume Park to sell my food to all the visitors at the Lightning Bug Festival. Stop by and see me. Just look for the stand with the large whiffle waffles floating overhead," said Madame Lumen as she headed back into her kitchen.

The family finished up eating and returned to their carriage so Aiden could run inside and retrieve their silver bag. It was time to start peddling their Silver Lilies.

"Where do we start?" asked Terrance, once Aiden had returned with the bag of lilies.

"There are lots of places to start. Father always let me pick the first place to go … so, why don't you two decide?" Aiden said in an encouraging tone.

The twins looked around for a moment and then looked back at each other. They smiled and blurted out in unison, "Ms. Goo's Potions Aplenty!"

"Ms. Goo's Potions Aplenty it is. Excellent choice!" Aiden exclaimed. "I know you're both all grown up now, but I want you to take my hands as we cross the street. Your big brother is overly protective of you because that's his job." He extended his hands and the twins gladly took them.

The family immediately headed to the north side of the square towards Ms. Goo's Potions Aplenty store. Without letting go of Aiden's hand, Theresa merrily skipped all the way there, stopping when traffic caused them to pause.

Just like all of the businesses in Illume, the shoppe was very quaint and charming. Ms. Goo's store was one of the most colorful places in the village due to the rainbow of colors present in her potions. For a village as small as Illume, Ms. Goo had a superb selection of potions.

"Greetings my Silverglade neighbors!" Ms. Goo exclaimed as the children entered her store. The potion brewer was covered in potion goo, as she always was. Although she made several of her potions herself, the majority of them were shipped in every quarter from outside the village. In a village like Illume she didn't have the proper resources to make a wide variety of potions, nor did she have quite the skills necessary to prepare the more advanced potions in her stock. "How may I be of service to you today? We have specials on friendship potions and magical scents going on all week. We also are giving away a free, small vial of lightning salve with every purchase. It's good for burns from those playful, little Lightning Bugs."

"No thank you, Ms. Goo," replied Aiden. "We are here for our family business today."

"That's right, Ms. Goo. Would you like to buy some Silver Lilies?" asked Terrance.

"They're ever so pretty!" added Theresa.

"Why yes, yes I would," said Ms. Goo.

The eyes of all three Siverglades were filled with joy. Aiden was especially surprised that they managed a sale on their first attempt. He and his father never had a sale on the first day before.

"Oh thank you, Ms. Goo! How wonderful! I mean ... how many would you like?" said Theresa, realizing mid-thought that she should try to act in a *professional* way since she was representing the family in their business.

"Let's see. I was just thinking last month about this, because that's when I used up the last of my Silver Lilies from three years ago. I purchased two dozen lilies from your father and Aiden here. I used them to add a special touch to some of my potions and they seem to work quite well. As a matter of fact, they made my potions even more potent. I think this time I'll go for four dozen. Do you have four dozen left?" asked Ms. Goo, knowing that they would. She was well aware that their father had never been able to sell an entire crop of Silver Lilies in Illume. Nonetheless, she acted as though they may have already sold their crop to make the children feel successful and motivated in their sales. She wanted them to do their lost parents proud.

"We certainly do," said Terrance.

Aiden reached into the silver bag and retrieved four dozen Silver Liles. He placed them delicately onto Ms. Goo's countertop. He learned from his father to have a delicate touch with the lilies, not for protection of the lilies but for *professional* effect.

"Now let me think. I believe last time I offered your father four green coins and fifty green pennies for two dozen Silver Lilies … so that would go to nine green coins now … and how about I make that an even ten green coins since you children have been so pleasant today and brightened up my store?" asked Ms. Goo, feeling a little sorry for the children with their lost parents.

"That's very generous of you," stated Aiden.

As Aiden collected the coins from Ms. Goo, the twins politely approached the other patrons of the store and asked them if they'd be interested in any Silver Lilies. One kind woman who was looking for a gift for her granddaughter purchased one Silver Lily from the twins for twenty-five green pennies.

When the twins returned to Aiden with the pennies and to retrieve a Silver Lily for the woman, Aiden whispered into their ears, "Well done. That's a very good deal you just did. Father would be quite proud of you both."

The twins quickly returned to the woman to deliver the Silver Lily to her. She seemed very pleased with her purchase, as she had never seen a Silver Lily prior to the beautiful pile that she saw laid out on Ms. Goo's countertop.

The family continued on that day visiting the various shoppes and businesses on the square. They managed to sell Silver Lilies to several travelers; however, they only made a total of eleven green coins and forty-two green pennies that day, as not all of the travelers were as generous as Ms. Goo or her patron.

The Village of Illume

Each evening that week the family paid a visit to Madame Lumen's stand in the North Illume Park. She was always anxious to hear their updates on sales. She didn't let them see how sad she was that they only sold two more bouquets of Silver Lilies by Saturday evening.

"Well, kids, tomorrow is Sunday and a new day. Let's see if we can make a good sale at the final day's events," said Aiden while they all relaxed in the family room of the carriage. The interior of the carriage looked much like their home, with each member of the family having a separate bedroom. Aiden had placed a portrait he had done of their parents over the fireplace in the family room as a surprise for the twins. Every night they spent time before bed looking at the portrait and praying for their parents' safe return.

"Even if we don't sell any lilies tomorrow, I won't be upset. That will just mean we'll have an even greater adventure traveling outside of Illume!" said Theresa. She and Terrance were both very excited at the prospect of leaving the village area. Neither one had ever traveled far outside of the village.

Aiden also was excited, not because he had never been outside of the village, but because it reminded him of many pleasant memories of his travels with his father.

"All right, you two, I think it's time for all three of us to be going to bed. We need to have plenty of sleep so we can be at our best tomorrow and sell these lilies," said Aiden.

Aiden led them off to their bedrooms and when they were ready he tucked both Terrance and Theresa into their beds. As he did, he tried humming a tune that their mother always hummed when she tucked them into bed. The twins were still excited from the idea of doing more traveling, so Aiden thought that his mother's technique would be a good way to calm down the twins ... and he was correct. The twins both quickly nodded off and dreamt of the stories that Aiden and their father had told them of cities far away from the Village of Illume and most especially of how pleasant their visit with Botania the Good Witch of Rootworth would be.

Chapter Three
Botania

The next morning they all rose out of bed early due to anticipation of meeting Botania.

The Silverglades departed from their carriage with their still-nearly-full silver bag. Theresa also carried with her some paper and a pencil, because she was determined to gather some new information about Glinda from Botania. She reasoned that one good witch would have to have considerable knowledge of other good witches, especially information about the most famous good witch in all of Oz, although Glinda was really a good sorceress rather than a mere good witch.

"Aiden, why can't we live in the carriage and live wherever we want? It's been awfully convenient to live right in front of Madame Lumen's Kitchen this past week," inquired Terrance.

"I agree. We should spend more time living out of the carriage. Just think of all the fun people we could meet every day while traveling! It's especially convenient today. All we have to do is go out our front door and we meet a good witch," said Theresa.

"That's an excellent thought; however, if we always lived on the road then we wouldn't have our farm to support us. It gives us just about everything we need, and the few things it doesn't provide it gives us the means to buy ... if we can sell these Silver Lilies, that is," said Aiden.

"Oh ... I didn't think about that. Well, maybe we can just spend a little more time traveling ... when the Silver Lilies don't need us and we have enough supplies from the farm to last us a while," stated Terrance, with an obvious drain on his enthusiasm present in his voice.

Madame Lumen was at the door waiting for the three Silverglades as they entered her restaurant.

BOTANIA

"Good morning, my Silverglade friends! You're just on time. Your breakfasts'll be floatin' out to you right about the time you get to your table," said Madame Lumen.

"Which table is ours?" asked Terrance.

"Why the one with the good witch sitting at it," said Madame Lumen as she pointed to the farthest back table along the side facing Luster Avenue. "My cousin, the Good Witch, is the lady wearing the floppy, pointed hat with the bird's nest in it. Just don't mistake her for tree!" said Madame Lumen with a big smile on her face.

Botania had arrived earlier in the morning, before the restaurant had opened so she could have a little chat with her cousin, Madame Lumen, in private. They had a confidential whiffle waffle spell to discuss. When Madame Lumen had warned the Silverglades to not mistake Botania for a tree, she meant it. The good witch's appearance made it quite evident to the children that her magical area of expertise was in nature spells.

As the children approached the table, Botania immediately arose and greeted each of them with a great, big hug. "Good morning to you, Silverglade children! My cousin has told me so many wonderful things about you all. It's a pleasure to meet you. I hope you don't mind, but I took the liberty of checking my Rose Mirror to see when you'd be arriving and I had my cousin arrange for our breakfast to be ready for you so you wouldn't have to wait with any grumbling tummies. And here it all comes now!" stated Botania as a small parade of whiffle waffles and bubbleberry juice appeared from the kitchen.

"It's a pleasure to meet you, too," said Aiden. "Thank you for your kindness. It's very good of you to meet with us."

"And thank you for anticipating us!" said the twins as they began to scarf down their whiffle waffles.

"My cousin tells me that you're selling Silver Lilies," said Botania.

"Yes, that's correct, Miss Botania," replied Aiden.

Chapter Three

"Oh, my dear, please call me Botania. We're all friends here. My cousin has told me so much about you all that I feel we've known each other for ages," said Botania. She was visibly pleased that Aiden had given her the courtesy of the title *Miss*; however, she preferred talking on the friendliest level possible with everyone she encountered. As a good witch, she had good reason to bring friendliness into almost any conversation. She also had a way to make most people around her feel instantly comfortable, which was in part due to a very subtle magic that surrounded her. "Now, I'm afraid that I'm not in the market to purchase your entire crop of Silver Lilies, but I think I can find some good use for about a dozen of them."

"I knew you'd be able to sell a few of your lilies to my cousin. A good witch of any quality will want to keep such a beautiful flower in her collection," said Madame Lumen.

"Did you say something about a Rose Mirror, Botania?" interrupted Theresa. Her curiosity for Glinda made her very curious about magical objects in general.

"Why yes I did, my young friend," replied Botania.

"May I please see it, I mean, if it's not too much trouble?" asked Theresa.

"I told you this young lady would be quite interested in your mirror. She has an interest in all things magic, especially if they relate to Glinda. You'll find little Theresa, and both of her brothers, to be quite brilliant," said Madame Lumen.

Botania reached into her rootgrass purse, made from a grass that is unique to the area of Rootworth, and pulled out a small hand mirror. The mirror looked to be made of branches from a rose bush, with the mirror surrounded by thorns and white roses. The handle was covered in thorns and looked potentially painful to grasp.

"I'd love to let you hold my mirror, young Theresa, but I'm afraid that I've yet to find anyone other than myself who can manage the Rose Mirror without coming to meet a nasty surprise from these thorns," said Botania.

"That's ok, Botania, I can see it from here. It's quite beautiful. Did you make it yourself?" asked Theresa.

"As a matter of fact, I did. I used an enchanted rose bush from my garden. I love roses and these were perfect for fitting into my purse, because they can be crushed and immediately spring back into shape," said Botania. She squeezed one of the roses to demonstrate.

"That's amazing!" said Terrance. "How does it work? What does it do?"

"Do you remember how I said I was able to see when you would arrive this morning? Well, that is what it does. It lets me gaze into the future, but only a little bit. The magic only works when it's not anything of great importance, things that won't have a major impact on the course of my life events," Botania said.

"You should ask Glinda the Good Sorceress to help you with that," stated Theresa. "She's marvelous when it comes to enchantments, but I'm sure you already know that."

"Yes, I do know that," said Botania with a sweet smile. "But that would be cheating, now wouldn't it, my dear Theresa? If I knew everything that was going to happen in my life then life wouldn't be very fun, now would it? We all need surprises in our lives. We have to accept both the good and the bad if we want to have happy surprises."

"We all do love surprises, now don't we?" asked Aiden of the twins. "Do you remember how happy you were when you saw the portrait of our parents I hung for you in the carriage as a surprise? What would life be like without surprises like that?

The twins nodded in agreement.

"Now, back to these absolutely stunning Silver Lilies. How much do you want for them? They must be quite valuable. Would you prefer some money, or would you rather have some magic? I must admit it. I do enjoy giving people enchantments that make their lives happier," said Botania.

"We would be pleased to accept either, but we were hoping that maybe you would have an unlosting spell you could use to help us

Chapter Three

find our parents. Mother and father became lost a while back and we very much wish to help them become unlost" said Aiden.

"The Rose Mirror! Couldn't you use the Rose Mirror to find where mother and father went when they become lost?" asked Theresa.

"I'm sorry, my dear little one, but this mirror can only show me the future," said Botania.

"That's ok, we understand," said Aiden.

"However ... maybe I can manage a little adjustment here," said Botania.

"Oh thank you!" exclaimed Terrance.

Botania carefully held the mirror in front of her and closed her eyes. She seemed to be in an intense state of silent meditation. After a moment, she opened her eyes and from her ring finger she flicked a small, green spark into the center of the mirror.

"My Rose Mirror, would you please be so very kind as to tell me where these dear children's parents, Mr. and Mrs. Silverglade, have become lost?" asked Botania of her Rose Mirror.

"They are outside of my sight. Magic prevents me from seeing," stated the top, center rose on the Rose Mirror.

"Oh dear ... it seems that there is some enchantment, or what-have-you, interfering here. Hmmm ... perhaps this will help," said Botania as she pulled out from her rootgrass purse a pinecone.

"Ah yes, the pinecone. We mustn't forget the pinecone," said Madame Lumen.

"What is that, Botania? Why would a pinecone help anything?" asked Terrance.

"It's a charmed pinecone from a hundred centuries ago. It knows just about everything there is to know about the past," said Botania.

The good witch held the pinecone up against the mirror and asked again, "My Rose Mirror, would you please be so very kind as to tell me where these dear children's parents, Mr. and Mrs. Silverglade, have become lost?"

"They are outside of my sight. Magic prevents me from seeing," stated the top, center rose on the Rose Mirror.

"Oh dear ... my magic is not going to be able to help you, I'm afraid. There is some powerful magic here, or else you're just not meant to know, yet. Hmmm ... I recommend ... living your lives to the fullest until your parents become unlost on their own. If you keep doing as you're doing, then you're going to have two very proud parents on your hands when they become unlost!" said Botania.

"We never thought of it like that. How wonderful! I know they will be proud of us," said Terrance.

"Maybe they just needed to spend some time being lost for a while as a sort of vacation. You're right, Botania. I'm sure they'll come back to us when they're ready," said Theresa.

All three children were very happy with this new perspective on their parents' lostness. If it wasn't time for their parents to become unlost yet then they were happy to accept that, as long as they knew their parents would eventually return, and they knew this in their hearts to be true.

"Thank you so much for helping us, Botania," said Aiden as he handed her a dozen Silver Lilies.

"Oh nonsense, I've done nothing," said Botania as she reached into her purse again and pulled out a small, blue sphere about twice the size of a marble. She held the sphere in her closed hand and she shut her eyes. She hummed a tune that was one of the most beautifully peaceful tunes the children had ever heard. When Botania stopped humming and opened her eyes, she placed the sphere into Theresa's hand. "This is a petrified blue berry from a petrified shuffle bush. If you're within one-hundred feet of your parents it will start to glow. If you're within five feet of them it will also start to hum the tune you just heard."

"Oh thank you, Botania!" said Theresa. "I was wondering ... did you learn this spell or any of your other magic from Glinda?"

"My sister here adores Glinda. And wouldn't you just know it, she's writing a book on her, too," said Aiden.

Chapter Three

"Is that so? I have to tell you I haven't had the pleasure of meeting Glinda more than a couple of brief times many years ago ... and I can't tell you what I do know of her, other than she truly is a good witch ... or good sorceress if you prefer. She does value her privacy greatly, and we also must do our best to respect that," said Botania.

"According to my research, you are correct: she does value her privacy ... but it's still nice to know a little about her," said Theresa.

"I have something else for you, my Silverglade children. I know that you little ones would like to do some traveling, yet you'd also like to sell your Silver Lily crop. I know where you should be able to sell your Silver Lilies while also enjoying a very scenic trip. Somewhere in the very southern part of Oz is Glinda's Silver Tower. They always have use for anything made of silver for their research there. Theresa, the people who live in the Silver Tower are a little like you. They enjoy research. Now, I can't tell you any more about the Silver Tower, but you should have an amazing journey there and you will just love the citizens of the tower. I'm sure you'll find it with ease, considering how very brilliant all of you are. Oh! Don't drink the water from the lake! That could quickly confuddle your brilliance and help you become lost, too," said Bontania.

"Oh, Aiden! May we please go to the Silver Tower? We could sell our Silver Lilies quickly and make our parents very proud of us. We might also be able to meet Glinda the Good Sorceress in person, so I might also be able to discover a little more information on her," said Theresa.

"It does sound like an interesting and fun adventure .... What do you think, Terrance? Should we venture to the south and find the Silver Tower?" asked Aiden.

"Yes! I think that would be a marvelous way to do some traveling and also make our parents proud of their children. I'd also like to see Theresa meet Glinda," said Terrance, who was somewhat excited at the prospect of his twin having the opportunity to meet the subject of her research hobby.

34

"Then I think, for the sakes of our mother and father, we should go to the Silver Tower and sell these Silver Lilies," said Aiden.

"How wonderful you children are!" exclaimed Botania.

"Indeed they are," added Madame Lumen. "Now, we should all be moving along. My cousin and I have some more chatting to do ... and some enchanting to work through. And I think it's about time for the parade to start."

Just as Madame Lumen finished her sentence the sound of music started. The sound came from the village square, where the band had assembled and was beginning its march towards the North Illume Park.

The Silverglades and both ladies quickly turned their attentions to the window. The band was large enough that the back end of the band was very close to their window.

"Oh look! They have Lightning Bellows and Thunder Drums!" exclaimed Terrance.

"I hope they have the Lantern Tree wood harp again this year. It's what I've been telling you about, Botania, in my letters. It's small but has a huge sound ... oh! There it is! I hope they play it soon!" said Madame Lumen, and not but a moment later the harp began to play. The sound was both thunderous and tranquil at the same time.

"What a beautiful sound!" exclaimed Botania, who was impressed by the creative use of nature in the instrument. "You know, that sound is only possible due to the magical properties of the Lantern Trees."

"I wonder if the sound would be better with some of our family's Lantern Trees. Ours are of better quality than the trees elsewhere in the region because we have Silver Water," stated Theresa.

"Oh, I'm sure they would make an even more thunderously pleasant sound," said Botania. "The extra magic in the wood would make harps like this one even more potent in their performance."

Chapter Three

"Let's go outside and watch the band up close!" exclaimed Terrance.

"Yes, you all go outside and enjoy the day! You have worked so hard this week, so why don't you just take the rest of the day off to enjoy the festival?" said Madame Lumen.

"I fully agree. I'm certain you will sell your crop at the Silver Tower, so there's no reason to worry about your lilies. Be festive and merry for today, and worry about tomorrow when tomorrow comes," added Botania.

At that, the cousins hugged the Silverglades and wished them a good day.

The Silverglade children spent their day watching the band and enjoying the various festivities of the event: lightning eaters, Lightning Bug dancers, enchanted Lightning Bug rides, and many specialty foods that were only available during the Lightning Bug Festival. They planned to meet up with Madame Lumen and Botania again that evening to enjoy the Lightning Bug Ballet, which was the culminating event of the whole week. This occasion was a gathering in the North Illume Park to watch all of the Lightning Bugs of the entire region come together and dance in a massive cloud just above everyone's heads. Every Sunday for the remainder of the summer the Lightning Bugs would do this; however, this was their first cloud dance for the season.

It was the final evening of the Lightning Bug Festival and the Silverglade children were waiting at the North Illume Park with Madame Lumen, Mr. Lumen, and Botania for the Lightning Bugs to arrive. They all sat in wooden chairs, with seat pads made from Botania's cushion bushes.

"Children, as we wait for our little insect friends to arrive, I have a small favor to ask of you, if you don't mind," said Botania.

"Botania, of course we don't mind. How may we be of service to our good witch friend?" said Aiden.

"Since you have unanimously decided to venture off to the south and find the Silver Tower, would you please deliver a letter from me to Lady Thorn and Lady Thistle? They are colleagues of mine who are very renowned within our circle of nature enchantresses, and I have several questions I've wanted to ask of them for a very long time now," said Botania.

"Just give us the letter and we'll gladly deliver it to them when we arrive at the Silver Tower. How will we recognize them?" asked Aiden.

"You will recognize them without trouble, my kind friend. And I must thank you. It is very difficult to send messages to the Silver Tower …," said Botania. The good witch reached into her rootgrass purse and retrieved a letter, sealed with wax and bearing her signet mark from her magic rootgrass ring. Botania handed the letter to Aiden and said, "I'm sure you wonder why a witch of my caliber isn't using magic to send this letter. My questions aren't all that urgent … they're more of the hobby persuasion. Besides, it would be disrespectful to send a letter to them out of the blue using magic without being close friends with them. Thank you so much for helping me. Here's a bag of chocolate moss candies for you. They'll be a terrific treat for the three of you during your journey to the Silver Tower."

"Thank you, Botania," said all three children in unison.

At that very moment a loud cheer erupted from the crowd. The Lightning Bugs were arriving! Tens of thousands of the insects quickly filled the night sky above the heads of the crowd. The cloud of Lightning Bugs started a mere five feet above the average festival-goer's head, although a couple of exceedingly tall individuals were an anxious-few inches away from the cloud.

The lightning harp began to play and the Lightning Bugs began to dance to its hypnotic hymn. The insects flowed like several, illuminated rivers in the sky. They danced in varying, swirling patterns within their self-contained cloud. As they danced, small bolts of lightning came from every bug; however, in various parts of the cloud larger and larger bolts erupted as the insects interacted with one another. The hymn came to life within the cloud of Lightning Bugs. The blue lightning from the bugs mixed with the

Chapter Three

many shades of green light emanating from the common green Lantern Trees and other green-glowing plants of the village and the park.

The dance went on for a full hour, during which time the only audible sounds from the crowd of festival-goers were in the form of non-word expressions of awe.

At one point during the dance the Lightning Bugs all converged in a giant, swirling funnel that was almost like a peacefully slow tornado. At the center of the funnel was a massive and continuous bolt of lightning that branched several feet outside of the cloud of Lightning Bugs. You could see several spectators ducking to varying degrees out of fear that the lightning might stretch out a little too far and give them a nasty burn.

Chapter Four
A Blue Tempest

The morning after the end of the Lightning Bug Festival, the Silverglade children made their departure from the Village of Illume. They pulled out of their week-long home in front of Madame Lumen's Kitchen and began their journey south, following Luster Avenue.

Aiden was at the reins of the carriage, as was most often the case since he liked to allow the twins to have their playtime, which was quite typically study time for them. Both twins were in the coach of the carriage sitting across from one another, with Terrance facing forwards and Theresa facing backwards. Theresa was reading a book on Lantern Trees and Terrance was reading a book on Lightning Bug dances. Aiden had purchased the books for his siblings as a surprise gift for during their journey to the Silver Tower.

At the edge of the village, Luster Avenue became a regular dirt road. From then on the road was named South Grace Road, which headed towards the southern tip of the country of South Grace. The four principle countries of Oz at that time were named Grace: South Grace, North Grace, East Grace, and West Grace. The names were given in ancient times after the last Great War in honor of the grace that was granted on the kingdom with the end of the war. Oz was shaped like a giant, star-like spiral. The greater arms stretched out towards the cardinal directions, with secondary arms stretching out at the intercardinal directions. These intercardinal arms were the smaller Favor countries: South-East Favor, South-West Favor, North-West Favor, and North-East Favor. These names were given due to the favors felt by the countries at the ending of the last Great War.

Aiden, Terrance, and Theresa had all agreed that they would follow the road and remain on it until some kind person gave them

Chapter Four

more specific directions to the Silver Tower. They were taught to trust kind strangers, but also to be weary of those who were undeserving of their trust. Erring on the side of respect was what to do when in doubt, as this always led to goodness in the end.

Once the carriage had reached the valley of the Southern Illume Mountains, where the Village of Illume was no longer visible except for a green glow to the north, the vegetation began to change. The road was surrounded by patches of woods and inclined-meadows. Various grasses, shrubs, and flowering plants found their home within this environment. Aiden's travels with his father enabled him to identify some of these plants: yellow sunfire-illusion flowers, gray-goose flowers, bobbing bacon bushes (which were quite edible), and maple smoke grass. The grass helped give a pleasant taste to the bacon from the bobbing bacon bushes. Lunch pail trees were abundant in all of the wooded areas, along with apple trees, mint tea trees, poncho trees, and sponge cake trees, all of which were starting to look rather tropical in appearance. The lunch pail trees came in three varieties. There were lunchmeat sandwich lunch pail trees, which came with various types of meat; there were pasta lunch pail trees, which came with various types of pasta; and there were hamburger lunch pail trees, which came with various types of hamburgers.

"Aiden, is it time to stop for lunch yet? My tummy is starting to notify me that lunch should be nearing," commented Terrance as he took a moment to pause in his reading and look around at the beautiful scenery.

"Yes, favorite brother of mine, my tummy is in agreement with your tummy," said Aiden. He then pulled the carriage over to the side of the road near a particularly large area of woods where there were many lunch pail trees from which to choose a meal.

"What is everyone hungry for?" asked Theresa as the three approached the lunch pail trees.

"Since we had so many sandwiches and hamburgers during the Lightning Bug Festival, why don't we try some pasta from one of these pasta lunch pail trees?" said Terrance.

"That sounds like a smart choice to me," said Aiden. "I'll pick us out some ripe lunch pails since I'm the only one who can reach these branches. Let's see if I can pick us all something good."

Aiden walked over to the pasta lunch pail tree that had the ripest lunch pails within his arms' reach. Without having to jump, Aiden picked out six lunch pails. "I think saving three for later in case we need a snack would be wise. Now ... which ones shall we eat now? This one looks like it wants to go to Theresa ... and this one looks like it wants to go to Terrance," said Aiden as he handed the twins one lunch pail each. "And this one looks like it wants to go to Aiden," said Aiden as he laid down the other three lunch pails to take back to the carriage later, after they finished their lunches.

Theresa had brought with her a picnic basket, and while Aiden had been picking the lunch pails from the tree she had retrieved a blanket from the basket. She and Terrance spread it out on the ground and the three of them opened their lunch pails together. Theresa opened her lunch pail to find a nice South Grace alfredo and penne pasta. Terrance discovered a nice South Grace parrot pepper and rigatoni pasta. Aiden managed to pick for himself a lunch pail containing some South Grace shrimp pasta pomodoro. All three lunch pails came with vinegar chips, chocolate cake, and chocolate milk, which happened to be favorites of the Silverglade children.

"This is a wonderful meal," said Theresa.

"Oh yes! This is one of the best meals I've had all week," said Terrance in agreement.

"We're sure to have many more good meals like this if there are as many lunch pail trees along the rest of South Grace Road," commented Aiden.

As the children were finishing up their meals, a small cloud started to form over their heads. The cloud was so small that it was hardly any bigger than the picnic blanket on which the children were sitting. The cloud was within the branches of the tree directly above the children's heads and was very thick. They were no longer able to see the sky or even the top of the tree above them.

Chapter Four

"That's odd. I've never seen such a brilliantly-blue cloud before," said Theresa as she looked up and noticed the cloud.

"Neither have I," said Terrance.

"Nor I," said Aiden.

All of a sudden a heavy rain burst forth from the cloud.

"It's blue! We're turning blue!" shouted Theresa.

"Let's hurry back to the carriage! Grab the blanket!" shouted Aiden. At that point the rain was so heavy that Aiden needed to shout to make sure the twins could hear him.

Theresa and Terrance quickly scooped up the blanket while Aiden went for the three, unused lunch pails. Everything under the tree was completely covered in blue by then.

As the Silverglades ran back to the carriage the blue cloud started to follow them.

"The storm's growing larger!" exclaimed Terrance.

"No, it's following us! Get onto the carriage and we'll try to outrun it!" shouted Aiden.

The twins quickly climbed into the coach of the carriage and Aiden jumped into the box. Aiden handled the reins with great vigor, which caused the carriage to accelerate very quickly.

"We're losing it!" exclaimed Terrance after just a few seconds. The cloud had suddenly stopped following them and hovered in place.

"Not so fast, trespassers!" said a scratchy voice from within the trees.

"Who said that? And look! It's coming after us again!" shouted Theresa.

Just then an old woman, who seemed to have very little concern over her personal appearance, flew out from among the treetops. She looked to be riding on top of her own small cloud. This cloud was just big enough for one person and was dark gray, almost black, in color. As the old woman on her dark gray cloud increased in her speed, so did the blue cloud.

"It's gaining on us, Aiden! Please go faster!" shouted Terrance.

"I can't! I'm afraid this is the fastest we can go!" shouted Aiden.

The old woman and her clouds were quickly approaching the children.

As Aiden tried to figure out a way to escape, a rather small bird of some sort flew very quickly past him, only a few inches from his head. He heard a delightful humming coming from the bird as it flew by.

"A hummingbird!" shouted Aiden.

The hummingbird flew directly into the blue cloud, causing the cloud to rapidly disperse.

"No! My beautiful tempest! What happened to my beautiful tempest!?" shouted the old woman.

The hummingbird then changed its course to fly directly at the cloud underneath the old woman. This cloud too dispersed as the hummingbird punctured it.

The old woman screamed as she fell and landed in a bobbing bacon bush, thanks to which she managed to land with only a few minor scrapes and bruises.

"Thank you, Mr. Hummingbird!" shouted Aiden. He didn't slow down the carriage just yet for fear of the old woman trying to following them.

The hummingbird had already turned around and quickly arrived back at the carriage and flew directly next to Aiden.

"You're very welcome. We hummingbirds from atop the mountains come down every time we see a traveler pass through, because Renée the Wicked Magiciènne uses her cloud to chase away anyone who trespasses on what she claims to be her land. It's really hummingbird land, but we lend this small part of the valley to her since a wicked warlock trapped her here years ago with an enchantment. Renée was unwise to send her cloud after a wicked warlock. The wicked magiciènne's reach ends at that glowing, blue lunch pail tree up ahead. I'll fly you there to make sure you're safe," said the hummingbird. Every word that the hummingbird said was spoken in a humming tone that was very melodic and pleasantly tranquilizing.

Chapter Four

As the carriage approached the glowing, blue lunch pail tree, Renée came to her feet and let out a loud shriek. She pointed her finger at the carriage and a small ball of fire flew out, headed directly towards the children and the hummingbird.

"Look out! Fire!" shouted Theresa.

The carriage had just passed the glowing, blue lunch pail tree in time. The small ball of fire was magically extinguished right when it approached the perimeter marked by the tree, preventing it from harming the children and the hummingbird.

"No worries, she can't touch you now. You're all safe, although I recommend we continue a little farther so we're no longer within the magiciènne's sight," said the hummingbird.

"I agree. Thank you so much for your help. You're a very kind hummingbird," said Aiden.

"We do appreciate your kindness towards us strangers in your land. But … are you sure she's a magicièrne? I would have guessed her to be a wizardess or witch. Her magic seems a little too powerful to be coming from a mere magicièrne," commented Theresa. Her studies of Glinda had given her good knowledge of judging magic, even though she had not met very many magic users in her young life.

"You are very perceptive, young lady; however, Renée is very deceiving. You wouldn't have had time to notice this, but she was wearing a tempest amulet. Although there are more powerful tempest amulets in the world, her amulet provides her with the power of a wizardess … at least when it comes to storms. That fireball was the making of her own magical abilities. It probably tired her greatly to send it at us," said the hummingbird.

"I think we're all glad that she's not able to do any traveling out of her small area of the valley," said Aiden.

"Very true, but what brings you young Illumians through the valley? I've never seen a group of Illumian children enter the valley alone before," said the hummingbird.

"We are traveling to the Silver Tower and we are following South Grace Road until we find it. How did you know we're from the Village of Illume?" asked Terrance.

"Your carriage gives it away. I can see that you have Lantern Tree wood from the Silverglade Family Farm. Their trees are quite unique to the area," said the hummingbird.

"We are the Silverglade family. That's why we have their trees. I was unaware that our trees are so popular among the hummingbird population," said Aiden.

"Oh yes, indeed they are! We find them to be quite pretty," said the hummingbird. "You say you are going to the Silver Tower? Then you are going in the correct direction ... although I do not know myself where it is located. I do know it's located somewhere to the south, and this is the best route to take if you want to go south."

"Thank you, Mr. Hummingbird," said Theresa. "What a wicked person that Renée is! Why would anyone ever want to attack us like that?"

"As you are young children from the Village of Illume I suppose you are used to all of the kindnesses of the villagers. There are many good and kind people, much like yourselves, in the world. Sadly, there are also a number of wicked people, like Renée, in the world. They care of nothing but their own desires. If you continue on your journey you will undoubtedly encounter more wicked people ... but be happy! Because you will also encounter many good people who will make your encounters with the wicked ones well worth it. Now I must be off. Good luck my Illumian friends!" The hummingbird quickly flew off, back to the top of the western mountain bordering the valley.

After Aiden had guided the carriage out of the valley onto the south side of the Southern Illume Mountains, he pulled the carriage over to the side of the road so the family could take a quick break.

"We must remember to thank Botania for enchanting this carriage with self-cleaning magic," said Aiden. "Now let's all jump into the carriage to clean ourselves off."

Chapter Four

One of the many pleasantries Botania had added to the carriage was a self-cleaning enchantment. This prevented any dirt or other unwanted nasties from detracting from the elegance of the carriage. The enchantment included a special effect with the entrance to the inner chambers of the carriage. When a person passed through the entrance hatch, all dirt and grime were removed from him. The children took advantage of this to remove the blue colors from themselves, the picnic blanket, and the three leftover lunch pails.

Once they were clean the children continued on their journey. Having cleared the Southern Illume Mountains, the children found themselves at the beginning of a large savannah. Although it was some distance away, the children could clearly make out a much taller mountain range that was further to the south.

After a couple of hours of travel, the Silverglades were only about a quarter of the way across the savannah.

It was now nighttime and the stars were beginning to come out. Aiden enjoyed explaining to Theresa and Terrance what all of the bright objects in the sky were. This was their first time ever having seen stars. The lights of their farm and of the Village of Illume always prevented the stars from shining through for the Silverglades to see. The children's eyes were fixed on the sky in amazement of the beauty of the tiny spots of light. Even though Aiden had been able to see stars before when he had accompanied his father on sales trips, he was still catching himself looking up at the night sky regularly as he drove the carriage. The lights were very different from those of the natural surroundings of the Silverglade's home.

"I think with everything we've experienced today that we should perhaps set up camp soon and take an extra-long night's rest. What do you two think about that?" asked Aiden.

"We agree," said the twins in unison.

"Let's go over there and camp next to that misty-looking gold tree," said Theresa.

"I believe that is a golden raintree," said Aiden. "I recommend that we not take up camp next it, because that mist you see is its golden rain and I don't have any desire to become waterlogged while I'm trying to sleep. The rain is very tasty so we'll have to collect some. How about we take up camp underneath that lunch pail banyan tree, or what about one of the monkey bread baobab trees?"

"I'd like to try some of that monkey bread, so let's go to the monkey bread baobab tree that's close to the golden raintree. That way Theresa can see it from up close, without getting soaked," said Terrance.

For dinner that evening the Silverglades feasted on monkey bread and golden raintree water. They spent a calm evening under the monkey bread baobab tree, with the rain from the golden raintree providing them with a very tranquil reverberation that helped them all fall to sleep quickly.

Chapter Five
The Artificer of the Cypress Savannah

Early the next morning, Aiden collected a jug full of the golden raintree water. Since Theresa had shown such great interest in it and all three of the children enjoyed its taste so much, Aiden thought it might be nice to have some saved for a later date as a special treat.

"All right! I have some golden raintree water saved for us and I'm ready to be off. How about you? Are you two ready to continue on with our trek to the south?" Aiden asked the twins as he returned to the carriage with the jug.

"Yes, Aiden, we're ready and excited!" replied Theresa as she reached for the jug from Aiden's hand so she could find a safe place for it inside the carriage. She then descended through the hatch.

Aiden jumped into the box of the carriage and took the reins in hand. He guided the carriage back onto the road and headed south.

After about a half-an-hour had passed, Theresa made an interesting discovery while examining the nature around her. "What's that incredibly large tree over there, far to our east?" she asked.

The tree was a cypress tree, and it towered over all of the other trees in savannah. In fact, it could have been as tall as the mountains in the distance, but that may have just been a visual effect of the open savannah.

"I see it, too. I don't know what it is, but it looks amazing," said Terrance.

"I don't know either, and it's seems to be the only one of its kind in the whole savannah. Probably some playful scamp planted it there for amusement. It certainly does look impressive in these surroundings," said Aiden.

In another one-and-a-half hours, the family came upon a strange looking monkey bread baobab tree.

The Artificer of the Cypress Savannah

"Look at that fascinating baobab tree. It has a copper wire wrapped around it," said Theresa.

The baobab tree had an especially thick trunk. The copper wire spiraled all the way to the top of the tree.

"Let's take a closer look," said Aiden. He slowed down the carriage and guided it over to the tree, which was about four-hundred feet off the west side of road.

The children exited the carriage and walked around the tree.

"Look at that," said Terrance, as he pointed towards a wooden door on the west side of the tree. "There's a door in the middle of the tree. I wonder if anyone's home."

Aiden walked up to the door, examined it for a moment, and gave a cheerful knock upon it. "I guess we'll see in a moment," he said.

After a few seconds the door quickly opened and there stood a woman wearing a pair of goggles with one blue lens and one yellow lens, a work apron, and a copper hair ribbon.

"Guests! Guests! Guests! How wonderful, wonderful, wonderful! Please do come in! My name is Mrs. Tinkermeyer and this is our home and workshop. Please forgive the mess and make yourselves at home! Do be careful! Watch the steps! To what do I owe the pleasure of this visit?" said the woman in a very excited and pleasantly-frenzied manner as she guided the children down the spiraling steps inside of the baobab tree. She was a very kind yet perpetually energized woman. She was the epitome of hyperness.

"It's a pleasure to meet you, Mrs. Tinkermeyer. My name is Aiden, and these are my brother and sister, Terrance and Theresa. We were just traveling through to the south on our way to find the Silver Tower to sell our Silver Lilies and my observant sister noticed the copper wire on your home," said Aiden.

"Copper wire? Oh my goodness me, I must have left it out when I spoke to Mr. Tinkermeyer earlier this morning. I must remember better to bring it inside when I'm done with it" said Mrs. Tinkermeyer. She clapped her hands and the copper wire quickly unwrapped itself from the tree and tucked itself back inside

49

Chapter Five

somewhere at the bottom of the staircase. "I must use it to boost the signal on my talker bellows so I can talk with my husband. He's away on sabbatical right now. He's doing research at the Copper Academy in North Copperton. It's some ways away, so I need to have a boosted signal. Now you say you are heading to the Silver Tower? How do you know where to find it? No one knows where it is! At least no one I've ever encountered has ever known where it is and in my circles that is a very popular tower. They do the best work on artifacts and other knickknacks in all of Oz. I'm an artificer, so I should know!"

"Excuse me, Mrs. Tinkermeyer, but what is an artificer?" asked Terrance.

"What an excellent question, my young house guest," said Mrs. Tinkermeyer just as the four were arriving at the bottom of the stairs. The room that they had entered was relatively large and was filled with workbenches, machines, and many different handiworks that were all of greatly varying sizes. "Do you see all of the inventions around our workshop? These are our inventions, although we call them artifacts. An artificer is a person who studies artifacts. Not only do Mr. Tinkermeyer and I study artifacts but we also invent them. It's our life. They are our children. We spend all of our time working on artifacts because they help us understand what life's all about!" said Mrs. Tinkermeyer as she raised her arms in a grandiose gesture to emphasize the profoundness of what she was explaining to the children.

"That's so wonderful, Mrs. Tinkermeyer. That copper wire you use to talk to your husband is obviously enchanted. Do you use much magic with your artifacts?" asked Theresa.

"Oh my goodness me, yes! I'm also a wizardess and Mr. Tinkermeyer is a wizard. We use magic in all of our artifacts. They wouldn't be very effective artifacts if they didn't have enchantments on them, now would they? Let's look at this for an example," said Mrs. Tinkermeyer as she led the children over to one of her workbenches. Lying on the workbench were several artifacts. One seemed to be a large spring attached to a block of carved banyan tree wood. Another was a cuckoo clock with green light on its top. Mrs. Tinkermeyer directed their attention to a small, rectangular piece of boabob wood with a mouth carved into it. "This little fellow isn't just a simple carving. We've enchanted it so when it comes close to a piece of monkey bread it will tell us if that bread is fresh. That just wouldn't work without magic!"

"That's a beautiful cuckoo clock you have there, Mrs. Tinkermeyer. It reminds me of the common Lantern Trees in our village," said Theresa.

"Ah, you children must be from the Village of Illume! That's where we obtained the lantern we used to power the cuckoo clock. That light on the top there is the central gem of the lantern. You know, those lanterns are quite valuable and no one seems to know it. Those gems are emeralds, with some magic added, of course. One emerald from a common Lantern Tree provides plenty of energy to power most artifacts we make," said Mrs. Tinkermeyer.

"They couldn't be all that valuable. There are so many of them in the village and on our farm," said Aiden.

"You'd be surprised! There are many people who'd love to get their hands on a crop of Lantern Trees. You could make a fortune on them!" exclaimed Mrs. Tinkermeyer.

A loud bonging sound suddenly filled the workshop.

"My bubbleberryroot juice is ready! Make yourselves at home. I'll be right back with some refreshments for us. Feel free to look around. And by all means, touch anything you'd like! Mr. Tinkermeyer and I love showing our artifacts to guests and we don't mind if you break something because that means we get to have fun putting it back together. We do enjoy a good tinkering!" said Mrs. Tinkermeyer and she headed out of the room through the north door.

"I have never seen such well-organized clutter in my life," said Aiden. As he looked around the Tinkermeyers' workshop he could see that there was very little unused spaced. There were parts and pieces spread just about everywhere; however, the keen eye, as was

Chapter Five

a characteristic had by all three Silverglade children, could discern a very orderly manner to the spread.

"The Tinkermeyers must be the best artificers in the world," said Terrance. He was in awe over the intricacies of the many artifacts that he saw.

"I think Glinda would enjoy spending time in this workshop. There are so many inventions here that she could help enchant," commented Theresa.

The children continued to poke around the room, enjoying hearing the various tinks, bonks, thumps, bumps, and chimes that came from the various artifacts as the children handled them, and in some cases, as the children merely passed by them.

Mrs. Tinkermeyer returned to the workshop after being gone only a few, short minutes. She carried with her a wooden tray with four glass mugs on top. Each one contained a brownish-goldish liquid that was bubbling just like the bubbleberry juice the children had enjoyed at Madame Lumen's Kitchen.

"This is my own, culinary invention," said Mrs. Tinkermeyer with a little pride audible in her voice. "Regular bubbleberry juice is made from bubbleberries taken from a bubbleberry bush. This bubbleberryroot juice is made from the roots of a bubbleberry bush. You'll find the taste to be quite unique and quite refreshing. Here, go ahead and try some." She handed each of the children a glass with obvious excitement shown in her eyes.

"It's delicious!" said Theresa.

"This is even better than regular bubbleberry juice! I didn't know the roots bubbled, too," said Terrance.

"Oh my goodness me, yes! The whole plant bubbles! You just never see the roots since they're underground, so you can't see their bubbles," said Mrs. Tinkermeyer.

"It's quite good, Mrs. Tinkermeyer. It tastes like ... like wintergreen and caramel ... with some other flavors, too," said Aiden.

"Mrs. Tinkermeyer, may I ask why your home is so hidden? I mean why is the front door pointed away from the road? You seem

The Artificer of the Cypress Savannah

to like having guests, so why wouldn't you make it easier for guests to find you?" asked Theresa.

"Of course you may ask, my young guest. You see, with all of the artifacts that Mr. Tinkermeyer and I produce ... well, there are some wicked people out there who would like to use them to do wicked things. We are artificers in order to make the world a better place. We only want good to come from our creations, so we keep hidden. All of our friends know exactly how to find us, so we're not very hidden from them. Most people who bother to walk around to the front of our home are walking about because they appreciate the scenery, and I don't think anyone who's looking around at the scenery to appreciate it is going to make for a wicked guest. You three are proof of that. You are all absolutely lovely children. Anyways, we are well-protected here because hardly any wicked people pass by this way, and when they do they are usually in a hurry to make it out of the Cypress Savannah. That's the name of this place. It's quite beautiful, isn't it?" said Mrs. Tinkermeyer.

"Oh yes, it's very pretty. Why is it called Cypress Savannah?" asked Theresa.

"Did you see that fantastically large tree way over to the east?" asked Mrs. Tinkermeyer.

"We sure did," said Aiden. "Theresa was the first to notice it and drew our attention to it immediately."

"That tree is a Montezuma cypress tree. It's the only one of its kind in this whole savannah. It was planted there a very long time ago by the Lady Thorn and the Lady Thistle, who are well-respected in the community of artificers. The tree is also a bit of an artifact, too. The Ladies crafted it so it could be transformed into a giant magnifying glass. It allows them to examine the savannah and neighboring regions. I have seen it transform twice during my many years living in the Cypress Savannah. It's a magnificent sight to see! Accordingly, we refer to it as the Magnificent Magnifying Montezuma Cypress Tree. The tree is also full of powerful protective magic. It's said that the tree will one day preserve the Cypress Savannah from the next Great War. That's why we are

Chapter Five

well-protected here. Wicked folks can tell that they are not wanted here. The Magnificent Magnifying Montezuma Cypress Tree will remove all wickedness from the entire savannah one day, and you don't want to be standing around here when it does if you're wicked, or else you'll be in for a nasty surprise. We'll be just about the only part of Oz that doesn't change, which is good because this whole area is a sort of goldmine for us artificers. There are so many superb resources for people like us here. We built our home right here in the middle of the savannah so we'd have the best access to all of the countless assets of the land," said Mrs. Tinkermeyer.

"Another Great War? I do hope that never happens. Wars are such terrible things," said Theresa.

"I'd love to see the Magnificent Magnifying Montezuma Cypress Tree at work being a magnifying glass. Do you think the tree will do one of its transformations while we're here?" asked Aiden.

"Oh my goodness me, no! It only just did it last year, so it most likely won't be doing any magnifying for several more years. You must come back and visit then! You can see the tree and meet Mr. Tinkermeyer. I know he'd enjoy meeting the three of you. He and I both are always excited to meet interesting, new people, such as yourselves," said Mrs. Tinkermeyer as she gave a little hug to Theresa, who happened to be the closest person to her. The Silverglade children could tell by now that Mrs. Tinkermeyer was a very loving person and enjoyed demonstrating it, which the children greatly appreciated.

"Excuse me, Mrs. Tinkermeyer, may I ask, did you mention Lady Thorn and Lady Thistle a moment ago?" asked Terrance.

"Why yes I did, are they friends of yours? I do hope they are. They are such wonderful Ladies. Do you know them? Oh, I do hope you do!" said Mrs. Tinkermeyer with excitement.

"No, I'm sorry, Mrs. Tinkermeyer, we don't; however, we do know of them. Botania the Good Witch told us a little about them and how they are colleagues of hers. She gave us a letter to deliver to the Ladies when we reach the Silver Tower. I was just wondering

The Artificer of the Cypress Savannah

if you could tell us a little about them, if you wouldn't mind," said Terrance.

"Would I mind? Not at all! Oh my goodness me! The Lady Thorn and the Lady Thistle are Senior Artificers in the Silver Tower of Oz. They have what may be the most important job there! They provide most of the materials used by all of the other artificers, including Glinda the Good Sorceress herself. They tend to the Great Garden. They have been known to make infrequent visits to the Cypress Savannah to retrieve some of the very rare resources that are available only here. The Ladies are incredibly knowledgeable of artifice, so they know exactly how to prepare all of the various resources needed for the research done in the Silver Tower. Their area of expertise in is nature magics. They know more than most artificers about plants and also about the earth, which is why they are so good with the garden yet also know a lot about gems and metals. They tend to surround themselves more with plants, though, because they love the sensation of being surrounded by life. They of course love the land, too, with all of its metals and gems, because that's what makes the plants grow. Through their relationship together they created rosewood rings for one another. Their skills are strengthened through the rings, as a matter of fact. Our artificer circles say that the Ladies are two of the most pleasant and charming individuals one could ever hope to meet. I don't doubt this either, considering how in love they are with nature. People who love nature are always nice guests. And you must tell them to come visit us when you meet them! We would love to have them as guests. We could give them help in recovering whatever resources they need from the Cypress Savannah. We are the experts on the savannah, since we've lived here longer than most anyone else. Yes, to answer your question you're about to ask, there are many other people living here. They're mostly hidden, too, but they're ever such nice people, but most aren't artificers. We even have our very own resident good witch, Coppernia. She is brilliant with copper magics, but she's been asleep for the past couple of decades, as she has needed to rest

Chapter Five

awhile after enchanting her Copper Fortress. It's such a beautiful artifact. It's a large fortress when it's in use, but when it's in storage, as it is for the time being, it would easily fit in the palm of your hand," said Mrs. Tinkermeyer.

"Wow, you sure do know a lot, Mrs. Tinkermeyer. I hope I can be as smart as you one day," said Terrance.

"Oh my goodness me! How very sweet of you to say, young Terrance. I'm not all that smart, I'm just old. You know more stuff about the world when you're old," said Mrs. Tinkermeyer.

"You don't give yourself enough credit, Mrs. Tinkermeyer. I've known a lot of people much older than you are and hardly any of them are as smart as you are. Thank you so much for telling us about the Ladies and the Cypress Savannah. Do you think you might be able to help us find the Silver Tower?" said Aiden.

"See, I'm not as smart as you think I am. I don't know where the Silver Tower is, other than it being somewhere south of here. No one knows where it is, although all of my many artificer friends would love to pay a visit to the tower. It's the coveted workshop for artificers. I wonder if Coppernia might know where it is. Too bad she's still asleep. If she awakens and she knows anything I'll let you know immediately. For now, just keep traveling south and I'm sure you'll eventually find it," said Mrs. Tinkermeyer.

"Thank you, Mrs. Tinkermeyer. I do hope Coppernia wakes up soon and can help us, but I know we'll enjoy our journey even if she doesn't awaken in time to help us," said Terrance.

"When we come back this way after we've been to the Silver Tower, could we visit with you again? I'd very much like to meet Mr. Tinkermeyer, and maybe Coppernia will be awake by then so we can meet her, too. I'd love to meet another good witch. I'm researching Glinda the Good Sorceress, so I have a fondness for all good magic users," said Theresa.

"Oh my goodness me, yes! Please do visit again! We always love good guests, such as yourselves. Oh! I have something for you that will help you find us when you return, since we're not all that easy to spot from the road, although you did a fine job of spotting us this time," said Mrs. Tinkermeyer. She then walked over to some shelves on the far side of the room and picked up a small object. When she returned she handed a tiny model of their home made from monkey bread baobab tree wood to Theresa. The model had a mild, copper glow to it.

"It's quite lovely, Mrs. Tinkermeyer. Is it an artifact? How do we use it to find you?" asked Theresa.

"It's quite easy to use, young Theresa. Do you see how it's glowing right now? It does that when it's within one-thousand feet of our home. If you need more specific directions than that then all you have to do is ask it and it will tell you. Mr. Tinkermeyer makes those for all of our friends. Just keep it safely guarded. We don't want any wicked people finding one of these little map artifacts and discovering where we live! But I'm sure we can trust three wonderful children like you to keep it safe," said Mrs. Tinkermeyer.

"Thank you so much for your gift and for your hospitality, Mrs. Tinkermeyer. We will most assuredly be back to visit you," said Aiden.

"Thank you, Mrs. Tinkermeyer!" said the twins in unison.

"It's time for us to be off. We need to keep heading south so we can find the Silver Tower," said Aiden.

With that, the children all hugged Mrs. Tinkermeyer and ascended the spiral stairs back up to the surface. Mrs. Tinkermeyer continued to be the wonderful hostess that she was by taking them right to their carriage and waving goodbye to them as they started again on their journey south along South Grace Road.

Chapter Six
Mr. Hairold Bunnymunch

Terrance was taking a turn driving the carriage so Aiden could have some time to relax and enjoy the views of the Cypress Savannah, although most of the time Aiden found driving the carriage to be rather relaxing.

"We may just have to pay some more visits to this savannah in the future ... when we have time away from the farm, that is. This place is so wide and open, yet there are plenty of interesting features to it," said Aiden. At that moment, Aiden was looking at a monkey bread baobab tree that was well off in the distance. He found it to be quite infatuating because of its odd shape. In the center of the trunk was a large whole, directly through which he could see the Magnificent Magnifying Montezuma Cypress Tree.

"What's that moving up ahead?" asked Terrance, as he slowed down the carriage and brought it to a stop. He didn't want to get any closer if the movement was from one of those wicked people that Mrs. Tinkermeyer had mentioned. Terrance was still a little unnerved from the encounter with the wicked magicièone.

Aiden redirected his attention from the baobab tree to the road ahead of them. He scanned the area for a moment but was unable to see any movement, other than the gentle movements of the trees and other plant life caused by the warm breeze. "I don't see anything. Where did you see something moving, Terrance? Are you sure it wasn't just an effect of this breeze?" replied Aiden.

"It's over there, on the west side of the road, about thirty feet ahead of us," said Terrance. "Look! There it is again!"

"I see it! It's ... it's something small, and it looks to be covered with white and gray fur. It's probably just an animal of some sort," said Aiden.

"I think I saw it munching on some of that grass ... maybe it's a bunny. It looks completely harmless to me. I'm going to go take a look," said Theresa. She jumped out of the carriage and skipped along the road over to where the animal had appeared. Terrance and Aiden were quick to follow.

"Excuse me. Hello? Is someone there?" asked Theresa as she approached the spot where she saw the animal.

"Yes, I'm here," said a tiny voice. A small head, covered in white and gray fur, popped out from within the grass. "My name is Mr. Hairold Bunnymunch. Pleased to make your acquaintance. What's your name?"

"I'm Theresa Silverglade, and these are my brothers, Terrance and Aiden. Pleased to make your acquaintance, too, Mr. Bunnymunch. May I ask why you are out here munching away on the grass in the middle of the Cypress Savannah?"

"Well I'm a bunnymunch, so love to munch on anything. We bunnymunches will eat just about anything, because everything is so tasty. We live here in the Cypress Savannah because we can be useful here. It's our job to keep unwanted plants from invading and from keeping the native plants from growing too much and crowding out the other plants. We're very careful about what we eat, because we don't want to cause anyone trouble. The others who live here in the savannah were pleased when we moved here a long time ago because they needed help with maintaining the savannah's beauty," said Mr. Bunnymunch.

"Is that how you're different from regular bunnies? I've never met a bunnymunch before." said Terrance.

"That's one of the ways we're different. We also prefer warmer climates than does the typical bunny and our kisses can heal small wounds. Some say that our kisses are very peaceful-making, too," said Mr. Bunnymunch.

"You look like you have very soft fur, Mr. Bunnymunch. May I please pet your back?" asked Theresa.

"Yes, you may, Miss Theresa. Bunnymunches enjoy being petted," said Mr. Bunnymunch as he hopped out of the grass towards Theresa.

CHAPTER SIX

Theresa reached down and petted Mr. Bunnymunch. His fur was as soft as the finest silk. "You have a very nice coat, Mr. Bunnymunch, but doesn't it get rather warm here in the hot savannah?" she said.

"Thank you, Miss Theresa. No, it doesn't get too warm for us bunnymunches. We like the warmth so much that our fur coats don't bother us one bit. What brings the three of you to the Cypress Savannah?" said Mr. Bunnymunch.

"We are on our way to the Silver Tower. We have a crop of Silver Lilies we hope to sell there," said Aiden.

"That's an excellent place to sell Silver Lilies. I'm sure they'll buy them from three nice children, like you. The tower is very lovely. Its land has many munchable plants that are very tasty, although I would never munch on them without asking permission first," said Mr. Bunnymunch.

"Have you been to the Silver Tower? Do you know where it is?" asked Aiden.

"We only know it's somewhere to the south. No one seems to know any more of its whereabouts than that. Any help you could give us in finding the tower would be most appreciated," added Terrance.

"Of course I know where the Silver Tower is! I could never forget a place with no many marvelous munchies. I would love to go there again. Even if I don't get permission to munch I'd love to see the Great Garden again and enjoy its splendor for a while," said Mr. Bunnymunch.

"Oh, Aiden! Why don't we invite our new friend to come along with us? He could be our navigator. We have plenty of room and he's quite small, so he wouldn't take up much space," said Theresa.

"What do you think, Mr. Bunnymunch? Would you like to join us on our journey? We could use the help and we'd love to have the extra company," said Aiden.

"That's very kind of you and I'd be happy to be your navigator. I've been to many places in South Grace, so I know the way very well, although the path is rather straight on to the south from here.

May I quickly pack a few items to take along with me? It will only take me a moment," said Mr. Bunnymunch.

"Of course, Mr. Bunnymunch. We'll wait for you at the carriage. It's just over there," said Aiden as he pointed back to the carriage.

Mr. Bunnymunch hopped off at a surprisingly fast pace. He had forgotten to mention to the children that bunnymunches are also terrifically fast. The children could see the grass divide very quickly in a small path as Mr. Bunnymunch hopped off to his home, which seemed to be quite a long way away.

By the time the children had walked the short distance back to the carriage, Mr. Bunnymunch had already returned. He carried a very small suitcase in his mouth.

"Where may I put my luggage?" asked Mr. Bunnymunch in a muffled voice.

"Allow me, Mr. bunnymunch," said Theresa as she took his tiny suitcase. "Follow me and I'll show you to your room."

When Theresa opened the hatch door on the floor of the carriage and started walked down the stairs, Mr. Bunnymunch was amazed.

"You have an enchanted carriage! How very splendid," said Mr. Bunnymunch.

While Theresa was showing Mr. Bunnymunch to one of the guestrooms, Terrance took the reins and started the carriage off back towards the south.

As the quartet traveled south, they had a pleasant chat about bunnymunches. Mr. Bunnymunch explained more about why bunnymunches are so fast and why they moved to the Cypress Savannah.

"Our quick, superfast hopping helps us to get to places with good munchies more quickly," said Mr. Bunnymunch. "We also had to be very fast hoppers where we used to live before the last Great War. We bunnymunches used to live in the north, in what is now called North Grace. Most of us moved south to the savannah because we needed a place to live that had less wickedness in it. We

Chapter Six

decided to take up residence in the Cypress Savannah because of the Magnificent Magnifying Montezuma Cypress Tree, which keeps out most of the wicked passersby."

"Mrs. Tinkermeyer told us all about the Magnificent Magnifying Montezuma Cypress Tree. It's such a fascinating artifact. I hope that one day we have the opportunity to see it transform into the magnifying glass," said Theresa.

"My bunnymunch friends and I take especially good care of the Magnificent Magnifying Montezuma Cypress Tree. A lot of our munching takes places right around the tree. If anything grows too tall around the tree it could obstruct the view of the magnifying glass, although such plants would have to be tremendously tall to obstruct the view of such a soaring structure … but we like to do whatever we can to be extra cautious to keep out any wicked people. They can cause terrible mischief, you know." said Mr. Bunnymunch.

"I'm very glad you have such a well-protected home, Mr. Bunnymunch. We had our fair share of time with a wicked magicìenne, and we would rather not encounter any more people like her, if we can help it," said Aiden.

"Most people in the world are good, but there are a number who are wicked, and you can't help that. It's just the way people are. Some choose to be good, like us bunnymunches, while others choose to be wicked, like the wicked magicìenne. I do hope she didn't cause you too much trouble. A wicked person with even a little magic can do a lot of troublesome things," said Mr. Bunnymunch.

"She did cause us some trouble, but we were able to manage things just fine, thanks to a kind hummingbird that came to our aid," said Terrance.

That night the children and Mr. Bunnymunch took up camp at the edge of the Cypress Savannah bordering the Majestic Moonlit Mountains, which were so named because of a magical haze that fills the sky every night and enhances the intensity of the moonlight over the entire range. This was also the tallest mountain range in all of South Grace. The mountains were so tall that there were no plants visible more than half the way up most of the mountains. The group felt that it was best to spend the night within the borders of the Cypress Savannah, since the area was safer than the mountains due to the Magnificent Magnifying Montezuma Cypress Tree.

Chapter Seven
The Tree Guard

The Majestic Moonlit Mountains were magnificently majestic even during the day. The children were in awe over the Majesty of the mountains. There was a power to the mountains, almost as if they were royalty of South Grace. In fact, some of the areas higher up in the mountains contained patches of what looked to be royal blue and purple pine snowcone trees.

"What is that man doing over there standing by that tree up ahead?" asked Terrance.

"I'm not sure. He looks like a military officer of some sort … and he seems to be guarding something, but I can't see anything to guard, other than the tree. Let's pull over and inquire of him," said Aiden, who was again driving the carriage. Aiden slowed down the carriage and brought it to a stop along road, about ten feet in front of the man. "Excuse me, sir. We're sorry to bother you, but my brother, sister, and I would like to know why you are standing here. Are you guarding something?"

"Am I guardin' somethin'? Of course I'm guardin' somethin'! What else would I be doing standin' here in the middle of the Majestic Moonlit Mountain Woodlands?" responded the man with a very official, yet rustic, tone to his voice.

"I do apologize if I have offended you, but may I ask what you are guarding? All we see are trees? Is there something hidden nearby we should be made aware of so we don't inadvertently disturb it?" asked Aiden in continuing his inquiry of the man.

"Of course you see trees. That's exactly what I'm guardin'! Do ya see me standin' in front of this tree? Wouldn't ya think I might be guardin' it if I'm standin' directly in front of it with my sword? I am a Tree Guard and I guard this tree," said the man, with his voice starting to change to a more civil and kinder tone once he stated his identity as a Tree Guard. "This is my friend, Wilma. She's a wanderin' wollemi pine tree ... although, come to think of it, I've never seen her do any wanderin', and I've been here some time and would've seen. I never leave her. I provide her with protection and she provides me with everything I need. She's the only one of her kind in this woodland area, so she needs protection and I've been assigned to give it to her."

"That does sound like a wonderful friendship you have with Wilma," said Theresa.

"Why yes, yes it is ... but wait!" said the Tree Guard, returning to his more official tone of voice. "Why would three young children be comin' through here on their own? You ain't working for that wicked witch are ya? I don't want any of that witch's friends comin' near Wilma!"

"No, we are definitely not friends of the wicked witch, Mr. Pommier!" said Mr. Bunnymunch as he jumped up through the door of the carriage floor.

"Well I'll be. Of course ya'all ain't friends of the wicked witch! Mr. Bunnymunch, my fine friend. How you be on this fine day? What brings you and these children through these here woodlands?" said Mr. Pommier, the Tree Guard, in a much friendlier tone of voice.

"I'm quite fine, thank you. We are on our way to the Silver Tower of Oz. My friends have some Silver Lilies to sell and we think they have a good chance of selling them at the Silver Tower. Hello, Wilma. How are you and Wilma doing, Mr. Pommier? Does she still make that scrumptious tea?" said Mr. Bunnymunch.

"We're fine, just fine, my friend. And of course she still makes her tea! Why don't the four of ya step out of your dandy carriage there and come join us for a nice little tea party? Wilma, my sweet, how 'bout whippin' up some of that fine tea of yours for our friend, Mr. Bunnymunch, and his young companions?" asked Mr. Pommier, talking to the tree as he would a dear friend.

In a small hole about chest-high in the trunk of the wandering wollemi pine tree there appeared five wooden teacups.

Chapter Seven

"Thank ya, my sweet," said Mr. Pommier as he reached into the hole and retrieved the cups of tea. He handed one cup to each of the children and placed one on the ground in front of Mr. Bunnymunch.

The children all sat down with Mr. Pommier underneath the wandering wollemi pine tree to enjoy their tea. She provided excellent shade from the sun without obstructing too much of the majestic view.

"Mr. Pommier, who assigned you to protect Wilma?" asked Terrance.

"Frankly, my young lad ... I don't rightly remember. I've been here so long that I've just become accustomed to being here. This is my home, here with Wilma, and I right like it. I especially like Wilma's food. She's very good at makin' things from apples. Oh! You must try her apple pie," said Mr. Pommier. He stood up and went over to the hole in the wandering wollemi pine tree and fetched five pieces of warm apple pie.

"That's very kind of you to keep up with your guardianship even though you can't recollect who sent you here," said Theresa.

"Yes, it's very responsible of you," said Aiden.

"This tea and pie are quite delicious! We could use a tree like Wilma on our farm," said Terrance.

"That will be very hard to do, young Terrance. Ya'see, this is the only wanderin' wollemi pine tree I've ever come across, so you're not likely gonna find one you can git to wander over to your farm," said Mr. Pommier.

"Would you please tell us more about the wicked witch? You said you thought we might be her friends, but we've never met any wicked witches ... unless you're talking about Renée the Wicked Magicìenne, although we're most assuredly not friends with her," said Theresa.

"Oh no, my young lady, it's not Renée. I know of her, and she's just a minor nuisance and nothin' more. I'm talkin' about a powerful wicked witch who had her black heart set on terrorizin' everyone in the Majestic Moonlit Mountains. She used her powers to turn the magic haze that you'll see overhead tonight into a thick storm that blocked out the moonlight, and also the sunlight durin' the day. The mountains didn't look very majestic back then," explained Mr. Pommer.

"If the sky isn't clouded with the storm anymore, then doesn't that mean the wicked witch has more than likely gone away?" asked Aiden.

"I've mentioned that to him before, Aiden, but he's very protective of Wilma and would rather err on the side of caution. You can never be too careful when wicked witches are involved," said Mr. Bunnymunch.

"Well, I reckon you're prob'ly right about that, Aiden ... but, as Mr. Bunnymunch said, I just can't take any chances with Wilma. The last time that wicked witch came around here she tried to set fire to my sweet Wilma! If it hadn't been for that good warlock, who came along just in the nick of time, I right sure would've lost my best friend. That's been several years now ... and come to think of it, it was that night the clouds turned back into the normal haze," said Mr. Pommier.

"Then I think you and Wilma are probably safe now, but how horrible that she tried to set fire to Wilma! The wicked magicienne tried to do the same thing to us, but a lovely hummingbird came to our rescue. I guess we both had unexpected friends come to our aid from wicked people. It's just not nice to send fire after someone to try to hurt her. Just because she's a tree doesn't make her any less important than anyone else," said Theresa.

"Quite right! Oh, I hate to think about what could've happened to poor Wilma, here. That wicked witch — and I never found out her name — kept shootin' fireball after fireball at Wilma. I was sure she and I both were goners. That storm was somethin' awful fierce that day. It was almost black as night! That good warlock had some real talent to him, he did. He blocked every one of those fireballs from touchin' my sweet Wilma," said Mr. Pommier.

"Do you know why she was attacking Wilma?" asked Aiden.

Chapter Seven

"Well ... no, I have no idea. I suppose it's just because she was a wicked witch. Those wicked witches will attack anyone and anything on a whim. They don't care about anyone but themselves. Wilma is the prettiest tree in the woodlands, at least in my opinion, so maybe the wicked witch was jealous of her or somethin'. Then again, maybe she was just attackin' everyone in the Majestic Moonlit Mountains. That storm really was mighty fierce that day, and from what I could tell it was at least that bad everywhere else in the whole mountain range. Now that I think of it, I'd bet that wicked witch was tryin' for a final assault on all of us mountain dwellers so she could be queen of the range. As far as I'm concerned, that job's already taken. Wilma is the Queen of the Majestic Moonlit Mountains, as far as I see her, and that means the wicked witch had no right to take claim to these mountains. Ya can't just take somethin' that's not yours without permission. It's just not friendly-like. It's not very neighborly. I don't mind someone livin' here in the mountains, cuz there's plenty of room for everyone, just as long as they show some respect to the rest of us," said Mr. Pommier.

"I do hope we never meet up with that wicked witch. I'm sure that good warlock got rid of her, though. He sounds like he was a good neighbor and wouldn't have stopped until the wicked witch was gone. Anyways, since that storm hasn't been around for some time, I expect that neither has the wicked witch been around," said Terrance.

A creaking sound started to come from the wandering wollemi pine tree and the tree began to shake, but only for a moment.

"Why thank you for the reminder, my sweet Wilma! That was Wilma remindin' me that in a few short minutes the herd of Sapphire Squirrels will be comin' through these parts, and you don't wanna be here when they come. Mind you, they're friends of ours and they never hurt any of the plants through here. They always give Wilma and me plenty of space, as a precaution. It's just that it gets mighty crowded and your carriage might git in their way. It would be right kind of ya if ya could move your carriage so they can run through without anything in their path," said Mr. Pommier.

"We'd be happy to oblige," said Aiden. "Come one everyone, let's get back into the carriage and be on our way. We need to keep heading south towards the Silver Tower. Thank you so much for your hospitality, Mr. Pommier. And thank you, Wilma, for being such a pleasant hostess to us. If you ever find your way wandering through the Village of Illume, please pay us a visit at the Silverglade Family Farm."

"Likewise, my young friends. You and Mr. Bunnymunch must come back and join us again for tea and pie. Now ya'd best be off right quick before those Sapphire Squirrels arrive. You take care! Bye now!" said Mr. Pommier.

The children and Mr. Bunnymunch quickly returned to the carriage and headed off towards the south, with Aiden again at the reins. The children and Mr. Pommier all waved as the carriage rode off into the distance, gently ascending a road up through the Majestic Moonlit Mountains with the faint rumbling of the heard of Sapphire Squirrels sounding from not too far away.

Chapter Eight
The "Good Witch" of the Majestic Moonlit Mountains

The Silverglade children and Mr. Bunnymunch had spent several days traveling within the Majestic Moonlit Mountains. Each night they had taken a little extra time to enjoy the Majestic beauty of the magic haze that enhanced the moonlight over the entire mountain range.

By now the four were very far into the mountains, although there was still no end to the mountain range in sight. Theresa was taking a turn at the reins this time.

"I do hope we don't go up so high into the mountains again. Yesterday was so very cold. It was quite pretty, but I prefer this warm weather down here in the valleys," said Theresa. She almost shivered at the thought of the cold that she had experienced the previous day.

"I think we are all in agreement with you, Theresa," said Aiden.

"Most assuredly! We bunnymunches do not like the cold. The warm air in these valleys is much more pleasing to us. There is also much nicer flora in these valleys. Some of my most favorite trees are in this valley. There's one right now!" said Mr. Bunnymunch, as he used his paw to point to the west side of the road. "That is called a Spectral Pandanus Tree. It catches the moonlight at night and glows a brilliant shade of turquoise as it releases the light, even during the day."

"Oh yes, Mr. Bunnymunch. That is a particularly nice-looking tree," said Theresa. "Is that a path I see just on the other side of it?"

"I do believe you are correct, my little one. Why don't you stop us just in front of it so we can see where it goes?" said Aiden.

Theresa stopped the carriage in front of the small road coming off of South Grace Road. The road went a few hundred feet into

The "Good Witch"
of the Majestic Moonlit Mountains

the woods and then took a turn to the north. The view of the road beyond that point was hidden by the thick forest.

"I think I see a meadow just starting right were the road curves … and … isn't that a lunch pail tree back in there?" said Terrance.

"Very good, Terrance! You are correct. That is a lunch pail tree. I believe it's a dessert lunch pail tree. They only produce lunch pails that contain dessert. Theresa, would you like to drive us there so we can pick a few lunch pails for ourselves?" said Aiden.

"With pleasure!" said Theresa.

Theresa guided the carriage slowly down the small road so they could look at the other trees and plants along the way. When they reached the lunch pail tree, Aiden jumped out of the carriage and proceeded to pick some ripe lunch pails. He retrieved enough so there were two dessert lunch pails for each one of them.

"I think Terrance was correct when he said he saw a meadow. Look! There's a small one just around this corner," said Mr. Bunnymunch.

After Aiden returned to the carriage, Theresa drove the vehicle further along the road and into the meadow.

"It's a cottage! This is someone's home," said Theresa.

The cottage was situated in the middle of the meadow, with the road ending directly in front of the cottage. Around the small edifice was a white picket fence. Enclosed by the fence was a yard with a small garden filled with a variety of flowers and multicolored trees. The cottage itself looked like it was completely covered with White Angel Lilies, which produced a magical, dream-like, white glow around the structure. The only surfaces of the cottage that could be seen were the white, wooden handle on the front door and several windows that remained mostly uncovered, except for a few, overlapping White Angel Lilies. The flowers were very attractive to the several species of butterflies and birds that were playing in the yard.

Chapter Eight

"We should knock on the door and see if anyone's home. I wouldn't want to find that we have stolen those dessert lunch pails by accident. If we discover that we have then we should immediately return them," said Aiden.

"That we must!" agreed Mr. Bunnymunch. "Miss Theresa, would you like to knock on the door for us?"

"Certainly, Mr. Bunnymunch," said Theresa.

All four of them went to the door of the cottage and Theresa knocked on the wooden area of the White Angel Lily vines that were covering the door.

The door opened and there stood a woman who was clothed in a stunning, white, silk gown with a pointed, white, silk hat on her head. Her hair perfectly matched the color of her clothing, although it seemed to be somewhat tucked up inside of her hat.

"Well, hello there, kind strangers. I was just about to sit down for nice lunch. Would you care to join me? It's no bother. I have as much food as I could ever need and I would love the company," said the women in a very gentle voice.

"Why thank you for the kind invitation, we'd happily join you, but first we need to confess to an accidental theft that we may have committed. Before we noticed your cottage here we took eight lunch pails from your dessert lunch pail tree. Had we seen your home and realized that the tree may have belonged to someone we surely would have first asked your permission. We do apologize if we have done you any wrong," said Aiden.

"Yes, we do apologize," said the twins in unison.

"Well, don't think anything of it, dearies. Those lunch pails are for anyone to take. You may take as many as you please. Now where are my manners? I haven't introduced myself to you, yet. My name is Lilibeth, and I am the Good Wizardess of the Majestic Moonlit Mountains," said the woman.

"It's a pleasure to meet you, Lilibeth. My name is Theresa Silverglade, and I am very excited to meet a good wizardess. These are my brothers, Terrance and Aiden. This is our friend, Mr.

The "Good Witch"
of the Majestic Moonlit Mountains

Bunnymunch. We are passing through on our way to the Silver Tower," said Theresa.

"The Silver Tower? Well, isn't that lovely. Please, you must come inside and join me for lunch. You must be exhausted from your journey, and you'll need to keep up your strength to make it through to the other side of these mountains. Please do come in," said Lilibeth.

The children and Mr. Bunnymunch entered the cottage. It was just as beautiful on the inside as it was on the outside. The walls seemed to be covered in some sort of white, silk fabric. There were several paintings on the walls of people who looked like they must have been relatives of Lilibeth. Various tropical plants were scattered throughout the cottage. Lilibeth escorted the Silverglades and Mr. Bunnymunch over to her dining table, which was sufficient in size enough to seat eight persons. It was rather large for the dimensions of her cottage, but it still fit into the home quite adequately. The table was covered with a white, silk tablecloth and was completely set with fancy, yet simple, mother-of-pearl dishes. At the center of the table was a bouquet of White Angel Lilies. On the sides of the lilies along the length of the table were two, silver candle holders that each contained a tall, white candle that looked to be made of Angel Bee's Wax.

Lilibeth snapped her fingers and the Angel Bee's Wax candles lit. They each had a magical, white flame that had an entrancing dance to it. Lilibeth then waved her hand over the table and a full meal suddenly appeared. The children and Mr. Bunnymunch had no idea what any of the food was, except for the white cupcakes that were packed high with white icing in the shape of White Angel Lilies; however, it all had a highly pleasing aroma to it and looked very appetizing.

"What a lovely meal!" exclaimed Theresa.

"And what a magnificent home you have, too, Lilibeth. You must take very good care of it," said Aiden.

Chapter Eight

"Well thank you, my kind strangers, but it's all in the magic. Certain things like cleaning are made a lot simpler when you know the right spells to use. Now let's all sit down and enjoy this nice meal together. Don't be afraid, just go ahead and dig in. There's plenty more if you turn out to be extra hungry. My magic can produce as much food as we need," said Lilibeth.

The children ate until they were full. Mr. Bunnymunch ate until he was no longer hungry. Bunnymunches are never full, but they don't like to be rude and overeat when they are guests in a person's home.

After their lunch, Lilibeth invited the four friends outside to her garden to sit and chat about their journey.

"Now children, please do tell me about your journey to the Silver Tower. Why are you going there? It's very brave of you to be traveling so far on your own ... and it's very nice of Mr. Bunnymunch to help look after you," said Lilibeth.

"We are on our way there to make our parents proud of us by selling our crop of Silver Lilies," said Terrance.

"Silver Lilies? I've never heard of those. I already have plenty of lilies here, so I won't be able to purchase any from you, but I'm sure you will have great success at the Silver Tower. They need all kinds of resources there for their research," said Lilibeth.

"We're also taking a letter from Botania the Good Witch to the Silver Tower. She asked us if we would deliver it to the Lady Thorn and Lady Thistle. They are her colleagues and she has some questions to ask of them," said Terrance.

"How very kind of you to deliver the letter for Botania. I'm sure she's very grateful for your assistance. Since you are doing a favor for her and delivering her letter, perhaps you could do me a small favor. I am in need of an enchantment unbinding, or disenchantment, spell. Could you please ask the residents of the Silver Tower if they could give you one to send to me? I'm sure they have an artifact they'd let you borrow and use on me," said Lilibeth.

The "Good Witch"
of the Majestic Moonlit Mountains

"You've been so very kind to us and provided us with an absolutely wonderful meal, so we'd be very happy to help you," said Aiden.

"Why would you need an unbinding spell? Can't you use your own magic to do that?" asked Theresa.

"Well, my dear, I'm only a wizardess, so although I can unbind weaker enchantments I'm not able to unbind the enchantment that a wicked warlock cast on me," replied Lilibeth.

"A wicked warlock? I thought it was a wicked witch who once lived in these mountains," said Theresa.

"There certainly was once a wicked witch who resided here, but there is also a wicked warlock who still lives here. He's hidden away and doesn't cause much trouble nowadays, but I very much would like to rid myself of this pesky little enchantment," said Lilibeth.

"What kind of enchantment is it? I hope it doesn't cause you any harm. We once encountered a wicked magicièҮne, and she tried to harm us. Magic should never be used to hurt others," said Terrance.

"The enchantment prevents me from going beyond my white, picket fence. I can't even use my magic to bring me one of those delicious dessert lunch pails from the dessert lunch pail tree down the road. The warlock has blocked my magic from working beyond the fence, too. Don't misunderstand me; I love my little home and my little garden. I have almost everything I need here, except for freedom. I would love to visit some of my family and do some traveling like the four of you are doing. If you could help me I'd be very grateful to you," said Lilibeth.

"Of course we'll help. As soon as we've sold our Silver Lilies we'll head back this way with great haste, and we'll have an unbinding artifact with us for you to use to regain your freedom. Everyone has the right to be free," said Aiden.

"Thank you so much. You've made me very happy. There's just one other thing. Please don't mention me to anyone at the

Chapter Eight

Silver Tower. It's not that I don't want them to know it's me, but I'm just afraid that the wicked warlock will somehow find out, and then he might figure out a way to prevent the unbinding artifact from working. I just want to be sure that the unbinding will work. You can never be too careful when it comes to a wicked warlock. I also have reason to believe that he made the enchantment so that it would worsen if I were to talk to another magic user about it or if anyone mentions my predicament to anyone in the Silver Tower," said Lilibeth.

"We completely understand, Miss Lilibeth. I'm a bunnymunch, so I know what it's like to be burdened by a wicked magic user. It's a terrible experience that I would never wish on anyone. We will do our best to find you an unbinding artifact at the Silver Tower so you can be free. We will also keep your secret so that wicked warlock won't find out and try to disrupt your plans to become liberated from his evil enchantment" said Mr. Bunnymunch.

"I would so much appreciate my freedom. Before the wicked warlock enchanted me I was able to use my magic throughout the Majestic Moonlit Mountains. I spent my time making the entire mountain range very pretty. If you think the mountains look good now you should have seen them back in the day when I was not restrained by this pesky little enchantment. My magic was known throughout the land because of my power to beautify everything. It's very difficult for me to have such a limited area for my magic now. There's only so much a wizardess can do with a land as small as this property. Although I have managed to keep this place very pretty and tidy with what limited access I have. One day I hope to travel all around the Majestic Moonlit Mountains and transform them back into the truly Majestic range that they once were when I was free," explained Lilibeth.

"Why don't we head out now so we can make sure to come back as soon as possible," said Mr. Bunnymunch.

"Yes, let's return to our journey. We have a lot of important tasks to do at the Silver Tower, so it's even more imperative that we arrive there as soon as possible. We will come back as soon as we can, Lilibeth," said Aiden.

"Thank you very much, kind strangers. But before you go, would you mind running over to that delicious dessert lunch pail tree and bringing me back one or two lunch pails? I've been wanting to taste one of them again for a long time now," said Lilibeth.

"We'd be delighted to help," said Aiden.

All three of the children quickly ran over to the dessert lunch pail tree and filled their arms with as many dessert lunch pails as they could.

"Oh thank you, my dearies. This should easily last me until you return … even if I eat them at every meal," said Lilibeth.

The children and Mr. Bunnymunch returned to the carriage. Aiden took the reins and prepared to depart.

"Will you all be able to find your way back here? This road can be very easy to miss," said Lilibeth.

"Don't you worry, Lilibeth. We will be able to find the road because of the Spectral Pandanus Tree located at the opening of the road. Mr. Bunnymunch pointed it out to us, which is how we found your home in the first place," said Aiden.

"Yes, I will be able to recognize it best of all, because Spectral Pandanus Trees are one of my most favorite trees. There's no way I could miss it on our way along the South Grace Road," said Mr. Bunnymunch.

Off went the carriage, past the dessert lunch pail tree and along the small road back to the South Grace Road.

The children decided that since Lilibeth was in such need of their help that it would be wise to pick up their speed a bit. They had been traveling at a casual pace so that they could enjoy the magnificence of the landscape in South Grace. Now they were going to go as fast as their carriage could manage for the remainder of the trip.

Chapter Nine

Weathered

Several more days had passed by, and the carriage had yet to clear the Majestic Moonlit Mountains. The range was quite massive. Aiden was driving the carriage as fast as he could; however, this was only one-quarter of the speed that the carriage was capable of doing. The Silverglade children and Mr. Bunnymunch were now traveling higher up in the mountains, although they were not at a cold altitude this time. South Grace Road was very winding at this stage of the journey, so Aiden couldn't take the carriage up to more than a quarter of its full speed for fear of going off the road.

The sky was beginning to turn dark, yet it was early in the afternoon. A storm was approaching.

"Aiden, I think I just heard thunder in the distance," said Terrance.

"So did I," said Theresa.

"And so did I. Let me know if you see a good place for me to pull over where we can take cover. This wind is picking up a bit and I don't want the carriage to be blown away, especially not while were hiding from the storm inside of it," said Aiden, partly in jest.

The wind quickly became fierce in its strength. Theresa and Terrance held on to the carriage out of fear of being blown away, although the wind was not yet forceful enough to carry them off.

A loud flash of lightning appeared just off the road to the right of carriage. It was accompanied by a deep booming and crackling. The Silverglades and Mr. Bunnymunch all jumped from the shock of the close lightning strike. A nearby tree had been struck.

"We need to find good shelter soon ...," said Aiden once he had taken a moment to recover from the fearfully-close lightning.

After a few minutes the group noticed a cave off of the side of the road.

"I see a cave over there, to the left," said Mr. Bunnymunch.

"That looks like as good a place as any, and I think the carriage will just about fit inside of it," said Aiden.

Aiden guided the carriage into the cave just in time. Immediately after they entered another loud crash of lightning was heard, making all four of them jump again. Quickly the rain started to pour down, accompanied by a very powerful wind that howled outside of the cave entrance.

"Why don't you all head inside of the carriage. I'm going to wait out here just to make sure the wind doesn't decide to come inside and do its mischief to the carriage," said Aiden, being the protective big brother that he was.

"I'm staying with you, Aiden. We can watch the carriage together. Besides, you might need my help in case the wind really does become bad," said Terrance.

"I'm staying outside, too. I'm not leaving my family alone, out in this storm. It's kind of scary, but I still find the lightning to be rather pretty … even if it does make me jump," said Theresa.

"Perhaps I will stay outside as well. I'd rather not be lonely inside the carriage all by myself," said Mr. Bunnymunch.

"You can sit with me, Mr. Bunnymunch. I'll be happy to pet you, if you'll let me," said Theresa.

Mr. Bunnymunch climbed up into Theresa's lap and laid down so she could pet him. Over the past few days they had become especially close friends, because she very much enjoyed stroking his silky-soft fur.

While they were waiting for the storm to subside, Aiden came up with a plan to calm everyone down, since he could tell that the twins weren't all that comfortable with the ferocity of the storm.

"Terrance, I have an idea. I think this would be an excellent opportunity to try some of those dessert lunch pails. Would you please run into the carriage really quickly and bring back four of the lunch pails for us?" said Aiden.

Chapter Nine

"Perfect!" said Terrance. He then quickly disappeared down through the door of the carriage floor. A moment later he reappeared with four dessert lunch pails in his hands, three of which he distributed to his brother, sister, and Mr. Bunnymunch.

Aiden's idea worked. It calmed everyone down very effectively. They all became used to the loud noises, because they felt safe being inside the cave with family and friends.

"Since we appear to have a lot of time on our hands, as this storm does not want to let up, I'd like to know what happened to your parents, if you're willing to discuss the matter with me. All I know is that they became lost and they now have their three wonderful children who are on a journey to the Silver Tower with the goal of making their parents proud … and helping out a few friends along the way," said Mr. Bunnymunch.

"The matter is fine to be discussed. Although we miss our parents, we do enjoy talking about them," said Theresa.

"They're only lost, so we know they'll eventually return to us. Botania the Good Witch told us so, which is why we're not all that worried about them … or even about ourselves, for that matter. We are just happy to know they will be returning to us. What happened to our parents is that they become lost one night. They went out one evening just after the harvest last year to take one of their usual walks in the Silver Lily field. Aiden saw them at the top of the mountain where the field is. He looked away for a moment and when he looked back they were gone. That's when they became lost. Although we do suppose it's possible they went down the far side of the mountain and became lost after that. Regardless of the precise moment when they became lost, they did become lost that evening and we haven't seen them ever since," said Terrance.

"Nor has anyone else. Maybe they were called away to some far off place where they were greatly needed and they couldn't tell us … or maybe they just don't realize they've been gone for as long as they have. They always did enjoy their walks and would sometimes stay out for many hours walking around the farm and the neighboring lands," said Theresa.

"Nevertheless, we aren't upset with them for being lost. It's not their fault. We're just happy, as Terrance said, they're coming back to us one day. We have each other for now, so we still have family with us at all times," said Aiden.

"We also have good friends, like Mr. Bunnymunch," said Theresa as she gave Mr. Bunnymunch an extra-nice scratching behind his ear, which caused him to close his eyes and thump his hind leg against the inner side of the carriage.

When Theresa was done scratching behind Mr. Bunnymunch's ear, he responded to their story, "I'm very sorry that your parents have become lost, but I'm also very happy for you that you're handling their lostness in such a mature manner. I can tell from what you've said about them during our time together so far that they love you immensely, so I'm sure they're incredibly proud of you for all you're doing ... especially with traveling so very far for the good of the family. They'd be so very pleased to see their children working together as you are to reach the Silver Tower of Oz, and helping so many new friends along the way."

Just then, a large gust of wind blew a small piece of wood into the cave. The wood landed in Terrance's lap.

"That's strange," said Terrance.

"What's strange? Are you ok?" asked Aiden, who was worried that his brother may have been injured by the flying debris.

"K-A-N-S-A-S ... Kansas. The piece of wood has the word *Kansas* written across it. What's a Kansas?" asked Terrance.

"I don't know. I've never seen a Kansas before. Maybe it's a type of wood," said Aiden.

"I think it's a person's name. The wood must have come from the sign of a store or shoppe and it bears the owner's name. Mr. Kansas or Mrs. Kansas is probably looking for the sign. It's pretty writing. I hope Mr. or Mrs. Kansas is able to make a new sign for the shoppe," said Mr. Bunnymunch.

The storm continued to rage right outside of the cave entrance. After several hours, the storm began to weaken, but it continued to rain. The group of four decided to spend the night in the cave.

Chapter Nine

Aiden had retrieved some rope from inside the carriage, tying one end to the carriage and the other end to a large boulder inside of the cave, which he did in order to prevent any wind from carrying off the carriage while they slept inside of it.

That night, all three children had very sweet dreams of their parents, because they had enjoyed sharing their story with Mr. Bunnymunch.

Chapter Ten
The Black and White Lotus Bog

Another couple of days had passed. The children and Mr. Bunnymunch had finally reached the south side of the Majestic Moonlit Mountains. What was on the other side of the mountains, they could not quite tell. The region looked as though it may be relatively flat. Aiden suspected it to be another savannah, since there were sporadic trees sticking up from the vapors. As they descended the final hill, a foul smelled began to fill the air.

"What is that horrible aroma?!" exclaimed Terrance.

"It smells of ... sulfur," said Aiden.

"This is the Black and White Lotus Bog. South Grace Road goes right through the center of the bog. The smell is bad, but it won't hurt you. Just hold your nose and breathe through your mouth. You also can't see the bog from this distance at this time of the morning due to the fog. When we get closer you'll be able to see where the road continues and how it's surrounded by bog on both sides. The carriage will remain quite safe if we stick to the South Grace Road. In fact, we're safe even if we fall off the road. All of the many people and creatures that reside within the Black and White Lotus Bog are very friendly and would surely help us at the first sign of trouble ... although they are very shy," said Mr. Bunnymunch.

"I do hope we have the opportunity to meet some of the residents of the Black and White Lotus Bog. A person could always use more friends," said Theresa.

"That's not likely to happen," said Mr. Bunnymunch as he twitched his nose in a mildly disgusted way, since he had accidentally inhaled through his nose rather than his mouth. "The residents tend to stay very hidden here. They still have some paranoia from the last Great War. If you look to the east, you can see the Kitten Kudzu Mountain.

Chapter Ten

"That's a very interesting mountain. How did it come to find itself in a bog?" asked Aiden.

"It's not a natural mountain, that's why. That mountain used to be the home of the Forgotten Wicked Witch, whose name everyone forgot after the last Great War. Her home was there. It's said that two great and powerful good sorceresses conquered the witch by burying her home under a large mountain of Kitten Kudzu, which purrs as it grows. The Kitten Kudzu also destroyed the illusionary army of the Forgotten Wicked Witch. She used her army to terrorize and control all of the bog, which wasn't a bog back then. The bog was created to help keep all wicked witches, wicked magicians, wicked wizards, and the like away from the black and white lotuses. The Forgotten Wicked Witch figured out a way to use the black and white lotuses to help create her illusionary army. Now the bog, and even this early morning fog, are toxic to all wicked magic users. They melt as soon as they touch it. Many ages ago legend says that all water would melt wicked witches, but an enchantment was created that protects them from most waters. This bog has an enchantment on it to restore the toxicity of these waters to wicked witches. Even with the protection of the bog, the people and creatures here are all still very afraid of wicked people, and don't like to leave their homes and hiding places unless it's necessary," said Mr. Bunnymunch.

"I think I can understand why they are paranoid; although I would most probably not have been able to understand were we to have never encountered that wicked magiciènne. I couldn't imagine what powerfully wicked things a wicked witch could do as compared to a wicked magicènne ... and I'd rather not think about it either," said Terrance.

"Do you know the names of the good sorceresses who created the Kitten Kudzu Mountain?" asked Theresa.

"I'm afraid I don't, Miss Theresa. Their names seem to have been forgotten along with the name of the Forgotten Wicked Witch ... so I guess you would be safe to call them the Forgotten Good Sorceresses," replied Mr. Bunnymunch.

The Black and White Lotus Bog

As Mr. Bunnymunch continued to tell the children about the Kitten Kudzu Mountain – like how the kittens would sometimes bat at the early morning fog – the four travelers entered into the Black and White Lotus Bog. Once they reached the bog itself they were able to see the strangely dark yet clear water of the bog. As far as they could see, which was limited due to the fog, there were black and white lotuses on the water. Along with the fog the flowers gave an eerie prettiness to the bog. Every so often they thought they saw momentary flickers of light coming from the black and white lotus flowers; however, the lights may have just been a false illusion caused by the water and the clearing fog.

A few minutes into their journey through the Black and White Lotus Bog, the friends began to hear an eerie clicking noise coming from in the distance.

"What's that clicking sound?" asked Aiden.

"No one knows what it is, but it is often heard near the bog," commented Mr. Bunnymunch.

"I don't like it. It's creeping me out," said Theresa.

The noise became louder and louder. It soon sounded as though it were coming from just a few feet away from the carriage. The clicking reverberated throughout the bog and sounded as though it were examining the friends.

"What's making the sound?! It's so close but I can't see anything!" cried out Terrance in fear.

"Aiden! Go faster!" shouted Theresa.

"No, Aiden. We'll be just fine. It does this to some people who pass through here, but it's completely harmless. It will stop in just a moment," said Mr. Bunnymunch.

"It's scaring my brother and my sister, so I'm going to get us out of here," said Aiden, not wanting to admit to the twins that he too was rather scared, since such an admission would probably increase their fear.

Before Aiden could accelerate the carriage, the clicking stopped.

Chapter Ten

"See, it was nothing harmful. It was just a noise. I think it has something to do with the bog gases, or whatever. It's nothing to concern you. Noises can't touch you," said Mr. Bunnymunch.

This was the last that the friends heard the eerie clicking sounds that day.

It took the travelers about half a day to cross the Black and White Lotus Bog, which led them to another mountain range, for which Mr. Bunnymunch was not aware of a particular name. Not once during their travels along South Grace Road within the Black and White Lotus Bog did the travelers see any signs of life, other than plants. Although the scariness of the Spike Trees caused the twins to think that they may have seen a few dark figures watching them.

By the time that the Silverglades and Mr. Bunnymunch reached the far side of the bog, they all smelled of sulfur. It was fortunate for them that Botania the Good Witch had enchanted the carriage with cleaning magic; otherwise, the carriage would also have smelled of sulfur. As soon as they were far enough up the side of the next mountain to be relatively certain that they were no longer in an area with air affected by the bog's aroma, they all jumped back into the carriage in order to take advantage of the cleaning enchantment, which quickly removed all of the sulfur scent from each of them.

Chapter Eleven
Lady Thorn and Lady Thistle

"Mr. Bunnymunch, if I might ask, when will we be venturing off of the South Grace Road? It seems to me that if most people don't know where the Silver Tower is to be located then it can't be seen from the South Grace Road," said Aiden.

Mr. Bunnymunch let out a tiny little giggle in response to Aiden's question. "That is a very good question indeed! Once we make it over this mountain, you will understand why most no one knows where the Silver Tower is located … even though the South Grace Road leads directly to the front gates of the Silver Tower of Oz, although it does extend a little further south from there."

"How can that be? Have so few people traveled this far south that no one knows what lies in this region of South Grace?" asked Theresa.

"Be patient, Miss Theresa, and you will see in a few minutes when we reach the other side of the mountain," said Mr. Bunnymunch.

As the carriage reached the other side of the mountain the curiosity of the children climaxed … especially because there was nothing to see but forest.

"I don't see anything here but a forest. Is this forest enchanted? Is there a secret path that we can't see?" asked Aiden, as he was confused since they had arrived on the other side of the mountain where Mr. Bunnymunch had said they would see why the Silver Tower's location was unknown to most people.

"This is a garden, not a forest!" exclaimed Theresa all of a sudden. "Look! There are a lot of plants growing among the trees and they look awfully well-organized for a forest."

Chapter Eleven

"That's right, Miss Theresa. This is a garden. These plants will only grow in the shadows of these umbrella trees," said Mr. Bunnymunch.

A very short way into the woods, Terrance noticed some large mushrooms that had copper-looking objects dangling from them. He approached them to further examine this oddity. As he kneeled on the grown he realized very quickly what the dangling objects were.

"Nails ... these mushrooms are growing nails. Mr. Bunnymunch, why would anyone grow mushrooms that produce nails?" asked Terrance.

"Why else? Because we need nails," replied a lady who seemed to have been tending plants on the other side of a large umbrella tree.

"Oh, that makes sense. Thank you, miss," said Terrance as he realized how obvious the answer was.

The lady was wearing clothing that made it obvious to anyone that she had a great love of plants. In fact, she looked like she could even be a plant herself. She was wearing what could be best described as a gown of fabric, thistle vines, although that did not quite describe the almost magical nature of her clothing. Atop her head was a tiara made of thistles that were in full bloom.

"You are very welcome, young Terrance. Most people who come across this garden never notice the nails growing from the mushrooms. You should be proud of yourself for your keen sense of observation," said the lady.

"We have always been proud of him for everything he has done," said Aiden, as he approached Terrance and the lady.

"Thorn, sweetie, it seems that our guests have arrived," said the lady.

"... and right on time," said another lady who had been tending to plants just beyond another one of the larger umbrella trees.

This lady was rather similar in appearance to the lady with the thistle tiara; however, this other lady had a theme of thorns to her attire, with a tiara of thorns atop her head instead of a tiara of thistles. The thorn tiara was in full bloom with white roses.

"Excuse me miss, but how did you know my name?" asked Terrance as he suddenly realized that he had not mentioned his name to the lady.

"We'll we've been expecting you, that's how I knew your name," said the lady with the thistle tiara.

"Of course you know our names! You are the Ladies Thistle and Thorn," said Mr. Bunnymunch.

"Mr. Bunnymunch, it is a pleasure to see you again. I was just collecting some of our munchmoss for you to have as a little snack," said Lady Thorn as she reached into one of her many hidden pockets and pulled out a small, wooden bowl. She placed the bowl on the ground in front of Mr. Bunnymunch.

"Oh thank you, Lady Thorn!" said Mr. Bunnymunch as he quickly began to scarf down the bowl of munchmoss.

"It's no problem at all, and please take the bowl, too. It was made just for you," said Lady Thistle.

Mr. Bunnymunch was quick to eat the bowl that was specially prepared for him. He found both the munchmoss and the bowl, which looked to be made of umbrella tree wood, to be quite appetizing.

"Now, unless my ears deceived me, I believe the young Theresa determined this to be a garden. She is indeed correct. This is the Great Garden. Lady Thistle and I tend to it, as we do adore nature," said Lady Thorn.

"Doesn't that mean we're near the Silver Tower of Oz?" asked Aiden.

"Of course you're near the Silver Tower of Oz," said Lady Thistle.

"That is where South Grace Road leads just before it takes you to the ocean. You just can't see the Silver Tower from here, yet," said Lady Thorn.

"… because this forest blocks the view of it from here," said Lady Thistle in finishing Lady Thorn's sentence.

Chapter Eleven

"Aiden, let's not forget the letter from Botania. She wanted us to present it to Lady Thistle and Lady Thorn for her," said Theresa.

"That's right. Thank you for the reminder, my little one." said Aiden. He quickly ran over to the carriage and retrieved the letter from underneath the cushion seat of the box. "This is a letter from Botania the Good Witch," he said, and he handed the letter to the Ladies.

The Ladies opened the letter together. They both smiled as they started to read it.

"Ah yes, these are very good questions our colleague has. We will prepare a response for her," said Lady Thorn.

"Will you be seeing her again? If so, we can save some trouble and some magic by sending it back with you," said Lady Thistle.

"We'd be happy to deliver your response to her. She has been very nice to us, so it would be no bother at all to retrieve her answers for her. I'm sure we'd all like to visit her again, too," said Aiden.

"Are you Ladies related to Botania? Is that why she thinks of you as colleagues?" asked Terrance.

"Related? Oh I do suppose to the average person we would all look to be related!" said Lady Thistle, as she and Lady Thorn both released a small chuckle.

"We are not blood related, but we are all practitioners of natural magics ... so I suppose in a sense ... we are related through our love for the land," said Lady Thorn.

Terrance also thought that the Ladies and Botania may have shared a similar plant ancestor, as the three women all bore striking resemblances to plants; however, Terrance wasn't about to state his thought out loud, in case it would offend any of the women.

"This is a very lovely garden you have here. Do you have any room for some Silver Lilies? Although I suspect you may already have some considering how big I expect this garden to truly be," asked Aiden. He wasn't about to forget the primary reason for which he and the twins made their journey to the Silver Tower.

"We'll take the entire crop," said the Ladies in unison.

Lady Thorn and Lady Thistle

The three children looked at one another with huge smiles on their faces. Terrance and Theresa quickly flung their arms around the Ladies and hugged them.

"Thank you!" said the twins in unison.

"You'll take the entire crop? That's wonderful! I mean ... thank you so much. I know you'll enjoy having them in your garden. They do add quite a splendorous sight to any homestead," said Aiden, as he tried to not act to overzealously excited. His father had taught him to never act too excited about a sale, because some air of professionalism should be maintained at all times. Aiden wondered if maybe this was perhaps an exception to his father's rule, because he could already tell that the Ladies didn't have much worry for the haughty, professional aspects of life; rather, they seemed to be more in touch with goodness and relationships instead of income.

"We certainly will take the entire crop, and although they will be very beautiful in the Great Garden, we and our many colleagues in the Silver Tower can think of quite a few uses for them in our antiquarian and contraptorix projects," said Lady Thorn.

"Terrance, my favorite little brother, would you please run back to the carriage and bring me the silver bag?" asked Aiden.

"Gladly!" said Terrance, and he ran off very quickly to the carriage.

"Yes, these Silver Lilies are probably more valuable than you might think," said Lady Thistle. She and Lady Thorn were perfectly honest people, so they weren't about to pay an unfair price to the Silverglade children for their lilies. The Ladies wanted to make sure that the children understood how very valuable their Silver Lilies were, although the Ladies themselves cared very little for financial matters. They valued life and goodness above all other things, which is why they were such good friends with Glinda the Good Sorceress. "I once saw a single Silver Lily sell for ten thousand green coins ... and that lily was not exactly in the best of conditions. You see, Silver Lilies contain the purest of magical silver."

Chapter Eleven

"Regular silver," continued Lady Thorn, "is very beneficial to magic; however, magical silver, particularly from such sources as Silver Lilies, is especially obliging to magical powers ... at least during this Age of Silver, that is. Your lilies are the healthiest Silver Lilies either one of us has ever seen. This is due to the Silver Water you have on your farm. It is the most natural source of nutrition for Silver Lilies, which is why your farm was enchanted so many years ago, but we'll discuss that enchantment at a later time." As Lady Thorn said this, the almost-invisible silver within the tiaras that the Ladies were wearing began to shine, but only for a moment, as the Ladies thought the beauty of the shining would most effectively express their point.

"We had no idea they were anything more than an interesting decoration," said Aiden. "We appreciate your honesty with us. We still don't need very much money for them. We'll be happy to give you our entire crop for much less than ten thousand Green Coins. We'd never be able to spend that much money!"

Aiden, Theresa, and Terrance were all impressed with the unexpected value of their Silver Lilies; however, they all were in agreement that they shouldn't accept more money than what they truly needed. Their farm allowed them to be very self-sufficient, so ten thousand green coins was more than they knew they could spend in their lifetimes.

"Nonsense! We'll gladly pay you for what they are worth. You spent the time carefully tending to your crop and you should be appropriately compensated. We have some money for you and a few items in trade, if you will accept them, back at the Silver Tower," said Lady Thistle.

"We insist that you spend the night, too. Take some time to rest after your very long journey. We have the most comfortable guestrooms in all of Oz at the Silver Tower. You will find them to be quite relaxing. You should really stay a few days before you head out again. That way you can be well-rested for your return travels," said Lady Thorn.

Lady Thorn and Lady Thistle

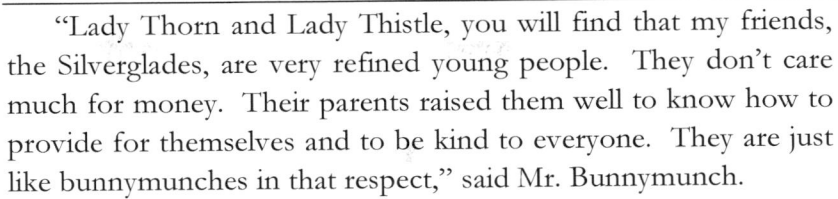

"Lady Thorn and Lady Thistle, you will find that my friends, the Silverglades, are very refined young people. They don't care much for money. Their parents raised them well to know how to provide for themselves and to be kind to everyone. They are just like bunnymunches in that respect," said Mr. Bunnymunch.

"That is why we have a very special form of payment for our new Silverglade friends. After some discussion with Glinda, we have decided to present young Aiden, Terrance, and Theresa here with a Green Coin Poinsettia. It's not like the typical money tree that so many greedy people want. A Green Coin Poinsettia provides you with exactly how much money you need. Not a penny more or a penny less," said Lady Thistle.

"Even so, the Green Coin Poinsettia could easily be abused by the wrong people, but we know you Silverglades to be of fine moral standards, so we know you can be trusted with this plant. You'll always have however much money you need – never more and never less," said Lady Thorn.

"We also have a few magical items that we believe will be of use to you on your journeys, but we will discuss those with you once we return to the Silver Tower and you've had a good night's rest," said Lady Thistle.

"That is so very kind and generous of you! And I do hope we have the opportunity to meet Glinda the Good Sorceress. I would so enjoy asking her a few questions, if she would be so kind as to answer them," said Theresa.

"You will have your opportunity, young Theresa," said Lady Thorn with a pleasant smile across her face.

"This Great Garden of yours was very easy to find. Is the Silver Tower hidden from here? I don't understand how so few people could know where it's located," said Aiden.

"That is an excellent question, young Aiden. Although we can't see the Silver Tower from here, it is not hidden at all. When we reach the edge of the forest, which is just down the road a short way, the Silver Tower will be a very obvious monument. Let us

Chapter Eleven

explain to you. Lady Thorn, my sweet," said Lady Thistle as she reached for Lady Thorn's hand.

As the Ladies' hands connected, their rosewood rings started to glow and the group was surrounded by a fantastic magical view of the Silver Tower and its surrounding lands. The view was absolutely spectacular, as it showed the massive Silver Tower surrounded by an even more massive garden. Aiden was certain that this garden was larger than all of the farms in Oz combined. The property of the Silver Tower that lied tucked away inside of the mountain range was larger than Aiden or the twins could have dreamed.

"This is an eagle's eye perspective of the Silver Tower. The Great Garden takes up nearly all of the land around the structure. The crescent-shaped lake that surrounds the inner part of the garden is called the Forbidden Lake. Don't drink from it, or you'll discover very quickly why so few people know of our location. There are plenty of Angel Fountains throughout the grounds where you can find plenty of drinking water. Even our plants don't drink from the Forbidden Lake. They know better and wait for our regular magical rain showers. And it's best to avoid the streams, too. Some of them are safe, but some are not ... and you don't want to be confusing the two. If you look in front of the Tower, you'll see the Forbidden Fountain. This is where all of the water within the lake comes from. The Forbidden Fountain produces the Water of Oblivion," said Lady Thorn.

"... which erases the memory of anyone who drinks of it," continued Lady Thistle. "If you drink the Water of Oblivion you will immediately forget where the Silver Tower is ... and you'll also forget just about everything else. This is only one of the many ways that Glinda keeps all of us safe here. Now, this whole area really is the Great Garden, even the meadows are part of the garden. We use this entire area to produce everything that we need, whether that be food, clothing, building material, or anything else that we artificers require. We are just like you Silverglades here: we are as self-sufficient as we can possibly be."

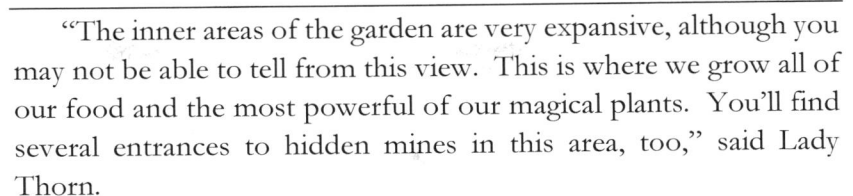

"The inner areas of the garden are very expansive, although you may not be able to tell from this view. This is where we grow all of our food and the most powerful of our magical plants. You'll find several entrances to hidden mines in this area, too," said Lady Thorn.

"We also have many animals that live throughout the grounds. Do remind us to give you a tour of the Meditation Park. I think you'll find it to be quite the amusing place," said Lady Thistle.

With that, the illusionary tour of the Silver Tower came to a conclusion.

"Shall we be on our way now? I'm sure you four would enjoy some time to spend in your rooms relaxing, and then you can join us for dinner. We always serve whatever you're hungry for here at the Silver Tower," said Lady Thorn.

"We have plenty of room in the carriage if you Ladies would like to join us for a ride," said Aiden.

"We would love to!" said the Ladies in unison.

The three Silverglades, Mr. Bunnymunch, Lady Thorn, and Lady Thistle all climbed up onto the carriage.

"Theresa, would you like to have the honor of driving us the rest of the way to the Silver Tower?" asked Aiden.

"Yes, please. I would very much like to have that honor!" said Theresa as she climbed up into the box with Aiden and started the carriage off along the South Grace Road, out of the forest and to the Silver Tower of Oz.

The carriage quickly exited the forest. The woods opened up to an enormous land full of the most exotic plants a person could ever hope to see. Just about every plant in the world could be found somewhere in the Great Garden. As the group continued towards the Silver Tower they realized how tremendously immense the area was and how massive the tower itself was. The ride to the Silver Tower from the edge of the forest took almost a full hour, although Theresa did not drive the carriage very fast, since they all were very taken by the picturesque Silver Tower grounds. She was also very cautious while traversing the bridges over the various streams, since

Chapter Eleven

she did not desire to have any incidences with the Water of Oblivion.

Chapter Twelve
The Silver Tower

The group stood at the gates of the Silver Tower. Mr. Bunnymunch looked straight up, because he was always amazed that from this perspective he could never see the top of the Silver Tower.

The gates opened to a large atrium, although nearly everything about the Silver Tower could be described as large. Inside, the atrium had several attached corridors. Every aspect of the interior of the tower was intricately crafted. The sky above the atrium looked as though it may have been an illusion, because never before had any of the friends seen a sky to be so brilliantly blue. The space was also filled with a variety of very unique plants.

"This is the Grand Atrium," said Lady Thistle.

"Go ahead and examine the plants. You'll be pleasantly surprised," said Lady Thorn.

"Quite so! This is just the beginning of the amazing things you'll see here in the Silver Tower," said Lady Thistle.

The children and Mr. Bunnymunch all approached the nearest tree and examined it closely.

"Isn't this a mist tree?" asked Aiden.

"That's correct, but look at it a little more closely," said Lady Thorn.

"I remember father telling us about mist trees when we were very young. The leaves are actually made of mist," said Terrance.

"Wait … is this … is this silver in the tree?" asked Theresa.

"That it is. If you examine every plant in the Grand Atrium you will find they are all made entirely of silver," said Lady Thistle.

"Even the mist in the mist tree is made of silver. That took some skilled enchanting on the part of two of our Senior Artificers," said Lady Thorn.

Chapter Twelve

The Ladies escorted their guests through the Grand Atrium and to the Center Corridor.

"It must have taken many years for your artists and craftsmen to find all the materials to build this tower," said Aiden as he looked around in awe.

"Not so, young Aiden. Everything you see is crafted from silver," said Lady Thistle.

"There's no paint, either. Everything is silver. The designs are just well-crafted so as to give the appearance of other materials," said Lady Thorn.

"You will also notice that this Corridor seems to be rather longer than the building allows for," said Lady Thistle.

"I was just going to ask about that. It looks to be impossibly long," said Terrance.

"That's because it is impossibly long … unless you take magic into consideration, of course," said Lady Thorn.

"The inside of the Silver Tower is roughly one-hundred-thousand times larger than the outside. If it weren't we just wouldn't have enough space for storage", noted Lady Thistle.

"Did you use Lantern Trees to build the tower?" asked Terrance.

"No, everything is definitely made of silver … with a few small exceptions. Although Lantern Trees are an obvious material to use to make something have more space on the inside, other materials can be enchanted to have the same effect," said Lady Thorn.

"Especially if you have a sorceress like Glinda on hand," said Lady Thistle.

About twenty feet into the Center Corridor were a series of doors. On each door was a large symbol shaped like an eagle in flight. The Ladies led their guests to the closest of the doors, which opened as they neared.

"Everyone inside, please. This will take us where we need to be," said Lady Thorn.

Everyone walked through the doors. On the other side was a small room that was about the size of a large closet.

"What type of room is this?" asked Aiden.

Before there was time for anyone to provide an answer to Aiden's question, the doors closed and then immediate reopened.

"Where did the corridor go?" asked Terrance.

On the other side of the doorway was no longer a corridor. Instead there was parlor room that looked to be suitable for royalty.

"That was an Eagle Room, and this is where you will be spending your evening hours for the week," said Lady Thistle. She and Lady Thorn then escorted their guests from the Eagle Room into the suite.

"This is one of our many guest suites. We're certainly not an inn, but we do insist upon being fully prepared for guests. Glinda requires every resident in the Silver Tower to be skilled in hosting," said Lady Thorn.

"This is the main parlor for the suite. There are bedchambers for each of you. There is also a nice kitchen area, of which you most probably will have little need if you join us for meals, and there is a nice balcony that overlooks the Great Garden," said Lady Thistle.

"Of course, all our balconies overlook the Great Garden. We just like to remind our guests so they don't forget to enjoy the view, which is rather impressive since we're on the one-hundred-seventh floor," said Lady Thorn.

"How did we arrive here so quickly?" asked Aiden.

"That's easy, friend Aiden," said Mr. Bunnymunch. "That was an Eagle Room. They take you wherever you want to go. You can tell them where you want to go, or they can just guess. They are very good at guessing, so you'll always end up where you need to be."

"The Eagle Rooms are located throughout the Silver Tower. We do as much walking as we can, but with the enormous size of the tower, sometimes magic must be used," said Lady Thistle.

"Otherwise, we'd spend all of our time walking around and we'd never get anything accomplished," said Lady Thorn.

Chapter Twelve

"How do we find the Eagle Rooms? Which doors are real doors and which are for Eagle Rooms?" asked Theresa.

"Excellent question! The Eagle Rooms are all marked with an eagle. You'll never miss them ... but if you do, just ask someone," said Lady Thistle.

"Everyone here is happy to help you. Now you all make yourselves at home. It's getting late and I'm sure you'll want some rest. Sleep tight and don't worry about bed bugs ... none of our beds are bugs," said Lady Thorn.

After having a good night's sleep and then joining the Ladies for a nice breakfast of chocolate fruits and puffin muffins, the Silverglades and Mr. Bunnymunch went on a grand tour of the Silver Tower, escorted again by the Ladies.

The Silverglades, Mr. Bunnymunch, Lady Thorn, and Lady Thistle all exited one of the Eagle Rooms and entered into what the Silverglade children thought to be an indoor forest.

"This is our personal greenhouse," said Lady Thorn.

"... and laboratory," continued Lady Thistle.

"This is the largest greenhouse I've ever seen!" said Mr. Bunnymunch.

"Is your laboratory ... greenhouse as large as the Great Garden?" asked Theresa.

"Although it may appear to be from here, it's not quite as expansive as the Great Garden. Much of this area our colleagues like to joke is just for mere pleasure. It's actually to make sure there's plenty of oxygen and mulch available to us," said Lady Thorn.

"Our experiments sometimes require very specific types of mulch," said Lady Thistle.

"Where do all of these paths lead?" asked Aiden.

"This one right in front of us leads to the center of our greenhouse," said Lady Thorn, as she began to lead the group along the central path of the greenhouse.

THE SILVER TOWER

The walk to the center of the greenhouse took about ten minutes. Along the way, there were many trees, shrubs, flowers, and grasses that the children and Mr. Bunnymunch did not recognize. They all found the laughing grass to be the most amusing of the plants along the central path.

At the center of the greenhouse was a large stone area with a platform and a circle of pillars. In the middle of the platform was an area of soil, at the center of which was a large hole.

"If you choose to venture through the pillars up ahead, please do be careful. There is an invisible oak growing and you might become a little bruised if you don't watch where you're going," said Lady Thistle.

"Avoid the hole in the center. You won't fall into it, but you might hit your head on the trunk of the invisible oak if try to look down in. And please do venture over to the basket by the invisible oak if you find yourself in need of a snack. That's our enchanted bread basket. It produces a honey oat bread that even the pickiest of eaters couldn't hate," said Lady Thorn.

"Back that way is where we are studying the effects of cloud snails on mist trees ... and over here we are trying to grow some moonflowers, which are related to sunflowers but aren't nearly as bright ... and back this way we have some artificers attempting to solve our problem with clockwork weeping willow trees. They keep laughing instead of weeping. It's quite funny at times, but it's just not logical," said Lady Thistle.

"What's that up above us producing all of the light?" asked Theresa.

"Isn't it the sun just shining through? ... oh ... wait ... the sun's over there ... so what's making the light? It's far too close to be another sun," said Aiden.

"Is it a reflection of the sun so your plants receive more light?" asked Terrance.

"That is our Brilliant White Rose Bush. It provides very healthy light for all of our plants. It has its very own greenhouse area up above because it's so very special and necessary," said Lady Thorn.

Chapter Twelve

"It doesn't just produce sunlight, either. It also can heal almost anything. It can even heal your very soul ... and the rosehip tea we make from it is just marvelous," said Lady Thistle.

"Let's head back to the Eagle Room. There's plenty more to see today and we don't want to be getting underfoot of the many workers we have here in the greenhouse," said Lady Thorn.

"I would love to have a laboratory like this! It's such a pleasant place to work. I'd never tire of being here," said Theresa.

"That's exactly how we feel," said the Ladies in unison.

The next Eagle Room took them to the Northwest corridor. This corridor was as tall as the tower itself. Up the sides of the corridor were the walkways and balconies for each of the several hundred floors.

"This is the Ancient Artifacts Research Facility. It takes up an entire wing because of its great importance," said Lady Thistle.

"This research facility looks more like a large city to me!" said Terrance.

"I bet all the ancient artifacts in the world are here," said Mr. Bunnymunch.

"No, not all of them ... but we can say with good certainty that the majority of them are located within this wing. Many can be found in other wings and laboratories within the Silver Tower because they are useful for the research projects of our various colleagues," said Lady Thorn.

As the group walked down the corridor, hundreds of artificers passed by them. Many of the artificers politely greeted the guests even though most of them were trying to make obvious haste to reach other parts of the Ancient Artifacts Research Facility.

"What are all of those creatures doing flying above us? Are they pets of some sort, or maybe helpers?" asked Terrance.

"Those are not creatures ... at least not in the living sense you mean, Terrance. They are all artifacts. They are the creations of our colleagues," said Lady Thistle.

"Some of them are also helpers. Some do interdepartmental deliveries and others wait here in the corridor until they see someone that needs help ... like if I drop this acorn," said Lady Thorn as she reached into one of her many hidden pockets, pulled out an acorn, and dropped the acorn on the floor. A small birdlike artifact that was made of copper gently glided down to the floor and landed right by the acorn. The metallic bird picked up the acorn in its copper beak, flew up to Lady Thorn's open hand, and carefully placed the acorn in her palm. The bird then flew back up to the higher altitudes of the corridor and resumed its aimless flight.

"Good afternoon Ladies, and guests of the Ladies. Have any of you seen my Discombobulated Diakonou Dodo? She flew off with my Petty Pocket Watch before I could properly install the last few gears," said an interesting fellow who himself resembled a thin bird. His hands were full of rolled up diagrams and charts, as was typical of the many artificers hurriedly traveling through the corridor.

"I have not seen a thing, Mr. Aves, but we've only been here a relatively few moments," said Lady Thistle.

"Excuse me, Mr. Aves, but I think I might see your Discombobulated Diakonou Dodo over there next to the door marked Ancient Gastronomics," said Theresa.

"Oh yes! That's it!" exclaimed Mr. Aves. He threw up his hands in excitement, causing him to drop all of his papers.

Theresa, Terrance, and the Ladies immediately helped Mr. Aves pick up his mess of papers. Several of the flying artifact-creatures descended to assist in picking up the jumble.

"I'll go catch the dodo!" said Aiden. He immediately ran off towards the Ancient Gastronomics Laboratory entrance.

"I'll help, too!" said Mr. Bunnymunch, who took off so quickly that there was a mild roar of air around him. He promptly cut off the dodo and guarded it in the few seconds that it took Aiden to run to the laboratory entrance.

Unfortunately, neither one of them arrived in time to prevent a young artificer, who hadn't noticed the dodo, from tripping and spilling the contents of the large jar that she had been carrying. The

Chapter Twelve

jar shattered and a river of small marbles rapidly flowed across the floor.

"Incoming!" shouted the young artificer. She quickly crouched onto the floor and covered her head.

A loud ruckus of machinery twirling and gizmo-ing descended on the corridor from above. The sound came from a massive flock of helper artifacts that had been hovering above the corridor and flew down to the floor in order to retrieve all of the spilled marbles.

The Silverglades and Mr. Bunnymunch saw that everyone else was taking up a similar position to that of the young artificer. The Silverglades quickly did the same. The Lady Thorn and the Lady Thistle were fast to cover the heads of Terrance and Theresa, although the Ladies knew that there really wasn't any danger. The rush of the artifact swarm flying by just wasn't all that pleasant and could be rather disturbing to people who are unaccustomed to the occurrence. Mr. Bunnymunch, due to his small size, felt relatively safe and decided to continue guarding the dodo so it wouldn't cause any further trouble.

All of the artifact-creatures working together only required a few seconds to pick up all of the marbles. They were quick to return each marble to the jar from which they had been spilled, after several of the artifact-creatures had together reassembled the jar.

The flock of artifacts casually returned to its hovering position over the corridor. Everyone hastily returned to their feet and continued on as they were, unfazed by the sudden swarming of the flock. Of course, the residents were used to such swarms as spills were not uncommon within the Silver Tower.

Once he had risen to his feet and had made sure that the young artificer who had tripped was unhurt, Aiden quickly picked up the Discombobulated Diakonou Dodo, which looked to be very discombobulated, and he removed the Petty Pocket Watch from its mouth. Aiden and Mr. Bunnymunch then ran back to rejoin the group, although Mr. Bunnymunch ran at a speed more comparable to Aiden's pace this time.

The Silver Tower

"Here's your Petty Pocket Watch," said Aiden as he handed the watch to Mr. Aves.

"Oh thank you both so much! I was very worried that my silly little creation here would ruin it before I was even finished crafting it," said Mr. Aves.

"Indeed! And here is your Discombobulated Diakonou Dodo ... that is still very much discombobulated. I don't think she knew what she wanted to do with the watch," said Aiden.

"Well of course she didn't know. I built her purely for amusement. That's why she's always discombobulated. She provides a lot of amusement for us ... but she does get herself into trouble once in a while, and that doesn't always bring about amusement when we're in a hurry," said Mr. Aves. "And thank you four for helping me pick up all of these papers. These messes are quite common here in the Silver Tower. We're always carrying around too much stuff, but that's a sign of a good artificer."

"That is very true, Mr. Aves! Our best artificers always tend to have a few too many items on them. If everyone knew how much Lady Thistle and I both kept in our pockets we may just get ourselves kicked out of the Silver Tower for being overzealous hoarders," said Lady Thorn in jest.

The next area on the tour was a massive library. The collection of books was so large that the end opposite of the Eagle Room from which the group entered the enormous hall was too far away for the average human eye to detect.

"This is the Library of Mr. and Mrs. Lexiconica. These two scholars amassed a huge compilation of books and other scholarly resources. They somewhat gave their lives in order to protect their ancient stash of books, which were the first deposits into the library when it was established," said Lady Thistle.

"They somewhat gave their lives to protect their books? They must have been very important books ... or they loved academia very much ... or both. And who would somewhat murder another person over books? That must have been one very wicked person

105

Chapter Twelve

indeed who somewhat killed Mr. and Mrs. Lexiconica for their books," said Aiden.

"Both is correct, and yes that person was very wicked. He was a wicked warlock who had very little appreciation for people who used knowledge for the benefit of others. The personal library of the Lexiconicas was the most impressive library of the time and was a highly valued resource for much of Oz. It was a very unfortunate day when the wicked warlock attacked. The Lexiconicas had a brief warning that he was coming to destroy their collection and they had just enough time to use all of their magical abilities to cast a protective enchantment over the library. This left them very weak ... and the warlock punished them for their spell casting," said Lady Thorn.

"It was a bunnymunch who warned them! I remember my grandparents telling me the story of the bunnymunch that risked his life to help save the Lexiconicas. He was almost somewhat killed, too, but he managed to escape just in time, and then he ran off and told a good witch what had happened so there would be someone to continue on with the work of the library," said Mr. Bunnymunch.

"That's exactly how the library came to the Silver Tower. It's a good thing too that the wicked warlock didn't gain access to the library, because there was powerful knowledge contained within the pages of some of those books that could have helped him to do some very terrible things ... even more terrible than the somewhat murdering of the Lexiconicas," said Lady Thistle.

"This is why this library is so important to us. It's not only very helpful in providing information to us, but it also serves as a reminder of both the good and the evil present in Oz. That's something a person should never forget. Now back to the Eagle Room with us, so we can continue on with the tour," said Lady Thorn.

Next was a corridor along one of the outer walls. One side of the corridor contained various doors. The other side seemed to be one, large piece of glass; however, it was really a transparent, silver wall.

"Down this hall we have one of our many staff lounges. We would love to take you in and show you around ...," said Lady Thistle.

"... but there was an unfortunate accident here the other day while one of our Able Artificers was attempting a new recipe that he wanted to share with his colleagues. The room is now filled with something that he described as 'bountiful blueberry baking batter'," said Lady Thorn.

"You'd best not stand too close to the door, or you may find yourself turning blue," said Lady Thistle.

"We've already had the experience of turning blue recently, and we would prefer not to experience it again ... so you will not be seeing any of us going near that door," commented Aiden.

"What's that sound I hear coming from further down the corridor?" asked Mr. Bunnnymunch.

"That is Clockworks. It's the laboratory where most of the research on clockworks is accomplished. It gets quite loud in there at times," said Lady Thorn.

"All the clockwork plants and monuments you see in this corridor were constructed in the Clockworks Laboratory. I'm particularly fond of the clockwork peach and pinecone tree. The peaches and pinecones are especially pretty come Christmas time," said Lady Thistle.

"Let's take a quick peek inside of Clockworks, shall we? It's a relatively quiet day in there, so we won't need to bother with the usual enchanted earmuffs," said Lady Thorn.

The group entered the Clockworks Laboratory through a giant, silver door. Immediately inside the room they were greeting by a ruby automaton.

"Welcome to Clockworks. I am the Ruby Automaton, at your service. If you have any questions please do not hesitate to ask," said the automaton.

CHAPTER TWELVE

"Thank you, Ruby Automaton. May I ask, what is an automaton? Are you alive or an artifact" said Aiden.

"I am an artifact, and not alive. An automaton is a type of artifact that is made to resemble a human or other creature and to provide mechanical service to its creator or owner," said the automaton.

"That's very interesting. Thank you, Miss Automaton," said Aiden.

"You are very welcome," said the automaton.

"It's very good to see that none of you are afraid of artifacts. You'd be amazed at the number of people who are afraid of a talking artifact for no reason at all. Some people are just silly and have to be afraid of everything," said Lady Thistle.

"We were raised better than that," said Theresa and Terrance in unison.

"Yes, our parents did a very good job, I believe, of teaching us right from wrong and how not to judge other people ... or artifacts ... just because we don't understand them," said Aiden.

The children and Mr. Bunnymunch were all captivated by the many artifacts around them. There were more clockwork artifacts than they could count. There were automatons of many shapes, sizes, and materials. There were clockwork garden tools, monuments, walkers, rollers, clothing, books, cabinets, flowers, and paintings ... just to name a few things. Aiden was pretty sure that he could see a clockwork worm crawling around on the floor, but he didn't say anything in case it would startle the twins.

"Theresa, you might find it even more interesting than the others would to know that this laboratory is run by Glinda herself. She is very adept at clockwork artifice," said Lady Thorn.

"That doesn't surprise me at all, but I would be very grateful if you could show me some of her work! Is she here right now? Would I be able to meet with her, even if it's just for a few seconds?" said Theresa with obvious excitement in her voice.

"I'm sorry, young Theresa, but today she is taking care of other important matters, such as her Clockwork Witch, and is not in the Clockworks Laboratory," said Lady Thistle.

"But don't worry, you will most assuredly have the opportunity to meet her during your visit with us this week," said Lady Thorn.

Just then, a flying clockwork squirrel landed on Aiden's shoulder. The Ladies looked at Aiden expecting him to be startled, but he wasn't.

"Hello there, little friend, and what is your name?" said Aiden to the squirrel that was twitchily scanning his face.

The squirrel responded in a series of squirrel chatters that sounded just like a real squirrel.

"You don't have a name yet? We'll have to think of one for you then," said Aiden.

"Oh, he's so cute!" exclaimed Theresa.

"May I hold him?" asked Terrance.

"I think we should give the clockwork squirrel and Aiden a moment to become better acquainted first ... but I must ask one thing: Aiden, were you able to understand the squirrel when it chattered just then?" said Lady Thistle.

"Well ... yes. I guess I did. When did I learn to speak squirrel?" said Aiden.

"Mrs. Cache, please come here," said Lady Thorn. She then waved to a woman who was digging through a nearby chest of various trinkets and knickknacks. "I think we've found a friend for your squirrel."

"Is that so? How marvelous!" said Mrs. Cache as she stuck her head out from in the chest. She then quickly scurried over to Aiden, who was now petting the clockwork squirrel that still sat on his shoulder. "My stars, you are the first person he's befriended since I built him. That would mean you are ... Aiden. Is that correct?"

"Why yes, yes I am. My name is Aiden. How did you know my name?" asked Aiden.

"My clockwork squirrel told me. He told me that his rightful owner, and one true friend, was named Aiden and you would come

Chapter Twelve

to collect him one day. Congratulations! You are now the owner of one clockwork squirrel. He requires no regular maintenance. He'll last forever, as long as you take reasonably good care of him. He's made of bronze-silver and he'll never rust or tarnish. I really don't have to tell you to take good care of him because I know you will. He told me so. You're the only other person besides myself that understands him, you know," said Mrs. Cache.

"I really like your new friend," said Theresa.

"I hope we can be friends with him, too!" said Terrance.

Aiden continued to pet the squirrel. He was quite mesmerized by the clockwork squirrel, which was well-evidenced by the smile on his face. "I think I'll name you ... Acorn," said Aiden.

"Acorn Silverglade!" said the twins in unison.

"Yes, Acorn Silverglade. That is your name, my new friend," said Aiden just as Acorn gave him a little squirrel kiss on the cheek.

"Now that you have found a clockwork companion, Aiden, let's head on down the corridor to Stoneworks," said Lady Thistle.

As the friends traveled down the corridor, Acorn remained on Aiden's shoulder. Their instantaneous amity was evident.

Very abruptly, the décor within the corridor changed from a clockwork theme into that of stone. There were several stone monuments and carvings of strange creatures made of basalt, granite, trachyandesite, rhyodasite, basanite, and various other stone types.

"This door leads to our Stoneworks Laboratory, but don't try opening it on your own. You might strain something," said Lady Thorn.

"Mr. Bunnymunch, do you see the dark stone with the symbol of Oz carved in it? Would you please step down on it for us?" asked Lady Thistle.

"Gladly," said Mr. Bunnymunch. When he stepped down on the stone bearing the symbol formed from the letters O and Z, the door to the Stoneworks Laboratory opened. The Silverglades and Mr. Bunnymunch were all a little surprised that the door made absolutely no noise whatsoever as it opened. They all presumed

THE SILVER TOWER

this to be an effect of magic, though, so their surprise quickly subsided.

Inside of the Stoneworks Laboratory the friends were met with an interesting situation.

"Lady Thistle, Lady Thorn, why is everything that's not fixed to the floor floating in the air?" asked Aiden.

Inside of the very large laboratory were hundreds of floating, stone artifacts. There were half-carved boulders, statues, orbs, and even a few stone trees. Many of the artifacts contained various glyphs that were unrecognizable to the children or to Mr. Bunnymunch. All of the artifacts were suspended in midair by an unseen, magical force.

"It would seem that either someone is testing out a levitation spell of some sort …," said Lady Thistle.

"… or has had a minor mishap of magic," continued Lady Thorn.

The latter of the two suggestions turned out to be true.

"My dear Ladies, and guests of my dear Ladies! I do ask for your forgiveness. We are experiencing a small error in enchanting right now. One of our Advanced Artificers has encountered a bit of a snag in his Levitating Leviathan Monolith artifact" said a stone-faced gentleman who acted as though he were a person of some authority in the Stoneworks Laboratory.

"Mr. Lithinos, it does look like your Advanced Artificer's spell has succeeded in producing levitating effects. Is that not what he had intended of his Levitating Leviathan Monolith?" asked Lady Thistle.

"Levitation was definitely his goal; however, he had only intended to levitate the monolith. Instead, he has managed to levitate everything else in the lab. We're just happy that the charm didn't levitate all of us, or else we may have had some other dilemmas of even greater urgency to handle!" said Mr. Lithinos.

"What's a leviathan?" asked Terrance.

"Good question, young guest of my dear Ladies. A leviathan is a magnificently large sea serpent. They're actually quite friendly,

Chapter Twelve

but they have come to have a bad reputation because of their large size … especially with respect to their large teeth," said Mr. Lithinos.

"We're ready to unbind! Take cover!" yelled an echoing voice from somewhere far back in the laboratory.

"You'd best be on your way right quick! We don't want to be around in case this unbinding spell is as effective as we all hope it will be. Please do forgive me, guests of my dear Ladies, for not being able to give you a proper tour of the lab," said Mr. Lithinos.

"That's quite all right. You're experiencing an emergency and we understand," said Aiden.

"Perhaps we can bring them by again later in the week once everything has been cleaned up from the unbinding," said Lady Thorn.

"We'd best be on our way now so as to not be in the way of all these floating monuments and other artifacts," said Lady Thistle.

The friends all quickly exited through the main, stone doors of the Stoneworks Laboratory. The doors closed behind them as soon as they were all clear of the entranceway.

"Will the unbinding spell be gentle with all of those stone artifacts when they land? I do hope that stone falcon isn't damaged when it lands. I rather liked it," said Theresa.

Before anyone had the opportunity to respond to Theresa's question, there came a very thunderous boom from the direction of the Stoneworks Laboratory. The entire Silver Tower was shaken by the roar. The Silverglades all fell to the ground, with Acorn leaping from Aiden's shoulder and landing gracefully on the floor. Mr. Bunnymunch was happy to be a bunnymunch, because he had much more stability due to his four legs and short stature. The Ladies didn't waver a bit with the shock of the entire Stoneworks Laboratory crash landing, because they had prepared themselves for the coming unbinding and accompanying earthquake. A small cloud of dust puffed through from underneath the stone doors.

"Don't worry, Theresa, there are various other enchantments at work within each of the workshops of the Silver Tower that prevent such accidents from being thoroughly destructive," said Lady Thorn.

"You must thank the builders of the Silver Tower for making the floor so durable as to be able to withstand an earthquake from such a powerful stoneworks crash," said Mr. Bunnymunch.

"Perhaps we should move to another area to avoid this dust cloud," said Aiden while still seated on the floor.

"Agreed," said everyone else in unison.

The Silverglades returned to their feet, and Acorn returned to Aiden's shoulder.

"Where are we going now?" asked Terrance.

"We are on our way to the Iron Laboratory," said Lady Thistle.

The friends all entered into another Eagle Room and instantly arrived in the Iron Laboratory. This workshop had an interesting feature to it, or more so lack of feature, that quickly caught the attention of Theresa.

"Why isn't there any silver in this room? All of the other laboratories had at least some silver in the walls or ceiling fixtures, but this one doesn't. Why is that?" asked Theresa.

"You are a very keen observer, young Theresa. Maybe one day you will become an artificer, because a good artificer must have a good sense of observation. There is no silver in here because Mrs. Ferrous, the Senior Artificer in charge of this workshop, requested that there be none present," said Lady Thorn.

"Although silver is a very valuable tool for artificers, it can interfere with certain projects that Mrs. Ferrous is doing with her iron, so Glinda was happy to oblige by allowing this workshop to be constructed of nothing but iron," added Lady Thistle.

"Is that another entrance stone?" asked Mr. Bunnymunch, indicating a circle of iron in the floor bearing the symbol of Oz on it.

"Almost. It's not an entrance stone, but an entrance iron. There's no stone in it, because it's made entirely of iron ... as one would expect for the Iron Laboratory," said Lady Thorn.

Chapter Twelve

"Would you care to open the iron doors for us, Mr. Bunnymunch?" asked Lady Thistle.

When the doors opened, a wave of heat bellowed out from the workshop.

"Why is it so hot in there?" asked Theresa.

"I would presume that it's due to the melting of the iron so the artificers can shape it into whatever they desire," stated Aiden.

"Absolutely correct! That's why we won't spend too much time in here. People who aren't used to this heat can easily become overwhelmed with heat exhaustion," said Lady Thorn.

"... and we certainly don't want that happening to any of you," added Lady Thistle.

"Mrs. Ferrous, we have guests of the Ladies Thorn and Thistle," announced an iron orb that was floating above head right inside the entrance of the Iron Laboratory.

"We should purchase an orb like that for the entrance of our home. I know we don't really need one, but I think it would be fun," said Terrance.

"I think that we can manage to live without one for the time being, favorite little brother of mine" said Aiden, smiling at his younger brother.

"Hello Ladies! And hello guests of the Ladies! Welcome to my workshop. Please make yourselves at home," said Mrs. Ferrous as she seemingly appeared out of nowhere. Mrs. Ferrous was wearing an interesting dress that was very formal yet also very much like a lab coat. Her dress looked to be very soft yet also looked to be made of woven, iron fibers. It was very appropriate for an ironworker and a woman of style, which Mrs. Ferrous was. Around her waist she wore a jewel-studded belt that had broad buckles in the back and several, small, iron objects attached to it. The iron objects looked to be charms of some sort.

"Good day to you, Mrs. Ferrous. We have brought you some visitors that would like to see your laboratory," said Lady Thorn.

"Might you have a moment to tell them a little about your work here?" asked Lady Thistle.

THE SILVER TOWER

"I always have time for friends of the Ladies Thistle and Thorn. It's a pleasure to meet you children, and it's a pleasure to meet you for a second time, Mr. Bunnymunch. Now, this workshop is where my artificers and I study iron. What a useful metal it is! We can do anything with it. Take for instance this iron statue of the Mayor of Baumville. With this statue, which we will be sending off to the Mayor next week, he will have the ability to make announcements to his entire town. We've enchanted the statue to project his voice whenever he speaks into this iron voice receptacle. And if you walk over here … we have a laundry iron. It takes the wrinkles out of your clothing without the use of heat. That way little ones can't accidentally touch it and burn their little hands on it. We do enjoy making things that keep people safe. Safety first!" said Mrs. Ferrous.

"Mrs. Ferrous!" said an exceptionally tall young man with hair that was permanently stuck up, most likely due to his past work with iron and lightning. "Excuse me, everyone. Mrs. Ferrous, you asked to see my Love Magnet once I was done with it. I've completed my work, although I don't know if it's quite as powerful as the Pink Diamond Ring. I'm going to start on my next project now: an iron fountain. It will have liquid iron, not water." With that the young man quickly returned to his workbench.

"Thank you, Anisotrope. I'll have this back to you later today once I examine it," said Mrs. Ferrous.

"What's a Love Magnet?" asked Theresa.

"This is a Love Magnet," said Mrs. Ferrous, holding up the Love Magnet in her hand. "It causes people to fall in love … or at least it's supposed to. This afternoon I'll be using my Magic Belt to help determine how good this Love Magnet is at creating such feelings of adoration."

"Is it just me or is it becoming hotter in here?" asked Terrance.

"I think you're right. It's becoming hotter every moment. Are you melting more iron, Mrs. Ferrous?" asked Theresa.

"Well normally that would be the cause of the heat; however, at this particular moment we are enduring heat from Soleil, one of our

Chapter Twelve

Master Artificers, who is experimenting on his Fire Poker. It produces heat on its own," said Mrs. Ferrous.

"Let's get these young ones out of here before they suffer from heat exhaustion, as they're not used to temperatures quite this high," said Lady Thorn.

"Although I find this temperature to be quite relaxing, I agree. I don't want my friends to suffer so I can relax" said Mr. Bunnymunch.

"Yes, somewhere that's a bit cooler would be nice to visit next," said Aiden, as he petted Acorn's head.

"Then on to the Master Silver Wing with us!" said Lady Thistle.

The friends headed out of the Iron Laboratory and walked to the nearest Eagle Room.

The Master Silver Wing was an impressive sight. The main corridor of the wing was a giant, indoor, tropical rainforest.

"This rainforest is, as you all may have guessed, made from the purest of silver. Everything from the soil to the leaves on the trees to the clouds up by the ceiling is all made of silver," said Lady Thorn.

"It doesn't look like silver, except for the shininess ... but I suppose that's due to the craftsmanship and magic used to create such splendors," commented Aiden.

"Is that a stream of Silver Water?" asked Terrance.

"That is correct, young Terrance. The meditation pool in the center of the forest is also filled with Silver Water," said Lady Thistle.

"This is one of the areas where we may end up planting some of your Silver Lily crop," added Lady Thorn.

"Those would look very lovely here in the rainforest," said Theresa.

"Let's take you to Madame Argentum's private workshop. It's just over here by the silver peacock statue," said Lady Thistle.

When the friends approached the entrance to Madame Argentum's workshop, the feathers of the silver peacock statue shone brilliantly for a moment and the workshop doors opened.

Inside of the workshop was Madame Argentum, who was sitting at one of her many workbenches.

"Come in! Come in! Are these your guests, Ladies? The Silverglades and Mr. Bunnymunch, if my memory serves me correctly? Please do come in!" said Madame Argentum in a very friendly tone.

"How are your Silver Shoes coming along?" asked Lady Thorn.

"I have several more months of work to do on them. These enchantments and grafts do take considerable time to do if you want to have a properly working pair of Silver Shoes," said Madame Argentum as she examined very carefully a small point on the toe of one of the Silver Shoes with her monocle.

"What do your Silver Shoes do?" asked Theresa.

"Presuming my enchantments work out the way I intend ... these Silver Shoes will transport whoever wears them to any location of her choosing. I've made them for Glinda. She says that down the road her great-granddaughter is going to have a friend who will have need of them. I believe the friend's name is Dotty ... or did she say Dorothy? Debbie? The name doesn't matter. She's going to need them and I'm going to make sure she has them when the time comes," said Madame Argentum.

"Everyone could do with a pair of those. I can think of a lot of people whose lives would be made a lot easier with Silver Shoes ... although I guess you can't make too many pairs since there would undoubtedly be those people who would abuse such a privilege. Imagine what would happen if a wicked witch were to get her hands on a pair of Silver Shoes ... or more so her feet in a pair of them," commented Aiden.

"I'm sure if a wicked witch were ever to find herself in possession of Madame Argentum's Silver Shoes that she wouldn't find herself to have such possession for very long," stated Lady Thistle with a pleasant smile.

"Madame Argentum, you might like to know that these young children have sold to us a crop of Silver Lilies of the highest quality.

Chapter Twelve

Perhaps you could use some in your research and experiments," said Lady Thorn.

"Silver Lilies!" exclaimed Madame Argentum. "I most certainly could use some! They would be just perfect for completing my Silver Slinking Sea and Sand Ship. It's a vessel that can travel across anything: land, sea, dessert, forest ... you name it and the ship can cross it. I need the lilies to make the enchantments be sufficiently effective to handle all environments."

"I'm so glad our Silver Lilies can be helpful to someone," said Theresa.

"If you ever need more of them, please let us know. We have crops available every year. Since the Ladies are giving us a Green Coin Poinsettia that will provide us with all the money we will ever need, we'd be happy to just give you the lilies whenever you want them," said Aiden.

"How very generous of you! But I will pay you. I can tell that you don't understand how incredibly valuable Silver Lilies are," said Madame Argentum.

"Even if they realized how valuable the Silver Lilies are, that wouldn't make their offer any different," said Mr. Bunnymunch. He wanted to make sure that Madame Argentum was aware of how genuinely kind the Silverglades all were.

"Ladies, will you be taking your friends by the Room of Magic Rings? I have a ring that needs returning and I would be greatly appreciative of someone who could handle the task for me, since I need to keep working on my Silver Shoes," said Madame Argentum.

"That happens to be the very next location on our agenda," said Lady Thistle.

"We'll be happy to save you the trouble," added Lady Thorn.

Mrs. Argentum then removed a ring from her finger and placed it into Lady Thistle's hand. The central stone of the ring was a large, brown diamond that had a very gentle glow to it, although the glow was difficult to detect with all of the shining silver in the workshop. Lady Thistle placed the ring onto Lady Thorn's finger for safe-keeping until they arrived in the Room of Magic Rings.

Chapter Thirteen
The Room of Magic Rings

"Please forgive us, but this is the least impressive room in the Silver Tower," said Lady Thistle.

"Mind you, at first it was quite impressive ... and you can still see some of that impressiveness if you look carefully between the cracks of all these boxes and shelves," said Lady Thorn.

The friends were now in the Room of Magic Rings. The room was incredibly long, yet it did not have much to it in terms of width, although it may have been as wide as it was long were the masses of boxes not present. This made things difficult when the friends had to pass by one of the many artificers looking for rings. There were too many boxes piled up to be able to see the walls. In fact, the children and Mr. Bunnymunch were all curious when Lady Thorn mentioned the presence of shelves, because none were in sight. They presumed them to be hidden among all of the boxes.

"Try not to bump into any of the boxes while we make our way through the mess. We don't want to cause any avalanches," said Lady Thistle.

"Why are there so many boxes here? What's in all of them?" asked Theresa.

"Does this room even have walls?" asked Aiden.

"The boxes are probably the walls," said Terrance.

"Is the cleaning staff on vacation?" asked Mr. Bunnymunch.

"These boxes are all filled with magic rings, of course! What else would you expect in the Room of Magic Rings?" said Lady Thorn.

"But why are there so many of them?" asked Theresa.

"A while back Glinda gave a seminar on magic rings and their enchantments ... and a few too many artificers decided that they

Chapter Thirteen

too needed to try out their skills at producing magic rings," said Lady Thistle.

"There was one day when seven-hundred-thousand-and-four magic rings were submitted to the storage space in the Room of Magic Rings. That's when we stopped trying to make sense of things and merely added an enchantment to the room that would retrieve any ring requested ... other than rings from the Rather Rare Rings Room, which is part of the Room of Magic Rings ... the latter of which is in of itself actually a few hundred rooms that mostly just run together and seem like one large room," said Lady Thorn.

As the friends walked through the seemingly endless span of boxes they encountered some areas where they were certain that avalanches had recently occurred and other areas where they were certain that avalanches could occur at any moment.

"How many rings are in here?" asked Aiden.

"Silly child! Numbers don't go that high," answered Lady Thistle.

"How are those boxes staying stacked so well above us without falling?" asked Theresa.

"Very carefully, young Theresa," said Lady Thorn.

"I think I see a chandelier a few hundred feet ahead of us, but it could just be the reflection off of some of the rings," said Aiden.

"I'm going to presume it's a chandelier. That way we can say we've seen something other than boxes and rings in the Room of Magic Rings," said Terrance.

After twenty minutes of walking, Terrance asked, "Is there an end to this room?"

"Of course there is! Or ... at least I think there's one. I remember there being one ... although that could have been another room I'm thinking of," said Lady Thistle.

"Perhaps Glinda replaced the end of the room with more storage space. Here we are! This is the entrance to the Rather Rare Rings Room on the left," said Lady Thorn.

"That's an entrance?" said Terrance.

The Room of Magic Rings

"It looks more like a small tunnel made of boxes to me," said Aiden.

"Well ... yes ... I do suppose it is a small tunnel made of boxes, but it does lead to the Rather Rare Rings Room," said Lady Thistle.

"How long is this tunnel made of boxes?" asked Mr. Bunnymunch.

"It's not very long, especially if you compare it to the main tunnel of the Room of Magic Rings. Look, you can easily see the door from here," said Lady Thorn as she pointed to a door that was about forty feet down the tunnel.

"Are there forty feet of boxes on the sides of the Room of Magic Rings?" asked Aiden, with some shock to his voice.

"I wish there were only forty feet of boxes on the sides of this room! That would make organizing this room an effort that could possibly be accomplished," said Lady Thistle.

"This door just happens to be a lot closer to us than most of the walls," said Lady Thorn.

"Please forgive our rudeness but we need to enter through the door first, or else it won't let us in. We have many safety features like that on rooms like this. We must take extra precautions with the more powerful magical artifacts in the Silver Tower," said Lady Thistle.

The door to the Rather Rare Rings Room opened on its own as the Ladies Thorn and Thistle approached it. The door was inobviously made of silver, with an image of a ring at its center.

Once the friends were all in the Rather Rare Rings Room, Lady Thorn removed the Brown Diamond Ring from her finger and placed it into her open palm.

"It's time for you to return to your home, little ring," said Lady Thorn.

The ring gently floated into the air and returned to its pedestal in the center of the room. The Rather Rare Rings Room was very museum-like in its structure. There were many hundreds of rings in the room. Some were in private display cases, such as the Brown Diamond Ring that Lady Thorn had just returned to its pedestal,

Chapter Thirteen

while others resided in shared display cases. Beside each display case was a sign that provided a description of the contents therein.

"This room has a very pretty rainbow color to it," commented Theresa.

"I think that's caused by all of the rings that are glowing. They seem to have a ring of just about every color in here," said Aiden.

"Yes, we do have quite a few rare rings in here with a variety of colors," said Lady Thistle.

"Is there something special about these rings in the middle of the room? They all seem to be stored in their own housings away from the other rings," said Mr. Bunnymunch.

"These are the rarest and most protected of our rings. I wouldn't recommend touching any of the cases if I were you," said Lady Thorn.

"They have some rather powerful enchantments and devices protecting them. In fact, there are a lot of artifacts hidden throughout this room that are not rings. They are all here to help protect the rings ... although it would be nearly impossible for anyone to make it this far into the Silver Tower without permission from Glinda, which she has granted to all of you," said Lady Thistle.

"All of the Diamond Rings you see in the central display area are especially potent in their magics. You can read a summary of all of them in the center illusiprojector," said Lady Thorn.

The friends all walked up to the illusiprojector, which was an intangible projection suspended in midair by illusion magic.

"White Diamond Ring – Power of Air and Light. Black Diamond Ring – Power of Darkness and Death. Blue Diamond Ring – Power of Water. Red Diamond Ring – Power of Fire. Green Diamond Ring – Power of Plants and Nature. Brown Diamond Ring – Power of Earth. Purple Diamond Ring – Power of Leadership. Pink Diamond Ring – Power of Love. Yellow Diamond Ring – Power of Friendship. Orange Diamond Ring – Power of Change. Ruby Ring – Power of Grace. Emerald Ring – Power of Citizenship. Sapphire Ring – Power of Intelligence and Wisdom. Ivory Ring – Power of Goodness and Healing.

Rosewood Ring – Our Little Secret," said Aiden as he read from the illusiprojector. "I can see why you would want to take extra precautions in protecting this room. These rings could be used to do a lot of good, but also a lot of bad," said Aiden.

"That is an unfortunate truth of this world. There is both good and evil, but I guess that's what helps us to learn how to be real people ... so it's perhaps worth the struggles," said Lady Thistle.

"Why does the Rosewood Ring have a description of 'Our Little Secret'? Shouldn't anyone in the Silver Tower be sufficiently trustworthy to handle knowing what the ring does ... or does no one here know what it does?" asked Theresa.

"There are a very few people who know what abilities lie within the Rosewood Ring, and everyone here can be trusted ... but there are wicked people out there who could use their powers to draw out the information from our colleagues and that would not be a good thing to have happen," said Lady Thorn, trying not to sound offensive in her maintaining of the ring's secrets.

"It's all right, though. No one here is offended. They all understand that this is not just for the protection of the ring but for their protection as well. If they don't know what it does then no one can go looking for them to try to force information out of them that they don't have inside of their heads," said Lady Thistle.

"In all of your rings, do you have any that are capable of removing enchantments from a person? We have a friend that is in need of such a ring," said Theresa.

"... or artifact," said Terrance.

"... or spell," said Aiden.

They had been waiting for the proper time to ask for help for their friend, Lilibeth the Good Wizardess.

"We most certainly do!" said Lady Thorn.

"Come back out into the main tunnel made of boxes and we'll pick out something good for you to take to your friend," said Lady Thistle.

"Thank you so much! Our friend will be most grateful," said Terrance.

Chapter Thirteen

The Ladies escorted the Silverglades and Mr. Bunnymunch back into the main tunnel made of boxes and led them to a box that looked just like all of the others.

"This is just one of our boxes of unbinding rings. Now tell us, what kind of enchantment does your friend need to be unbound?" asked Lady Thorn.

"We're not quite sure what all the enchantment does to her, but we know for certain it prevents her from leaving her home," said Aiden.

"Hmm ... we'll give you a more powerful ring then just in case to make sure it can remove the enchantment properly," said Lady Thistle as she and Lady Thorn began rummaging through the box together.

"Ah! Perfect! This should do the trick ... and if it doesn't ...," said Lady Thorn. She handed the ring to Theresa for safekeeping. The artifact was rather plain-looking in texture, but was composed of an attractive gold.

"... just come back and we'll give you something with a little more oomph to it. When you want to use it on someone else you can say the words 'weeble-weeble-bind, weeble-weeble-free' and think of your friend. You can also just place the ring on your friend's finger and let her say the words herself," continued Lady Thistle.

"This is very kind of you to do," said Theresa.

"We're always happy to help! Now this particular ring we can't outright give to you. This is on loan, but you may use it for however long you need it," said Lady Thorn.

"Then just return it to us at your earliest convenience. No need to go out of your way to return it too promptly. A few years will be fine," said Lady Thistle.

"A few years? I'm sure we'll be able to return it long before then," said Aiden.

"My sweet Lady Thistle, why don't we also take this opportunity to reduce this clutter a little by giving our friends some rings that will be much greater use to them on their journeys than they will be to us sitting in these boxes collecting dust?" said Lady Thorn.

"I was just thinking that very same thought, my sweet Lady Thorn. Children, would you kindly hold out your hands for us?" said Lady Thistle.

The children held out their hands. When they did, three rings from far off locations within the Room of Magic Rings floated into their hands – one ring each.

"Oh thank you, Ladies! They're so very pretty!" said Theresa.

"You're quite welcome, but we must also thank you for helping us reduce our clutter ... although these rings will be particularly useful for you, so they will definitely not be clutter for you," said Lady Thorn.

"What do our rings do?" asked Aiden.

"Your ring is called Irkin's Ring of Sneezes. The ring stops all of its wearer's allergies, if he has any, and can stop anyone he's touching from sneezing. He can also use the ring to cause someone nearby to sneeze. It can be an amusing little artifact if used right," said Lady Thistle.

"Theresa's ring is called Hilaritiènne's Ring of Laughter. With it you can make anyone within your sight laugh. This may sound rather worthless, other than at parties, but you'd be surprised at what you can accomplish with a little laughter. Humor is a powerful tool!" said Lady Thorn.

"Terrance's ring is called Illumina's Ring of Light. Your ring produces a mild yellow light equivalent to about three candles in strength ... or at least that's what we've seen it do so far. The light brings a mild presence of goodness into the room, so it can take care of any fears you may have in a dark place. Since you are from the Village of Illume, I suspect that you have spent little or no time in complete darkness, which is why nearly everyone from your village is afraid of the dark. This ring should help with that if you ever find yourself in a situation where you are afraid because there isn't enough light," said Lady Thistle.

Chapter Thirteen

"And Mr. Bunnymunch, don't think we have forgotten about you!" said Lady Thorn. At that moment a fourth ring floated to her from yet another far off location within the Room of Magic Rings.

Once the ring had landed in the palm of Lady Thorn's hand, she waved her other hand over the open palm of Lady Thistle and a long piece of thread appeared in the open palm. Lady Thistle then magically wove the thread into a small necklace, to which Lady Thorn attached the ring. "Since rings are rather difficult for bunnymunches to wear we have transformed this into a necklace you can manage more easily."

"How wonderful! I've always wanted a handsome necklace like this!" said Mr. Bunnymunch.

"Your ring, Mr. Bunnymunch, is called Lionora's Mighty Roaring Ring. With it you can let out a mighty roar whenever you need to make your presence known," said Lady Thistle.

"That will be very handy, since we bunnymunches are very easy to miss. Even when we are speaking to someone we often go unnoticed," said Mr. Bunnymunch.

"Let's make our way back out of the room. You all have had plenty enough exercise for one day and it's another twenty-five minutes for us to make it back to the exit," said Lady Thorn.

"By the time we return you to your rooms it will be nearing time for dinner. We do hope you will join us for dinner in the Grand Dining Hall. Tonight's menu is anything you want," said Lady Thistle.

Chapter Fourteen
Glinda of Oz

The Silverglades and Mr. Bunnymunch were relaxing in the main parlor of their guest suite having just returned after joining the Ladies Thorn and Thistle for a very filling dinner. Acorn looked to be fast asleep on Aiden's shoulder, although Aiden was unsure if a clockwork squirrel could actually sleep ... but maybe this was a way for Acorn to rest his squirrel gears. The three children had decided to try something new this evening and eat some Wheeze Mush. This delicacy was provided by the Ladies, in so much as they grew Wheeze Mush plants themselves. The dish looked rather unpleasant, although its undesirable appearance was not nearly as undesirable as its din. The first bite of Wheeze Mush for each of the children had been the most difficult because the food sounded as though it were gasping for breath, and when it was touched by silverware the wheezing sounds doubled in magnitude. Fortunately for the children, the flavor of the Wheeze Mush was well worth the visual and auditory discomfort.

"Do you think we should ask the Ladies Thorn and Thistle to sell us a Wheeze Mush plant? I sure would enjoy eating more of it regularly when we return home," said Terrance.

"I wouldn't mind that myself; however, I'm not sure if mother and father would appreciate a farm full of plants constantly gasping for a breath of air. It could become annoying very quickly, and we wouldn't want to get on their nerves once they become unlost," responded Aiden.

"The Ladies' Wheeze Mush plants can be a little distracting at times, I must admit," said a voice coming from the direction of the Eagle Room off of the main parlor of the suite.

Walking towards the children and Mr. Bunnymunch from the Eagle Room was a stunningly magnificent woman, dressed in a

Chapter Fourteen

glimmering white gown that must have been made of the finest of silver fabric. Although she had never before seen this woman, Theresa immediately knew the identity of their visitor.

"Glinda!" exclaimed Theresa.

"It's a pleasure to meet you, Theresa ... and also you, Terrance, Aiden, and Mr. Bunnymunch. Please forgive me for not having greeted you when you first arrived at my Silver Tower, but this is a particularly busy time for me and I am not afforded many occasions within my schedule to act as the good hostess that I should be," said Glinda.

"Lady Thorn and Lady Thistle have been especially good hostesses to us. We have all been very impressed by the hospitality of everyone here in your Silver Tower. You also shouldn't be sorry for not being able to act as a hostess. There was no way for you to know that we were coming, since we never scheduled our visit with you or with anyone else from the Silver Tower," said Aiden.

"But I'm sure you knew we were coming, didn't you, Glinda? You are a powerful sorceress, so you must know whenever someone is coming to visit you." said Theresa.

"Magic is not something that I use at all times merely because I have the capability to use it, Theresa; however, I do often know in advance whom my visitors are going to be," said Glinda as she smiled at Theresa.

"You probably have artifacts that tell you, so you don't have to waste your own magic, right?" asked Terrance.

"That may well be, Terrance. That may well be. Now the reason for my visit is to make sure that you have been well taken care of, and by the looks of things it seems that you have. The Ladies are my best and most trusted hostesses, so I knew you would have no problems finding the comforts of home here in my Silver Tower. You have been very kind to bring us your Silver Lilies, so if there is anything else I can do for you please let me know ... although I do see by the rings on your hands, children, and around your neck, Mr. Bunnymunch, that the Ladies have been generous to you already with some of our magical artifacts," said Glinda.

"We already have more than we need, so we just thank you for letting us remain here and rest a while before we begin our return journey home," said Aiden.

"There is one thing ... a question ... if you don't mind," said Theresa.

"And what might your question be, Theresa?" asked Glinda.

"Why did you build this tower?" asked Theresa.

"That is a very good question, and I'll be happy to answer it. I was raised around artifacts and the skills of artifice. My family has been fascinated by the study of artifacts, and of course the related magics, since long before I first set foot in Oz. When I was a young girl, not much older than yourself, Theresa, I was gifted a Ruby Ring from my father. The ring is a family heirloom, and artifact, that has been handed down for many generations. Each generation adds to the enchantments of the ring, so it was a most wonderful gift indeed from my father because it gave me a brilliant connection to all of my family members who came before me. It helps me to feel their presence and love in my life whenever I wear it," said Glinda.

"The ring must be very powerful if everyone in your family has enchanted it," said Aiden.

"Well, in my family we do have a special talent for enchantments, so there is some evident power to the ring. Now since that ring came into my possession, I have always felt the strong desire to continue my family's work in artifice. When I was a little older I came upon the idea of constructing an institute where artifice could be studied by all of the greatest artificers of the Land of Oz together. Studying artifice within a family setting gave me special insight into understanding the benefits of practicing such academic skills with others in an open and friendly environment; thus, I came to found the Silver Tower. This is a place where the most talented and serious of artificers can come together and work collectively to study the field of artifice and bring advancement to goodness in the world through our fastidious work," said Glinda.

Chapter Fourteen

"Isn't the Ruby Ring in your Rather Rare Rings Room? I think I recall it as granting its wearing the gift of grace, although I could be remembering another ring ... perhaps one of the Diamond Rings," said Theresa.

"Your recollection is accurate, Theresa. Grace is the primary gift to the wearer of the ring; however, there are many charms on the ring that help grace to be realized in the wearer in a great number of ways. Also, those Diamond Rings were all crafted by my parents. They spent many years crafting and enchanting them. They are quite powerful and very valuable to me, as they are a special part of my family's heritage," said Glinda.

"Wasn't the Ruby Ring used in the last Great War?" asked Mr. Bunymunch.

"It was, and it was very much needed. But that story is for another time, as I am needed back in one of my workshops. I have several projects that require my attention this evening, so I will now leave you Silverglades and Mr. Bunnymunch to relax and enjoy the rest of your evening," said Glinda.

This was the only time that the Silverglades and Mr. Bunnymunch saw Glinda during their visit to the Silver Tower. On the day that the Silverglades departed from the tower, the Lady Thorn and the Lady Thistle traveled in the Silverglade's carriage with their guests to the edge of the Great Garden as a farewell to their new friends. The brilliance of the sun shining off of the Silver Tower prevented them from noticing Glinda waving to them from her private balcony that was located at the top of the tower.

Glinda thought to herself as she waved goodbye, *My new friends are true and honest citizens of Oz; however, they are about to learn the hard lesson that not everyone who seems to be a true and honest citizen of Oz really is one. I will have the Ladies look in on them regularly to make sure the children and Mr. Bunnymunch are all right. Their new rings and Acorn will be very valuable to them in the coming days. Together, through friendship, they will succeed in overcoming a wicked situation ... and perhaps make a new and unexpected friend in the process.*

Chapter Fifteen
The Return to Lilibeth

The friends had greatly enjoyed their visit to the Silver Tower of Oz. It had now been several days since they had departed from the Silver Tower and they were making their way back to Lilibeth the Good Wizardess. Since the weather was bright and sunny, they were all sitting on the carriage together enjoying the scenery. This time it was Terrance who was taking his turn at the reins of the vehicle. Theresa was taking a moment to care for the Green Coin Poinsettia that the Ladies had given to them. She thought that the sunlight would do the plant some good and would more than likely be even healthier than the Silver Lantern Tree light under which the poinsettia had been growing since their departure from the Silver Tower.

"Let's keep our eyes open for that Spectral Pandanus Tree. It will show us exactly where the road is to Lilibeth's cottage," said Aiden.

"She's going to be so happy when we bring her this ring!" said Theresa, who was wearing the ring alongside her Ring of Laughter.

"I'm happy that we not only have the opportunity to help Lilibeth but that we'll also be going back to the Silver Tower once she's done with the unbinding ring! I want to experience another rain shower in their tropical rainforest made of silver. That was very nice of them to let us spend so much time playing in the rainforest," said Terrance.

"I have a feeling the artificers enjoyed the break from their daily work to see two, fun-loving children enjoying their artifact-filled rainforest," said Aiden.

"There's the Spectral Pandanus Tree just up ahead!" said Mr. Bunnymunch. From this distance only a small glowing object was visible, but Mr. Bunnymunch could tell that it was the Spectral Pandanus Tree marking the road to Lilibeth's cottage.

Chapter Fifteen

As Terrance drove the carriage along South Grace road and prepared for the turn onto Lilibeth's road, he had to be reminded by his older brother to not drive like a race-carriage driver. Aiden was very understanding of Terrance's enthusiasm over arriving at Lilibeth's cottage with a cure for her wicked curse.

Lilibeth was waiting for the friends at her front door when they pulled up to her cottage, since she could hear their carriage coming up the road and she had a feeling that it was the Silverglades returning to her with some disenchantment magic. Since they had been her only visitors in a very long while, it really only could have been the Silverglades and Mr. Bunnymunch who were arriving.

"Welcome back, my Silverglade children and friend Mr. Bunnymunch. I've been anxiously awaiting your return. I very much would like to again venture over to my dessert lunch pail tree and gather some dessert for dinner with my own hands," said Lilibeth.

"Lilibeth! We have something very special for you!" said Theresa.

"It's from the Silver Tower and it's going to get rid of your terrible curse!" said Terrance.

The twins quickly ran to Lilibeth and greeted her with a big hug.

"What is it you have for me, my dearies? Is it a potion? I do like a good potion," said Lilibeth.

"It's an unbinding ring," said Aiden as he, Mr. Bunnymunch, and Acorn all arrived at the front door a moment later than the twins had, since the three of them had been able to control their enthusiasm a little better than had the twins.

Theresa quickly removed the ring from her finger and placed it onto Lilibeth's finger.

"How does it work?" asked Lilibeth with an unsubtly-hidden restless tone to her voice.

"You wear it as you are right now and say the words 'weeble-weeble-bind, weeble-weeble-free' ... I suspect you also may have to think about the curse you want to have removed from yourself, but

I could be incorrect," said Theresa, trying to be has helpful as she could in getting the ring to work.

"If this ring isn't strong enough to help you then we were directed to return to the Silver Tower so we can be given an even stronger one, although this one supposedly should be enough, according to two expert artificers of the Silver Tower," said Aiden.

"We should tell you that this ring is merely on loan, so we must eventually return it," added Mr. Bunnymunch.

"I'm sure that won't be a problem at all," said Lilibeth.

Lilibeth took a moment to examine the ring. The whole while she had a very large smile on her face.

After a moment she spoke the magic incantation, "Weeble-weeble-bind, weeble-weeble-free."

Immediately a gentle glow surrounded Lilibeth. When the glow subsided, Lilibeth released a large sigh, as if she were cleansing her soul.

"I must thank each one of you for your gift to me. The ring has worked and I am now free ... very free ... to go to my dessert lunch pail tree ... and do anything else my heart desires," said Lilibeth.

At that moment a small gray cloud began to form over their heads. Within a few seconds raindrops began to fall from the sky. After a few more seconds there was no sunlight left in the sky at all.

"Oh no! What a horrible time for a storm!" exclaimed Theresa.

"Just as we were having a wonderful time! We need to celebrate Lilibeth's liberation from that wicked curse," said Terrance.

"Lilibeth, what's happening to your pretty lilies?" asked Bunnymunch.

Mr. Bunnymunch was the first to notice that the lilies were all falling off of Lilibeth's cottage. Within seconds the vines began to wither and wilt. All of the plants in Lilibeth's garden soon followed after. The cottage quickly gained the appearance of an old, abandoned ghost cottage where nothing could live, plant or otherwise. Slowly the grassy area outside of the fenced-in property began to die. There was a slowly expanding circle of dead plants

Chapter Fifteen

that looked to be spreading out from the cottage ... and the children all felt a strong sense of dread.

Lilibeth began to cackle.

Aiden could sense that something was definitely wrong and he slowly reached for the children. "I think we should head back to the carriage."

Lilibeth stretched her arms above her head and a sparkling mist of blackness rained down on her from her hands. Her clothing became dark black and she transformed into what was obvious to all of the friends as something very wicked.

"A wicked witch!" yelled Mr. Bunnymunch.

"Run to carriage everyone!" yelled Aiden, as he placed himself between the Lilibeth and the twins.

Aiden jumped quickly into the box of the carriage once he had helped everyone into the coach. He then fiercely pulled at the reins and the carriage took off.

"Not so fast, my pretties!" screeched Lilibeth.

She pointed her finger at the carriage, which came to such an abrupt stop that everyone flew out of their seats and Aiden almost tumbled out of the carriage completely.

"You didn't think you'd be able to escape from the Wicked Witch of the Majestic Moonlit Mountains, did you? You must let me thank you properly for gifting me this ring ... which you will never be returning to the Silver Tower," said Lilibeth.

The children, Mr. Bunnymunch, and Acorn all looked at Lilibeth with great fear. Suddenly the ground began to shake and the cottage started to transform into stone and enlarge.

Just then, Lilibeth began to laugh and sneeze uncontrollably. This gave the friends a few seconds to make their escape.

Aiden again fiercely pulled at the reins of the carriage and they quickly made their way around the corner and onto the road back to South Grace Road.

As the carriage turned the corner from the small road onto South Grace Road, a large ball of black fire flew past the friends, barely missing them. Aiden took the carriage to its top speed.

Thirty minutes passed before anyone dared to look behind them. Since the black fireball had narrowly missed them, no other wicked magic had been sent in their direction and no sign of the Lilibeth the Wicked Witch had been seen ... other than an expanding storm in the sky above, which they knew to be a concoction of the Wicked Witch.

Everyone had been too afraid to speak during their rapid departure from Lilibeth's cottage ... or what had once been Lilibeth's cottage.

Aiden stopped the carriage for a moment so they could all catch their breaths.

"Look, everyone. There's a large castle to the South that wasn't there before," said Aiden.

"I think that's the castle of the Wicked Witch. She used her magic to turn her cottage into an evil, stone castle. It looks like it's probably haunted, too," said Mr. Bunnymunch.

"What ... what happened? How could the ring from Lady Thorn and Lady Thistle make the curse worse like that?" asked Theresa, still partially crying from fear.

"I don't think it made the curse any worse. I think we may have been tricked and we removed a good enchantment from a wicked witch," said Aiden.

"What are we going to do?" cried Terrance.

"I don't know ... but we'll think of something. For now ... let's just keep heading north, back towards home ... and keep thinking of what we can do to fix our mistake," said Aiden.

"We can't blame ourselves for this. We did something good. We helped a person we thought was in need, and that is never the wrong thing to do. Something horrible may have resulted, but our hearts were in the right place" said Mr. Bunnymunch.

"Theresa, I think you and I had the same idea there. That was very quick thinking of you to use Hilaritiènne's Ring of Laughter on Lilibeth to make her laugh. I used my ring to make her sneeze.

Chapter Fifteen

She was too distracted to catch us. You should be very proud of yourself for your quick thinking," said Aiden as he hugged his sister.

"Look above us. It's like a wave of gloom coming from the castle. It's going to take over all of Oz!" said Theresa.

"I don't think she's powerful enough to do that ... at least not with the Silver Tower around. Although I do think she will attempt to take over the Majestic Moonlit Mountains again ... and I think it was Lilibeth who reigned over them before. She's the wicked witch that Mr. Pommier, the tree guard, told us about," said Aiden.

"Oh no! I hope she doesn't attack Wilma the wandering wollemi pine tree again!" said Theresa.

"We need to warn Mr. Pommier, so he can be ready to protect his tree friend," said Terrance.

"We should head to them straight away," said Mr. Bunnymunch.

"That's exactly where I'm taking us first," said Aiden.

Chapter Sixteen
An Army of Friends

It had only taken the Silverglades and Mr. Bunnymunch about a day's worth of time to reach the edge of Lilibeth's storm, which had stopped expanding outwards from Lilibeth's castle. Mr. Bunnymunch informed the children that he suspected the Wicked Witch was busy using her magic for some other wicked purpose and would restart her expansion of the storm as soon as she could. They all agreed with him.

By the time the carriage had reached Wilma the wandering wollemi pine tree, there wasn't a cloud in the sky. This was very pleasing to the friends because they knew that this meant Lilibeth was not yet ready to regain her full dominion over the entire region of the Majestic Moonlit Mountains. They also didn't have to constantly wear their heavy raincoats. Every night they watched the sky to make sure that the magic haze that made the moonlight over the Majestic Moonlit Mountains look so very Majestic was still above them and not replaced by wicked storm clouds.

"I see Wilma! She looks like she's still well-protected and safe," said Theresa as the carriage approached the spot where the friends had visited with Mr. Pommier and his tree friend, Wilma.

"Does anyone see Mr. Pommier?" asked Aiden.

"No, I don't see him anywhere," said Terrance.

"I don't see him, either. I hope Lilibeth hasn't kidnapped him!" said Mr. Bunnymunch.

Aiden stopped the carriage as near to Wilma as he could so they could search for any signs of Mr. Pommier.

"Mr. Pommier! Are you here? We have some very urgent news to share with you!" shouted Aiden.

"Don't be gittin' yourself in such a fuss … I'm right here," said Mr. Pommier. "I was just takin' my rest period. I like to take my catnaps on the other side of Wilma. That way I don't gotta deal

Chapter Sixteen

with any passersby who might see me and decide to take advantage of my unconsciousness ... although I'm still a fierce guard even in my sleep. Still don't wanna encourage shenanigans, though."

"Mr. Pommier, we have horrible news for you! Something ... something very bad has happened," said Terrance.

"Well go ahead and tell me, I'm listenin'. I'm sure it's not as bad as ya think. I've heard a lot of bad things in my day, so I'm sure whatever this is isn't so bad," said Mr. Pommier.

"You and Wilma are in danger. We ... have accidentally released ...," said Aiden, as he paused to look at the twins, "... the Wicked Witch of the Majestic Moonlit Mountains."

"What!? Oh no! Oh no! Oh no! Wilma, did you hear that? The Wicked Witch of the Majestic Moonlit Mountains is back!" exclaimed Mr. Pommier.

"We are so sorry, we didn't mean to ... we thought we were helping a good wizardess, but we were wrong," said Theresa, half crying.

"She tricked us into thinking she was a good wizardess trapped by a curse, but it wasn't a curse. It was a good charm to make her a good person and prevent her from causing mischief," said Mr. Bunnymunch.

"Can you help us figure out what to do? How can we help protect Wilma?" said Terrance.

"That witch is very good at trickery, so don't be worryin' yourselves. It's not your fault. Now ... I ... must stay here and protect Wilma! The Wicked Witch will come soon. Has she started her wicked thunderstorm yet?" said Mr. Pommier. His voice wavered a little as he mentioned the storm, because he greatly feared it as a sign of the Wicked Witch's power.

"Yes, but the storm stopped growing a few days ago. Mr. Bunnymunch thinks she's using her magic on something else wicked for now but will make it grow more soon," said Aiden.

"That's good ... no, that's bad ... but it's good for now, 'cause we're safe 'til the storm comes. The wicked thunderstorm marks what she likes to think is her territory, and she rarely leaves her territory. Wilma, my dear, now would be a very good time for ya to decide to do some wanderin'. Maybe we could wander together up north, far away from the Wicked Witch of the Majestic Moonlit Mountains," said Mr. Pommier.

They all looked at Wilma and waited for her to show a sign of response to Mr. Pommier, but she was not ready to respond.

"She doesn't look like she's going to do any wandering today, Mr. Pommier. We will stay here and help you protect her," said Aiden.

"No ... I think ... I think what's best to do, although Wilma and I do appreciate your willin'ness to stay ... what's best to do is for you to find help. Ya see, all of us together are no match for a wicked witch! We must have help," said Mr. Pommier.

"Should we go back to the Silver Tower and ask for help?" asked Theresa, with some hesitation in her voice. She was a little afraid to think about how the Ladies and Glinda might react when they found out that a wicked witch had been released with an unbinding ring on loan from the Silver Tower.

"I don't know ... maybe ... maybe ... maybe we should try to work this out without bothering them just yet. I know if we put our heads together we can figure out a way to take care of our own problem. We need to learn to fend for ourselves better. We can't just go running off to the Silver Tower whenever we have a problem," said Aiden.

"What about the Tinkermeyers? They are always looking for problems to solve and they are ever so friendly. I've known them for years and they enjoy solving problems for their friends. I'm sure they can help us figure out what to do," said Mr. Bunnymunch.

"The Tinkermeyers! Mrs. Tinkermeyer was so very kind to us and we do need to visit her again. Let's ask her if she and her husband can help. He should be returned from his sabbatical by now," said Theresa.

"Maybe they have an artifact we can borrow. We need to work out our problems ourselves, but maybe we can buy an artifact from them that could help us. I don't think our magic rings are nearly

Chapter Sixteen

strong enough to get us much of anywhere with un-unbinding that enchantment on Lilibeth," said Aiden.

"Lilibeth? Who's that? Is that the name of the Wicked Witch? We never found out her name. We just knew she was wicked and hates everyone," said Mr. Pommier.

"Yes, Mr. Pommier, Lilibeth is the name of the Wicked Witch of the Majestic Moonlit Mountains," said Mr. Bunnymunch.

"Let's go to the Tinkermeyers straight away and see if they have any artifacts we could borrow," said Terrance.

"All right, let's be off. Mr. Pommier, we will return soon with help. We'll try to be back before Lilibeth's wicked thunderstorm arrives ... but we don't know when that will be, so we can't make any guarantees," said Aiden.

"Don't you be worryin' about us. We'll be just fine for now. I don't think she'll be after us immediately ... but don't take too long, 'cause she'll eventually come for Wilma."

***

The Silverglades and Mr. Bunnymunch were quickly back on their way towards the north. They arrived in the Cypress Savannah that night and arrived in the region of the Tinkermeyers' home the next morning.

Theresa had the tiny model of the Tinkermeyers' home in her hand, ready to notify Aiden as soon as it began to glow. That was how they would know if they were approaching the baobab home of the Tinkermeyers.

"It's a good thing Mrs. Tinkermeyer gave us that artifact, or else it might be rather difficult finding their home among all of these nearly identical baobab trees," said Aiden.

"For travelers not from the Cypress Savannah that may be true, but for us natives each tree and each plant has its own, unique appearance. You won't miss the home of the Tinkermeyers with me on the lookout," said Mr. Bunnymunch.

"I'm so glad you're here with us, Mr. Bunnymunch!" said Theresa.

"As are we all," said Aiden.

"Their home is just up ahead," said Mr. Bunnymunch.

A moment later the artifact began to glow, indicating that they were very close to the home of the artificers of the Cypress Savannah.

"Is that it? I remember their baobab tree was a bit fatter than the others," said Theresa, pointing to a baobab tree located to the north-west.

"That's it, Miss Theresa. Good eye!" said Mr. Bunnymunch.

This time the Silverglades didn't have the advantage of there being copper wire wrapped around the tree, as had been the case when they first discovered the Tinkermeyers' home.

As soon as they arrived at the tree, they all ran out of the carriage to the baobab tree in which, or really under which, the Tinkermeyers lived. Aiden arrived first and knocked on the door.

"Oh my goodness me! It's my Silverglade children! And I see you've met Mr. Bunnymunch. How are you all? Please do come in! Mr. Tinkermeyer is here and he'll be so excited to finally meet you! I've told him all about our visit. And is that a clockwork squirrel I see following you, Aiden? How did you ever come across such a wonderful artifact? The Silver Tower, perhaps?" said Mrs. Tinkermeyer with very excited energy.

"Yes, Mr. Tinkermeyer, we did adopt Acorn into our family while at the Silver Tower ... but we have some bad news to share with you," said Aiden.

"And we could really use your help!" said Terrance.

"Do you have any artifacts that we might be permitted to borrow or purchase to help us un-unbind an enchantment on a wicked witch?" said Theresa.

"An artifact that can un-unbind an enchantment ... no, we don't have anything capable of doing that. And what's this about a wicked witch? There aren't any here in the Cypress Savannah ... unless they're just passing through in great haste. Did you forget we're well-protected from wicked people here?" said Mrs. Tinkermeyer.

Chapter Sixteen

"It's the Wicked Witch of the Majestic Moonlit Mountains. We accidentally unbound an enchantment on her that was making her good and stopping her from doing wicked things," said Theresa.

"Do you have any artifacts that could help us? Do you have anything that could place a new enchantment on her to stop her wickedness?" asked Aiden.

"Oh my goodness me! That is a predicament you have found yourselves in. It also doesn't sound like you to help a wicked witch like that, so I must presume she tricked you. Wicked witches are like that, you know. Let's go consult Mr. Tinkermeyer," said Mrs. Tinkermeyer.

"She did trick us. We thought she was a good wizardess. The enchantment made her do good things and made her look like a good wizardess, too!" said Mr. Bunnymunch.

"Most likely she was a good wizardess thanks to that enchantment, but there was a little wickedness in her that let her trick you into bringing out all of her wickedness again. Enchantments can be very hard to use and sometimes they are not quite complete in doing what a person intends for them to do. That's a lesson you learn very quickly as an artificer that's trying to enchant an artifact," said Mrs. Tinkermeyer.

The friends arrived in the parlor of the Tinkermeyers' home, where Mr. Tinkermeyer was sitting in his favorite chair, watching an illusionary fire dance away in the fireplace.

"Mr. Tinkermeyer, I have some guests here for you to meet. You know Mr. Bunnymunch already, but here are the Silverglade children I told you all about. We also have Mr. Acorn here. He is the newest member of the Silverglade family ... and he just happens to be a clockwork squirrel from the Silver Tower," said Mrs. Tinkermeyer.

"The Silverglade children? How marvelous to finally make all of your acquaintances! I've heard so many good things about you from my wife and have been cheerfully anticipating a visit from you all. Now where is this clockwork squirrel? Is that him there hiding behind this young man?" said Mr. Tinkermeyer, gesturing towards Aiden, around whose leg Acorn was looking.

"Yes, this is Acorn. He's a bit shy around new people," said Aiden.

"My husband, we have a situation at hand and our friends here could use our help," said Mrs. Tinkermeyer.

"We don't want to be a burden. We were just wondering if you had any artifacts we could use to stop a wicked witch. It's our fault she's free from an enchantment that was making her good and we need to work things out as much as we can on our own, so we can learn to be independent," said Aiden.

"Learn to be independent? That's a good thing to do, but you must also learn to trust your friends and know when to ask for help. Good people always help each other," said Mr. Tinkermeyer.

"Quite right! That's how the world is meant to be. Good people help others. It's why good people are here," added Mrs. Tinkermeyer.

"Tell me, my friends, exactly how did this wicked witch become freed from this enchantment of goodness?" asked Mr. Tinkermeyer.

"We were loaned a magic, unbinding ring by Lady Thorn and Lady Thistle. It was used to remove the enchantment from Lilibeth – she's the Wicked Witch of the Majestic Moonlit Mountains. We're so sorry, but we thought we were helping to set free a good wizardess," said Theresa.

"And we thought she'd remain a good wizardess and not turn into a wicked witch," said Terrance.

"Hmm ... Lilibeth ... the Wicked Witch of the Majestic Moonlit Mountains. We are familiar with her wickedness. Not that we've met her personally, but one of our friends came across her some time back and did not appreciate her wickedness one bit. I think Mrs. Tinkermeyer and I may be able to help, wouldn't you agree, my wife?" said Mr. Tinkermeyer.

"Yes, my husband. Children, may we please see the ring? We may be able to study its powers and figure out a spell to un-unbind

Chapter Sixteen

the enchantment, although with a ring powerful enough to unbind an enchantment from a wicked witch we will more than likely require the assistance of some of our more powerful colleagues, since a good wizard and a good wizardess like the two of us are no match for a wicked witch of Lilibeth's caliber," said Mrs. Tinkermeyer.

"Unfortunately, Lilibeth still has the ring. We barely managed to escape from her. There was nothing we could do to remove the ring from her hand," said Aiden.

"Let's get packing!" said Mrs. Tinkermeyer.

"Yes, we will need some supplies!" said Mr. Tinkermeyer.

"Why pack? Where are you going? Did we upset you? We are very sorry if we did ...," said Aiden.

"Oh my goodness me, no! You didn't upset us. We are packing so we can go with you to find Lilibeth and take that ring away from her. Even if we can't figure out how to un-unbind the enchantment, she still shouldn't have that ring. Her wickedness would cause her to do many terrible things with it," said Mrs. Tinkermeyer.

The Tinkermeyers quickly disappeared into their workshop and began to pack very loudly, as there were many supplies that they needed to collect and those supplies were nearly all made of metal and other loud, clanky materials.

As soon as the Tinkermeyers were packed, the friends all gathered into the carriage headed again to the south, towards Lilibeth's castle. Terrance had taken the time to inform the Tinkermeyers about the situation with Mr. Pommier and Wilma. The Tinkermeyers asked that they pay a quick visit to Mr. Pommier and his tree friend to assess the situation there before they arrived at the castle, which was an easy task to accomplish since the carriage would pass right by Wilma on the way to find Lilibeth.

The friends were all very pleased when they arrived back at the wandering wollemi pine tree that there were still no clouds in sight, since that would mean Lilibeth was extending her wicked thunderstorm and her territory ... placing Mr. Pommier and Wilma in immediate danger.

"That was a very quick trip!" said Mr. Pommier, who was standing guard in front of Wilma very diligently when the carriage arrived.

"Mr. Pommier, my name is Mr. Tinkermeyer, and this is my wife, Mrs. Tinkermeyer. We are here to ask you if you know why Lilibeth would want to attack your wandering wollemi pine tree. Does she have a particular reason to hate Wilma?" said Mr. Tinkermeyer.

"Good to meet ya both, Mr. and Mrs. Tinkermeyer. No, there's no reason I can reckon for her to hate Wilma ... but then again a wicked witch doesn't need a reason. She will attack anyone she wants. That's how wickedness works: it doesn't need a reason to do wicked things," said Mr. Pommier.

"We thought that perhaps coming here we'd be able to find something that would cause the Wicked Witch to attack you first ... but my detector here isn't finding anything," said Mrs. Tinkermeyer. She was holding a small, copper compass in her hand and seemed to be examining the area with it. She and Mr. Tinkermeyer had crafted the Artifacts-and-Magics Compass some time ago to help them track down artifacts that they could study.

"We should continue on towards Lilibeth's castle then," said Aiden.

At that moment, Wilma began to shake her branches.

"No, Wilma. I need to stay here, by your side, and protect you. I can't go with them," said Mr. Pommier.

Wilma continued to shake her branches.

"What's she saying?" asked Theresa.

"She's sayin' I need to go with ya. I can evidently protect her better if I go with ya. I guess ... I need to listen to her. She's earned my trust and I've earned hers over the years, so I'm going to do as she says. Wilma, darlin', you're gonna be fine. We'll stop the Wicked Witch and then we'll be back together in no time," said Mr. Pommier.

Chapter Sixteen

Suddenly apples began to appear in Wilma's branches and they fell to the ground. Wilma was very careful to not drop any of them directly on her friends.

"Why thank ya, Wilma! I would miss eatin' your delicious apples if I didn't have them every day," said Mr. Pommier.

"Let's put them all in here," said Mrs. Tinkermeyer, opening a small sack that she had in her pocket.

The friends quickly placed the apples in the sack, which happened to be bottomless, and then quickly jumped into the carriage for their departure.

Mr. Pommier couldn't stop waving as they left. This was the first time he had been without his tree friend an ages.

"It's like we have our own little army now," commented Terrance.

"It's the Army of South Grace," said Mrs. Tinkermeyer.

"This army of friends is determined to defeat the Wicked Witch of the Majestic Moonlit Mountains, so she should be preparing now for defeat because she doesn't have a chance!" added Mr. Tinkermeyer.

"I never thought I'd be part of an army. We bunnymunches aren't very good at fighting," said Mr. Bunnymunch.

"I don't think fighting is what's going to make us a good army, Mr. Bunnymunch. We need to outwit a wicked witch, and I'm sure you'll be invaluable to us because you know an awful lot about this area," said Aiden.

"Being good is important, too, isn't it? If that's so then you're perfect for the army, Mr. Bunnymunch, because you're a very good person and friend," asked Theresa.

"Exactly so! Goodness will defeat wickedness," said Mrs. Tinkermeyer.

Chapter Seventeen
The Good Warlock

The Army of South Grace was a day into its next journey south along South Grace Road. It had not yet reached the front edge of the Lilibeth the Wicked Witch's thunderstorm, which made traveling easier for the army. This was also a good sign that Lilibeth was not yet ready to reclaim all of the Majestic Moonlit Mountains for herself.

The first night together as the Army of South Grace, the friends had a splendid time together, at least as splendid of a time as was possible with the thoughts of a wicked witch in everyone's mind. The Tinkermeyers had brought along with them a small artifact that they had devised in order to put on an illusionary fireworks display. They never wanted to risk causing a fire during a dry season. Since the army was very careful to hide its presence from Lilibeth, the friends had the illusionary fireworks display inside of the carriage where there was plenty of space for a small display. The twins noted how the fireworks were almost as nice as the dancing of the Lightning Bugs in the Village of Illume. An outdoor fireworks display even in the middle of the day would have quickly caught the attention of the Wicked Witch. Even the carriage was a matter of concern. During a sunny day the carriage did not stand out all that well under the tree cover with the Majestic Moonlit Mountains; however, at night it was like a beacon. Being made from Lantern Trees, the carriage was a very luminescent vehicle. Travel at night was simply not possible.

"I do hope it remains bright and sunny for the rest of the day. I don't want to see any of those wicked thunderstorm clouds," said Theresa.

All of the members of the army were sitting on the outside portion of the carriage, with Aiden and Mr. Tinkermeyer sitting up front in the box.

Chapter Seventeen

"I hope so, too. That wicked thunderstorm will turn everything cold, and bunnymunches don't favor the cold much at all," said Mr. Bunnymunch.

"Aiden, if ya want us to stay hidden very well then I expect we should be takin' the Lapis Lazuli Lane. There's a road to the west just up ahead, Weepin' Willow Way, that'll take us right to Lapis Lazuli Lane. Both roads are well-hidden from view, thanks to the many willow, fog, blanket, and fuzzy trees," said Mr. Pommier.

"That's a very good idea, Mr. Pommier. How do we find Weeping Willow Way? It must be hidden since we didn't see it during our previous travels this way," said Aiden.

"Ya didn't see it because it's hidden underneath a weepin' willow tree. Unlike the road, the tree's easy to find. It's the only weepin' willow on all of South Grace Road," said Mr. Pommier.

"We didn't hear any weeping willow trees before," said Theresa.

"We were probably distracted before and didn't hear it," said Terrance.

"I agree with Mr. Pommier. We should take Weeping Willow Way to Lapis Lazuli Lane. There is a friend of the bunnymunches there I'd like to say hi to, if there's time. Maybe he can even help us. He's always been very kind to us bunnymunches. Sometimes he comes to visit us in the Cypress Savannah, and he brings us lots of yummies when he comes!" said Mr. Bunnymunch.

"I think I see it now. It's on our right, to the west. Do you see it, Aiden?" said Mrs. Tinkermeyer.

"I do now, Mrs. Tinkermeyer. Thank you. Mr. Pommier, how do we get to the Weeping Willow Way if the tree is blocking it?" said Aiden.

"The tree isn't blockin' the road … at least not exactly. Just take us through the branches and you'll find the road underneath it," said Mr. Pommier.

Aiden did exactly as Mr. Pommier said, although the rest of the army was a little worried that they might become caught up in the thick, dangling branches of the weeping willow tree. Once they made it through the edge of the branches, they could see on the ground that there was a dirt road. Aiden guided the carriage through the branches to the other side of the tree, where Weeping Willow Way stretched out before them.

"And here must be Weeping Willow Way. Well done, Mr. Pommier!" said Mr. Tinkermeyer.

The glow from the carriage was more evident on Weeping Willow Way. It was fortunate that the weeping willow trees prevented the carriage's glow from being visible for very far.

"Mr. Pommier, didn't you say these were *weeping* willow trees?" asked Theresa.

"That they are, Theresa. That they are," replied Mr. Pommier.

"Then ... why aren't they weeping?" asked Theresa.

"They do seem to be awfully quiet for weeping willows," said Mr. Bunnymunch.

"Well of course they're not weepin' right now. It's their nap time. Even trees become tired and need to rest. Don't ya think ya'd become tired if ya spent most of your time weepin'?" said Mr. Pommier.

"I suppose I would," said Theresa.

"I'm glad they're not weeping right now. I don't think I'd much enjoy hearing a forest of trees weep today," said Terrance.

"I'm with you, my favorite little brother. We don't need any sadness around us right now. I'd rather not hear the weeping either," said Aiden.

"How soon are they going to wake up?" asked Terrance.

"Oh, I suppose they'll be wakin' up in a few days. They're just takin' a short nap," said Mr. Pommier.

"A short nap? Being asleep for a few days sounds more like a coma to me, and not a nap," said Aiden.

"You're thinkin' about human naps. Trees can nap for months at a time, so a few days is a very short nap indeed," said Mr. Pommier.

The army continued for about an hour along Weeping Willow Way, without the sound of any weeping to be of disturbance to the army.

Chapter Seventeen

"What's that up ahead?" asked Terrance, pointing to where the trees and road suddenly seemed to disappear.

"It looks like fog to me," said Mr. Tinkermeyer.

"That must be from the fog trees Mr. Pommier mentioned," said Aiden.

"The fog trees are especially dense in this part of Lapis Lazuli Lane. That fog is right where Weepin' Willow Way and Lapis Lazuli Lane meet. Take a left, towards the south there," said Mr. Pommier.

"Everyone help me listen for others traveling along this road. We don't want to have any accidents, and I can't see far enough around these corners," said Aiden as he carefully steered the carriage onto Lapis Lazuli Lane.

Aiden successfully negotiated the turn, with all of the members of the army paying very close attention to the two roads with their eyes and ears.

"I think I see a cottage over there ... right along the left side of the lane," said Mr. Tinkermeyer.

"Good day, travelers! What brings you through these parts?" said a voice from a shadow that appeared on the front porch of the cottage.

"Good day to you, too, sir. We are on our way south to take care of an urgent matter of a wicked witch," said Aiden.

"A wicked witch? There are no wicked witches in the Majestic Moonlit Mountains ... at least not anymore. Are you sure it's not just a wicked basic conjurer? We do have a few of those living about, but they tend not to cause much trouble since we have so many good people here to discipline them. My name is Del, and I am the Good Warlock of the Majestic Moonlit Mountains, so I should know ... I manage to keep pretty good track of these things," said Del.

"Excuse me, Mr. Del ...," said Terrance.

"Please, just call me Del," said Del.

"All right, Del, we really do have a matter of a wicked witch. You see, we accidentally freed the Wicked Witch of the Majestic

Moonlit Mountains from an enchantment that was protecting everyone from her and made her good. We are traveling south to her castle so we can un-unbind the enchantment and make her good again," said Terrance.

Aiden pulled the carriage up to the front of Del's cottage so they could see Del without having to strain their eyes to filter out the fog. When they arrived at his cottage they realized that the cottage was not so much a cottage as it was an extraordinarily small, stone castle.

"Oh my goodness me, your home is very attractive," said Mrs. Tinkermeyer.

"Thank you very much, Mrs.....?" said Del.

"... Tinkermeyer. Mrs. Tinkermeyer. And this is my husband, Mr. Tinkermeyer. These are our friends, the Silverglades: Aiden, Theresa, Terrance, and Acorn, the clockwork squirrel. This gentleman in the guard's uniform is Mr. Pommier and this small, fuzzy friend of ours is Mr. Bunnymunch," said Mrs. Tinkermeyer. She seemed to take pride in having the privilege of introducing her friends, as she was very happy to have them all as friends.

"It's a pleasure to meet you all, and it's especially good to see you again, Mr. Bunnymunch ... but how did you all unbind the enchantment on Lilibeth? Surely she isn't free. I haven't seen any signs of her wicked thunderstorm yet, which I'm sure she'd try to make again. She does have a fondness for her storms," said Del.

"It's all our fault. We thought we were helping when we brought her an unbinding ring from the Silver Tower ... but she turned into a wicked witch instead when she used it. We're terribly sorry and we are doing our best to restore the enchantment," said Theresa.

"Well, I do thank you for your honesty ... and for that you should be commended. Some days with the lack of honesty in the world I ... I just ... well never mind, we need to concentrate on Lilibeth now and unwickeding her," said Del.

"Do you know how the enchantment was placed on her before?" asked Mr. Tinkermeyer.

Chapter Seventeen

"Of course I know how. I did it," said Del, very matter-of-factly.

"So you were the kind warlock that helped Wilma and me when that witch tried to burn down Wilma! I'd like to shake your hand, good sir. Wilma and I can't thank you enough for comin' to our rescue," said Mr. Pommier. He walked right up to Del and shook his hand as if the two hand been longtime friends.

"Wilma? Who's that? Oh! Is she that lovely wandering wollemi pine tree? My sister never should have tried to burn down such a charming tree," said Del.

"What? Did you say your *sister*?" asked Aiden.

"Yes, my sister. Lilibeth is my sister, which is why I felt it my responsibility to put an end to her wickedness. Please, do come inside and we'll discuss the matter over a nice meal," said Del.

The inside of Del's castle was full of Poofle art and Poofle furniture, which made sense to Mr. Pommier since Poofle Trees were common to the south in the area of Lapis Lazuli.

"Please, help yourself to whatever food you like. I can always make more with my magic. I do enjoy the company of good folks and bringing food to my friends, as Mr. Bunnymunch is well-aware," said Del.

"Del, since you are the expert in these matter, what do you recommend we do to restore that enchantment on your sister?" asked Mr. Tinkermeyer.

"Couldn't you just re-enchant her?" asked Theresa.

"The first enchantment was terribly difficult to place on Lilibeth, and it will take considerable time and effort to place another one on her. Her powers are substantially greater than mine, although she is certainly not a wicked sorceress, for which we should all be very thankful. There was a time when such an enchantment would never have been necessary. Many years ago, Lilibeth truly was a good witch. One day she made a small, yet innocent, error with one of her spells. She wanted to correct what she had done and thought that a small black magic spell would help, since any good magic would have taken a considerable amount of time to work ... but once she cast that one black magic spell she couldn't stop. There were side effects ... and in order to counteract those side effects she turned again to black magic. Each black magic spell she cast led her further down the road to wickedness ... and she became the Wicked Witch of the Majestic Moonlit Mountains," explained Del.

"Oh my goodness me! That must have been very hard on you to see a member of your very own family go down such a dark path and become wicked. We feel very sorry for you, Del," said Mrs. Tinkermeyer in the most comforting voice she could manage.

"The whole family was devastated. When I finally figured out how to bring her back to goodness ... or at least a resemblance of goodness ... I acted. This time I will need to find a more permanent enchantment if I can. May I ask, what had you intended to do when you reached Lilibeth? Surely you don't have the power to re-enchant her? The Tinkermeyers are the only ones among you that have magical ability, but you are only a wizard and wizardess ... not nearly powerful enough. Your artifacts that I sense on you are no match for Lilibeth either," said Del.

"The Tinkermeyers, the wonderful artificers and good people they are, had planned to examine the unbinding ring and figure out how to use it or how to construct a new artifact to un-unbind the enchantment," said Aiden.

"They are very good at artifice, so I'm sure they can do it!" said Theresa.

"Hmm ... that is a plan ... and there is at least a small amount of potential there ... so ... yes ... yes, do go ahead with that plan ... however ... I will still work on re-enchanting her myself. We must work together on multiple fronts to make sure she doesn't take control of the Majestic Moonlit Mountains again," said Del.

"Then we welcome to the Army of South Grace!" said Terrance.

"The Army of South Grace?" asked Del.

Chapter Seventeen

"We are the Army of South Grace, a group of friends that are using wit instead of fighting might to bring the Wicked Witch back to goodness," said Mrs. Tinkermeyer.

"How very excellent! I happily accept my membership in your army. Now … you should all head towards Lilibeth's castle and continue on with your mission. In the meanwhile, I'll work on an enchantment," said Del as he pulled a brilliant-white ribbon out from his pocket and twirled it in his hands. "While you're at her castle, try to find out what her plans are. I expect that it will take the Tinkermeyers some time to properly examine the unbinding ring, so we will plan to meet in twenty-eight days at the Poofle Inn. You will find the Poofle Inn in the Village of Poofle. Mr. Bunnymunch can lead you there. He knows where to find the village. You will be well-protected there, because there are enough good witches and warlocks in the village to keep Lilibeth away. When we meet, we will discuss our progress and figure out if either of our plans will work," said Del.

"That sounds like a superb battle plan to me. I'm confident that one, if not both, of our plans will bring success," said Mr. Tinkermeyer.

"I have another question for you, Silverglade children. When you were at the Silver Tower, did you have the opportunity to meet Lady Thorn or Lady Thistle? I ask because they are great role models of mine and I'd love to one day meet them," said Del.

"Yes! Everyone seems to love Lady Thorn and Lady Thistle. They were our hostesses for our entire visit there. They are very lovely ladies and good friends of ours now. You should come with us to the Silver Tower once we un-unbind the enchantment on your sister. We need to return the unbinding ring to them because it's only on loan to us for a while," said Theresa.

"My word, you are friends with the Ladies? Well … yes, I'd most happily join you when you return to the Silver Tower, if it wouldn't be an inconvenience to you. I'm not surprised that an unbinding ring from the Good Ladies Thorn and Thistle unbound my enchantment. They are most powerful sorceresses, you know!

Second only to Glinda herself. And you are incorrect when you say everyone loves them ... the villagers of the Iron Village don't much like the Ladies, although they certainly do not hate the Ladies outright. Those people founded their village a few ages back on the principle of the superiority of iron. They believe the Ladies' magic to be corrupted because they practice all different sorts of nature magics, not just iron magic, which is a form of nature magic," said Del.

"You seem to know a lot about the Ladies for someone who has never met them ... although that makes sense since you consider them to be your role models. Have you spent a lot of time studying them?" asked Aiden.

"Most assuredly! Did you know that before they met they were only good wizardesses? Their strong relationship together is what made them sorceresses. Their love for one another is a potent source of power, just as is the love of any good relationship. Their magics intertwined and grew. Some of us suspect that together they may even be as powerful or more powerful than Glinda! I'm sure you realize how astounding that would be if it were true. And I'm also sure the Tinkermeyers would love to have the opportunity to study the Rosewood Thorn Ring and the Rosewood Thistle Ring. Those are the magic rings of the Ladies Thorn and Thistle. I have yet to become acquainted with an individual that knows the true powers of the rings, but I suspect that they are representative of the amazing relationship the Ladies have with one another ... so they should be quite powerful artifacts indeed. The ladies made the rings for each other, you know. Yes ... quite powerful indeed," said Del.

"They didn't seem like powerful sorceresses to us when we met them. They seemed like very friendly good witches. We didn't see them use their magic very much, though," said Aiden.

All three Silverglade children were reluctant to believe that they could have met such powerful sorceresses without knowing it.

"I suppose that the rumors could be just that ... rumors. But it's nice to believe that people as nice as the Ladies might have great

Chapter Seventeen

power. Good people deserve good power. They can handle it better," said Del.

Since there was still most of the day left, the army decided to return on its way south along Lapis Lazuli Lane, which would take the friends to the castle of the Wicked Witch of the Majestic Moonlit Mountains. Mr. Pommier and Mr. Bunnymunch were both hoping that there wouldn't be any sightings of fog sprites along the way ... but, of course, they couldn't mention the fog sprites out loud.

Chapter Eighteen
The Road to Lilibeth

"**M**r. Pommier, didn't you tell us before there were many weeping willow trees, blanket trees, and fuzzy trees along this lane?" asked Theresa.

"There all around us, m'dear," said Mr. Pommier.

"Well ... where around us are they? I don't see any of them," noted Theresa.

"I haven't seen anything but fog trees, myself," said Terrance.

"Of course ya haven't seen anythin' but fog trees. The fog from the fog trees is too thick for us to see all of the other trees. You're also seein' a number of fog bushes, too ... but it can be very difficult here to tell the difference b'tween fog trees and fog bushes," said Mr. Pommier.

"That makes a lot of sense to me ... since I can barely see any of the road, myself," said Aiden.

"Oh my goodness me, this isn't too pleasant on my lungs, either. The humidity isn't very nice for my breathing ... but I'm just glad I didn't bring any artifacts that are prone to rust," said Mrs. Tinkermeyer.

"Terrance ... do you have your Ring of Light with you?" asked Aiden.

"Yes I do. I never take it off ... although I rarely use it. I do like to play with it a little at night, just for practice in case I ever really do need it," said Terrance.

"Although your ring most likely won't be of any help to our lungs, it might be of help to me and our speed. Could you try producing some light along the road in front of us? It might help me see the road better," said Aiden.

"I'm not sure ... but I can try," said Terrance. He crawled to the front of the carriage, the box, and sat down next to his brother.

Chapter Eighteen

Terrance then pointed his ring at the road in front of them and closed his eyes, in order to concentrate on illumination. A ball of light appeared a few feet in front of the carriage. Terrance opened his eyes and smiled, proud of his achievement. He had not yet tried to project light before. When he practiced using his ring at nights in his bedchambers within the carriage he had only tried making light appear directly from Illumina's Ring of Light.

"Very good, Terrance! Excellent job. Now could you please try to bring the light a little closer to the surface of the road? That will make it illuminate the road more than it illuminates the fog," said Aiden, who was very proud of his brother for helping.

"That is quite a handy little artifact you have there. Mrs. Tinkermeyer and I may ask you if we can borrow it sometime so we can study it," said Mr. Tinkermeyer.

"I think I can take us a little faster now that I can see the road ahead of us a little better. The faster we make our way to the Wicked Witch's castle the better. We need to stop her. This makes me think of father's fairytales about fog he'd tell us whenever there was a fog on the family farm. He'd always talk about being careful to not go outside because we could find ourselves in the midst of a swarm of mischievous fog sprites. He just wanted to keep us inside and protected so we wouldn't go off and accidentally fall into the Silver Water we have on our farm," said Aiden.

"Oh Aiden ...," said Mr. Pommier.

"Uh-oh ... Aiden ... they aren't a fairytale ...," said Mr. Bunnymunch.

"'Uh-oh'? Why 'uh-oh'? Is there a problem?" asked Aiden, confused as to the nervous looks on his friends' faces.

"Did your father mention to you that you should never say their name if you are in their land?" said Mr. Bunnymunch.

"No ... no he didn't ... are you saying they're real? Even so, I'm sure they aren't all that mischievous," said Aiden.

"You said their name ... so you're about to find out. They are attracted to anyone who says their name among the fog trees and

158

fog bushes of their home ... and Lapis Lazuli Lane is home to many of them ...," said Mr. Bunnymunch.

No one said anything for a moment. The army members looked all around themselves very carefully, searching for fog sprites.

"What's that fluttering sound? ... it almost sounds like dragonflies," said Theresa.

"Oh my goodness me, I hear it, too. I think that perhaps Aiden should increase our velocity a tad bit," said Mrs. Tinkermeyer.

All of a sudden the carriage took off at full speed.

"Aiden! She didn't mean to go that fast!" said Terrance.

"It's not me! I didn't do a thing! I ... I can't steer or anything!" said Aiden as he fought with the reins inconsequentially.

"It's the sprites ... just sit back and try to relax. Maybe if we ignore them the pesky little things will go away. Be they ever so mischievous, they tend not to hurt anyone," said Mr. Pommier, who looked oddly relaxed for being in a runaway carriage that could run into a tree or other passerby at any moment.

"Help!" screamed Theresa as a fluttering noise sounded to go right past her ear.

"Don't worry, m'dear. It won't do anythin' to ya. He's just flyin' by ya to be a bother. Try to think of somethin' else," said Mr. Pommier.

Mrs. Tinkermeyer began to hum a pleasant little tune in an attempt to get the children's minds off of the many fluttering fog sprites that were diving down through the fog by the heads the army members ... and to also get her own mind off of the disturbing sounds.

"They aren't going to crash us are they?" asked Aiden.

"I doubt they'd allow that to happen. They like to annoy, not harm," said Mr. Pommier.

"I consider scaring people to be a form of harm, so they should reconsider their mischievousness!" said Mrs. Tinkermeyer, who then continued with her pleasant humming.

The fluttering began to subside and the carriage came to a stop.

Chapter Eighteen

"What happened? I can still hear some fluttering ... but the carriage stopped? Are they waiting for something?" asked Aiden.

"I'm not sure ... they usually don't just stop like this," said Mr. Pommier.

A small figure, about only four inches in height, with wings like a dragonfly and a body like an elf calmly flew down in front of Aiden. "The fog ends just up ahead, so we can't take you any further. Thank you for stopping the Wicked Witch of the Majestic Moonlit Mountains," said the fog sprite, who then quickly disappeared back into the fog.

"Well I'll be ... they were helping us. How very nice of them. That just goes to show you not to judge a person before you take the time to understand the situation. Thank you for helping us, fog sprites! Please forgive us for being afraid! You were only helping!" said Mrs. Tinkermeyer.

"Why were they flying so close to us?" asked Terrance.

"The air felt warm and magical when they flew by me, now that I think of it. That must have been how they made us move so quickly," said Mrs. Tinkermeyer.

"I quite agree. They had to be very close to us for their acceleration magic to work in order to take such a large object to that speed. Yes, very kind of them indeed!" said Mr. Tinkermeyer.

Aiden had complete control over the carriage again, so he started them off on their way once more. In just a few seconds they were out of the fog ... but now underneath the wicked thunderstorm of the Wicked Witch.

"Look! I can see the weeping willow trees, blanket trees, and fuzzy trees now! They are very exotic. It's a shame we're in Lilibeth's wicked thunderstorm now ...," said Theresa.

"Those little fog sprites just shaved an hour or more off'a our travel time. I never woulda thought ...," said Mr. Pommier.

"They probably fear the Wicked Witch as much as anyone else. Fog sprites aren't wicked ... they are just mischievous. There's a big difference between the two, although sometimes that difference isn't so easy to see," commented Mr. Bunnymunch.

"Mr. Pommier, how far are we from Lilibeth's castle?" asked Aiden.

"If we keep up a good pace then we should be arrivin' in a quarter-hour at the Village of Lapis Lazuli. From there it should take us about another quarter-hour. If ya look through those trees you'll see one of the towers of her castle," said Mr. Pommier, as he indicated towards the south-east.

Chapter Nineteen
Lapis Lazuli

The trees of Lapis Lazuli Lane came to an abrupt end at twin boulder-mountains, one on each side of the road. The boulder-mountains were filled with lapis lazuli. Aiden drove the carriage through the stone passageway. On the far side of the twin boulder-mountains, the Army of South Grace found itself on the edge of the Village of Lapis Lazuli.

The town was impressively decorated with lapis lazuli stones and various woods and decorations from the unique plant life in the surrounding forests. The town sat on the edge of a plateau, under which there was a mine entrance, which almost looked like the town's master gateway.

"Oh my goodness me, this town is strangely quiet. Whenever I've heard stories of Lapis Lazuli, I've heard of a very welcoming people who are busily working on their many lapis lazuli crafts and what-have-you. This seems awkward," said Mrs. Tinkermeyer.

"It's this darn storm. The Wicked Witch uses it to bring gloom to everythin' so no one wants to be outside. It's so depressin' to see!" said Mr. Pommier.

"I think I see someone over there," said Aiden, pointing to one of the shoppes.

"Let's park this carriage and ask if anyone has heard anything about Lilibeth. It wouldn't hurt to get as much information as we can on her before we arrive at her castle," said Mr. Tinkermeyer.

Aiden parked the carriage in front of the shoppe where he saw a person entering. The army then entered the building together. Inside they found that it was the town's general store.

"Greetings visitors! I'd wish you a good afternoon, but it's not a good afternoon and it's not going to be. This wicked thunderstorm is not good for business and it's putting everyone in a right nasty mood. My name is Angelique and this is my family's general store. What can I do for you today?" asked Angelique. She was a short woman who had a lot of energy to her.

"We are looking for information on the Wicked Witch of the Majestic Moonlit Mountains. Her castle is near here and we thought maybe someone could tell us a little about her before we pay her a visit," said Aiden.

"I can tell you plenty about that mean witch! First, I wouldn't recommend paying her a visit. I wouldn't recommend that at all! She's wicked right down to the core. This wicked thunderstorm is all her fault, just like it was last time. Right after this storm started, everyone in this extraordinary village of ours became depressed ... and then people started becoming all nasty and unfriendlylike. It just gets on my nerves that a wicked person like her can send us an unwanted storm and ruin everyone's day," said Angelique.

"That's just why we're here. We want to put an end to her wickedness and bring back the peacefulness of the Majestic Moonlit Mountains," said Theresa.

"Do you know anything about the Wicked Witch's plans? Do you know how she plans to take over the Majestic Moonlit Mountains?" asked Aiden.

"It's this wicked thunderstorm. She uses it to make everything all gloomy and make people not care to stop her. I suspect she may be using other magics, too, but I'm no witch, so I don't know much about those things," said Angelique.

Just then, a loud crashing sound came from the far corner of the general store.

"Why can't you open!?" shouted a voice from the direction of the crash.

"Oh dear ... not another one. Please excuse me. People are just very temperamental with this storm overhead ...," said Angelique as she quickly headed off in the direction of the ruckus.

"Let's make our way over to the mine. We should try not to be in Angelique's way while she's trying to deal with an unruly patron and cleaning up a mess," said Mr. Tinkermeyer.

"Why should we go to the mine?" asked Terrance.

Chapter Nineteen

"If this town is being affected by the storm as badly as Angelique claims it is then I would expect the normal busyness at the mine to be ... well ... nonexistent. Let's see if I'm right," said Mr. Tinkermeyer.

As the army made its way over to the entrance, the friends all noticed that the inhabitants of the town were peering at them from their windows.

"This is very creepy ...," said Theresa as she held close to her older brother's side.

"These people are most assuredly bewitched," said Mr. Tinkermeyer.

"Why do you say that? How do you know it's not just sadness from all this storminess?" asked Mr. Bunnymunch.

"Sadness wouldn't make them stare at us in such an accusing way. They are looking at us like we are trespassers who should not be here. This village is normally very friendly, and it would take a lot more than mere sadness to make these people so paranoid," said Mrs. Tinkermeyer.

"Ouch!" Aiden cried out.

"Aiden! What is it!? Are you ok!?" asked Theresa, who held on to her brother even more tightly.

"Something hit me on the head," said Aiden as he rubbed his head where he had been impacted.

Acorn jumped off of Aiden's shoulder and picked up the stone that had hit Aiden on the head. Aiden leaned down and took the object from Acorn's hands.

"A lapis lazuli stone ... oh my goodness me," said Mrs. Tinkermeyer.

"Someone threw a rock at my head ... how rude!" said Aiden. He then placed the stone in his pocket and petted Acorn on the head.

"I don't think we're very welcome here. Let's hurry up and leave. Maybe everyone will be nicer once we un-unbind that enchantment," said Terrance.

"I agree with Terrance. Once we look at the mine, we need to leave. This place is very scary ... especially with all this thunder and rain," said Theresa.

"It should only take a moment to examine the mine ... and I don't think we'll find anyone else who is as friendly as Angelique here. She seems to be the only one who's unaffected by the wicked magic in this village. We'll leave very soon, children," said Mr. Tinkermeyer.

The army stood at the entrance to the mine, where the friends could hear the echoes of the miners hurriedly collecting lapis lazuli.

"This doesn't make sense. I would have thought that with all of this gloominess there wouldn't be anyone in the mine ...," said Mr. Tinkermeyer.

"Maybe working in the mine gets their minds of the storm," suggested Mr. Bunnymunch.

A pinging noise began to sound from somewhere within Mrs. Tinkermeyer's pockets.

"Oh my goodness me ... it's the Artifacts-and-Magics Compass ...," said Mrs. Tinkermeyer.

"What is it saying, my wife?" asked Mr. Tinkermeyer.

"Quick! Quick! Quick! Everyone ... lie down on the ground. We don't want to hurt ourselves. Mr. Bunnymunch, run as fast as you can *right now*. Acorn, you run, too. The magic shouldn't work on you." said Mrs. Tinkermeyer.

"What? Why should we lie down?" asked Aiden.

"Don't think. Just listen to Mrs. Tinkermeyer and do as she says," said Mr. Tinkermeyer.

A very loud swishing sound came as Mr. Bunnymunch vanished from sight, with Acorn quickly following behind him, although the clockwork squirrel couldn't manage to achieve a speed as fast as a bunnymunch could. The rest of the army quickly lied down on the ground ... just in time to fall into a deep sleep.

Lilibeth then appeared at the entrance of the mine, looking very proud and pretentious. "Take them to the castle! I want them

Chapter Nineteen

placed in the dungeon. I must thank them for bringing me my ring," said the Wicked Witch.

Chapter Twenty
The Castle of the Wicked Witch

"Mr. Acorn, I'm over here," said Mr. Bunnymunch.

Mr. Bunnymunch had hurried out of the village by way of the twin boulder-mountains through which the members of the Army of South Grace had entered the Village of Lapis Lazuli together. Since he was a bunnymunch he was able to run significantly faster than Acorn, although Acorn was still faster than any squirrel due to his clockwork nature. Mr. Bunnymunch was hiding among the branches of a fuzzy tree. He poked his head out so Acorn could see where he was, and Acorn ran to join him, hidden among the branches.

"What happened? Why did Mrs. Tinkermeyer tell us to run away?" asked Mr. Bunnymunch.

Acorn tipped over on his side and looked to suddenly fall asleep.

"They fell asleep?" said Mr. Bunnymunch.

Acorn quickly returned to a standing position and nodded.

"Why did they fall asleep? Wait … Mrs. Tinkermeyer said something about magic. She said that it wouldn't affect you. Maybe … maybe the Wicked Witch cast a spell on them and put them to sleep," said Mr. Bunnymunch.

Acorn nodded and chattered in affirmation of Mr. Bunnymunch's statement.

"That is not good … although it was a very wise thing that the Tinkermeyers brought along their artifacts. That compass of theirs must have given Mrs. Tinkermeyer warning of what was about to happen. I think she said before that it detects artifacts and magic. What are we going to do? … we are just a bunnymunch and a clockwork squirrel … so I suppose the only thing we can do is try

Chapter Twenty

to find out what her plans are for them and then go find Del. He will know how to rescue our friends. Let's go see what Lilibeth's doing to them," said Mr. Bunnymunch.

Mr. Bunnymunch cautiously poked his head out of the fuzzy tree first, to make sure that there was no one wandering about looking for them. He slowly exited from his hiding place within the fuzzy tree branches.

"Come on out, Mr. Acorn. It looks like we're alone," said Mr. Bunnymunch.

Acorn quickly joined his friend out in the open. He twitchily looked around just to verify that they were not being watched.

"Did you see if Lilibeth was taking our friends anywhere?" asked Mr. Bunnymunch.

Acorn twitched in the direction of the castle.

"The castle ... I guess we'll have to make our way there and figure out what she's going to do with them," said Mr. Bunnymunch.

Acorn began to twitch in a downwards direction to try to indicate something to Mr. Bunnymunch.

"What? Something is down? ... I don't understand," said Mr. Bunnymunch.

The clockwork squirrel hurriedly dug a small hole in the ground and jumped into it. He peaked his head out to see if Mr. Bunnymunch understood.

"We need to go underground?" asked Mr. Bunnymunch.

Acorn ran back to the fuzzy tree and began to shape the fuzzy branches. After a few seconds he made several small poles out of the fuzzy branches and stood behind them. He held on to the fuzzy poles as if he were trapped.

"They're in a prison! ... or ... no ... they're in a dungeon. That's where they are. They're in the castle dungeon!" said Mr. Bunnymunch.

Acorn twitched excitedly to let Mr. Bunnymunch know that he was correct and their friends were indeed being taken to the dungeon of the Wicked Witch's castle.

THE CASTLE OF THE WICKED WITCH

"Thank you, Mr. Acorn. I'm so glad you're here! Let's go find our friends," said Mr. Bunnymunch.

The two companions ran off quickly towards Lilibeth's castle. This time Mr. Bunnymunch matched Acorn's pace so as to not inadvertently lose his friend.

It only took them a few minutes to arrive at the castle, since they were able to travel in a more direct line through the woods and they were both quite fast at running.

When they arrived at the castle, Mr. Bunnymunch noticed right away that the fortress was even larger than he had remembered. He wasn't sure if this was because of his distance from the castle the first time or if Lilibeth had used her magic to further grow the structure's size, just like she was doing to her wicked thunderstorm.

Mr. Bunnymunch and Acorn remained hidden behind a tree on the edge of the woods, close by the castle. All of the trees and plants around the edifice looked to be dead, save for the dessert tree.

"I think … that … maybe … we need to get inside …," said Mr. Bunnymunch.

Acorn twitched his tail in the direction of the large castle entrance.

"That's a good idea, Mr. Acorn, but I think we need to find a way to enter that's less obvious. We don't want the Wicked Witch to see us, and I'm sure she has all of the entrances well-guarded. She has a few guards up in her towers watching, so we'll need to be careful no matter what. Maybe there's a secret entrance somewhere that she doesn't keep guarded …," said Mr. Bunnymunch.

The clockwork squirrel grabbed up a nearby twig and began to nibble on it. He paused to look at Mr. Bunnymunch, and then nibbled again, and then paused again. He was trying to tell Mr. Bunnymunch another suggestion for entering the castle.

"Munching! Of course! That's what we bunnymunches do best! I take it that clockwork squirrels are also rather good at munching?" said Mr. Bunnymunch.

Acorn twitched in acknowledgement.

Chapter Twenty

The two friends ran quickly to the closest wall of the castle when there weren't any guards looking in their direction.

***

"Hello ... hello ... is anyone else there?" said Aiden in a rather quiet voice, just in case there was anyone around who shouldn't hear that he was now awake.

The dungeon cell was very dark. In fact, there was no light at all. There seemed to be hay covering the floor, but Aiden wasn't certain since there was no light to allow him to see what exactly was covering the floor.

"I'm here, Aiden," said Theresa.

"Me too," said Terrance.

"Me three," said Mr. Pommier.

"Me four," said Mrs. Tinkermeyer.

"Me five ... and I believe that's all of us, since our two, smallest friends looked as though they managed to run away before that sleeping spell took hold of us," said Mr. Tinkermeyer.

"Is everyone ok?" asked Aiden and Mrs. Tinkermeyer in unison.

"Where are we ...?" said Theresa as she reached in the direction of Aiden's voice to try to find him.

"Oh my goodness me, I don't know. I can't see a thing. Perhaps young Terrance could help with that ... presuming he still has his ring with him. All of my artifacts seem to have walked off," said Mrs. Tinkermeyer.

The cell filled with a soft, magic glow emanating from the ring on Terrance's hand.

"I have my ring," said Terrance.

"It looks like all three of us still have our rings ... and it looks like no one was hurt," said Aiden as he reached out and held on to his brother and sister, who were shaking from fear of the dark. It was the first time any of the Silverglade children had ever experienced darkness. Coming from the Village of Illume they had grown accustomed to being surrounded by light at all times of the day and night, thanks to all of the glowing plant life. Even when traveling with their father for Silver Lily sales, Aiden had always been around the glowing Lantern Tree carriage during the nighttime, so he always had light around him.

"The Wicked Witch must not have seen your rings ... and there must not be any guards around here since I didn't hear any movement outside of this cell when Terrance turned on his light," said Mr. Tinkermeyer.

Mr. Pommier worked his way over to the bars of their shared cell and carefully pressed against them. "The bars aren't lookin' to give ... we're stuck here for now ... but look over there on the table," said Mr. Pommier.

The army members all moved towards the cell bars to look around the corner where Mr. Pommier was pointing.

"Those are all of our artifacts!" said Mr. Tinkermeyer.

"Too bad Acorn and Mr. Bunnymunch aren't here. Either one of them could easily squeeze through these bars and make their way over to your artifacts," said Aiden.

"Theresa, Terrance ... do you think either one of you could try squeezing through the bars. It'll be a tight fit, but it may be worth a try," said Mrs. Tinkermeyer.

Both Theresa and Terrance situated themselves to move sideways through the bars ... but unfortunately they were both too big to fit.

"I'm sorry everyone, I'm just too big," said Theresa.

"So am I," said Terrance.

"No worries ... it was still worth the try," said Mrs. Tinkermeyer.

"Perhaps we could tear some fabric from our clothing and make a lasso of sorts to use to drag some of the artifacts over here. A couple of them could get us out of here in a jiffy," said Mr. Tinkermeyer.

"Wouldn't they make a loud noise when they hit the floor?" asked Mr. Pommier.

"Oh my goodness me, yes, they would. Thank you for pointing that out, Mr. Pommier. That was very smart of you. The last thing

Chapter Twenty

we want to do is attract attention to ourselves while we plan our escape," said Mrs. Tinkermeyer.

"Maybe Aiden could use his Ring of Sneezes to make one of us sneeze. Then they'd have to open the door to check on us to make sure we're not sick," said Theresa.

"That's a wonderful thought, young Theresa, but I doubt any wicked witch would care about one of us being sick," said Mrs. Tinkermeyer.

"Although she might take some enjoyment from it, I'm sure," said Mr. Tinkermeyer.

"Shh! Everyone be quiet! Do ya'll hear that sound?" asked Mr. Pommier.

"It sounds like something small scraping up against the wall," said Terrance.

"That's exactly what it sounds like to me, too," said Mr. Tinkermeyer.

"I think it's coming from up there," said Aiden, pointing high up on the wall opposite the cell bars.

"It's getting louder," said Theresa.

"What is it? It almost sounds like … the stone wall is being eaten by a small animal …," said Mrs. Tinkermeyer.

"Look! There's light! Up by the ceiling!" exclaimed Aiden, although rather quietly so as to not alert any guard's attention.

"I see teeth … it's … Mr. Bunnymunch and Acorn!" exclaimed Theresa in a whispered shout.

"It's us, all right! We'll have you out of there in just a few seconds," said Mr. Bunnymunch.

Mr. Bunnymunch and Acorn were eating through the stone walls at an unimaginable pace. In a moment there was enough room for a person to fit through the hole.

"How magnificent! You two are true friends. How did you ever find us in here?" asked Mr. Tinkermeyer.

"We could hear you talking when we passed by looking for a good spot to munch through the wall," said Mr. Bunnymunch, who was feeling glad that he and Acorn both had exceptionally good hearing skills.

"Mr. Pommier, would you mind going up first. Being a professional guard, you're the obvious choice to go out first so you can keep guard on the other side of the exit to make sure we aren't seen," said Aiden.

"Of course! Happy to oblige," said Mr. Pommier.

"No, we can't leave the castle just yet. We need to collect our artifacts and then we need to make our way to Lilibeth and take that unbinding ring of hers," said Mr. Tinkermeyer.

"Mr. Bunnymunch, Acorn, could you jump down here and munch your way through these bars for us, please?" asked Mrs. Tinkermeyer.

The two munchers jumped down into the cell and ran to the bars. Mr. Bunnymunch started munching away on the lower parts. Acorn looked at Aiden and gave out a little squirrel chirp. Aiden immediately understood and walked over by the cell door. Acorn jumped up on Aiden's shoulder and began munching away at the upper parts of the bars.

"Help me hold these bars so they don't crash to the floor and alert the guards," said Mr. Pommier.

The Tinkermeyers and the twins took hold of the bars that Mr. Bunnymunch and Acorn were munching on and placed them carefully on the hay-covered floor once they were completely munched through.

In moments there was plenty enough space for the army to leave the cell and make its way over to the large table covered in the Tinkermeyers' artifacts. The Tinkermeyers then carefully returned their many artifacts to their various pockets, pouches, and sacks.

"I think it may be safe for us to just use the stairs to escape from the dungeon. There aren't any guards around, so Lilibeth must be pretty sure that we aren't going to escape. We should use her presumption to our advantage," said Mr. Tinkermeyer.

"Terrance, keep your light on low for now. We'll need to use it to see until we reach the lighted, upstairs of the castle. We just don't

Chapter Twenty

want it to be too bright, because that might attract the attention of someone wicked," said Mrs. Tinkermeyer.

The army quietly ascended the dark stairwell. At the top of the stairs was a long hallway that extended to both the right and the left. The hallway was filled with paintings of various dark locations in Oz. The army guessed that Lilibeth had most likely placed them there to remind her of the "pleasantness" of wickedness in other parts of Oz.

"Mr. and Mrs. Tinkermeyer, since you two seem to know more about what you are doing, would you mind being our leaders? I'm not really sure where we should be going," said Aiden.

"Oh my goodness me, nor do we, but we'll still be happy to lead," said Mrs. Tinkermeyer.

The Tinkermeyers led the army to the left, although that was a random choice of directions. Mrs. Tinkermeyer had tried to use their detector to get an idea of where the ring and Lilibeth might be, but there were too many magical artifacts around the castle to know what was what.

At the end of the long hallway was another staircase.

"I think we should go up these stairs. My guess is that Lilibeth will like to spend time on that balcony or near the windows of her uppermost tower. Wicked Witches enjoy looking out on the suffering that they cause, so upstairs is our best bet for finding her and the ring," noted Mrs. Tinkermeyer.

The stairs spiraled upwards. The army was very careful as it passed by doors on each level of the castle before arriving at the top floor, which was where Lilibeth's very private bedchambers were located.

Mr. Pommier peered around the corner of the doorway to check for guards, but there were none. With Mr. Pommier's ok, the army entered the grand hallway of Lilibeth's private bedchambers.

"Mrs. Tinkermeyer, behind which of these doors do you think we'll find the unbinding ring … and the Wicked Witch?" asked Aiden.

"Oh my goodness me, I couldn't tell you ... but I have an idea," said Mrs. Tinkermeyer.

"I can see your creative juices flowing, my wife. What do you have concocted for us in that brilliant mind of yours?" said Mr. Tinkermeyer.

"Opening the doors one at a time and looking inside may not be very wise for us to do, because if we are incorrect on our first try and there are guards on the other side ... we won't have time to check the other rooms, because we'll be too busy running away," said Mrs. Tinkermeyer.

"Then let's split up into four groups and each group take a door," said Mr. Pommier.

"That's exactly what I had in mind. Mr. Tinkermeyer and I can use our magic to open all of the doors at once. Whoever sees the ring or Lilibeth first should shout out to the rest of us ...," said Mrs. Tinkermeyer, before she was interrupted by twitching and chattering coming from Acorn.

"Wait, and I'm sorry to cut you off Mrs. Tinkermeyer, but I think Acorn has another idea that will be less likely to draw attention," interrupted Aiden.

"He does, and I think I will be assisting," said Mr. Bunnymunch.

"You will indeed. Acorn and Mr. Bunnymunch are very good munchers, so they can munch small holes in the walls where the Wicked Witch and her guards won't see. They can then check out the rooms and tell us which one has the unbinding ring inside it," said Aiden, interpreting Acorn's squirrel chattering to the rest of the army.

"Oh my goodness me, that sounds like a wonderful plan! Good job, Acorn. I never would have thought of that," said Mrs. Tinkermeyer.

"I'm sure your plan would have worked, too, Mrs. Tinkermeyer!" said Terrance.

Chapter Twenty

"Why thank you, Terrance, but I think Acorn's plan has a better chance of not getting us caught before we can find the unbinding ring," said Mrs. Tinkermeyer.

Acorn hurried over to the room furthest to the right, with Mr. Bunnymunch taking the room furthest to the left. They both began munching as quietly as they could. It took them only a few seconds to munch holes large enough for them to enter into the rooms. The two, small, army members disappeared through the munched holes.

Mr. Bunnymunch soon returned from the hole that he had munched. "The room is a glorified closet filled with clothing for the Wicked Witch, but there is no sign of the unbinding ring in it … unless she left it in the pocket of one of her coats, which I very much doubt she'd be so scatterbrained to do," said Mr. Bunnymunch, who quickly moved on to the next room to munch a hole in the wall.

"I wonder where Acorn is. What's taking him so long? I hope he's ok," said Theresa.

"I'm sure he's fine. He's probably being thorough to look everywhere," said Mr. Tinkermeyer.

Mr. Bunnymunch then appeared from his second munched hole and said, "Nothing in there either. The room was mostly empty as far as I could tell, other than a table with a few chairs around it. Has Acorn had any luck yet with his rooms?"

"He has yet to return from the first room," said Mr. Pommier.

"I hope he's ok. Maybe you could check on him, Mr. Bunnymunch?" asked Terrance.

"Sure thing!" said Mr. Bunnymunch. He quickly munched the hole larger that Acorn had started, since bunnymunches are a little bigger than clockwork squirrels. Mr. Bunnymunch disappeared through the twice-munched hole.

A minute had passed and there was no sign of either Acorn or Mr. Bunnymunch.

"What's happened to them? We should all go in and rescue them!" said Theresa, sounding very concerned for her friends.

THE CASTLE OF THE WICKED WITCH

"No we need to give them time. We don't want to disturb them and get them caught. If anything were happening we would have heard a commotion by now ... so I'm sure they're both just fine and need a few more minutes," said Mrs. Tinkermeyer, although she was just as worried as Theresa was. She thought that maybe they had encountered a trap that prevented them from leaving the room, or the Wicked Witch had discovered them and had captured them both.

After a couple more minutes, both Mr. Bunnymunch and Acorn scurried through the twice-munched hole. Acorn had a small, gold object in his mouth. He quickly ran to Aiden and climbed up on Aiden's shoulder.

Aiden put his hand out in front of Acorn's mouth and received the gold object from him.

"Good job, Acorn and Mr. Bunnymunch! They found the unbinding ring," said Aiden as he held up the unbinding ring for everyone to see. "Mrs. Tinkermeyer, I think you should take this for safekeeping.

Mrs. Tinkermeyer took the ring from Aiden and placed it on her finger, where she knew she wouldn't easily misplace it.

"We're sorry for taking so long, but the case where the Wicked Witch was storing the ring was awfully difficult to munch through. Acorn was trying as hard as he could, but he needed my bunnymunch teeth to break through whatever that case was made of," said Mr. Bunnymunch.

"Good for you both. Your teamwork paid off," said Mr. Tinkermeyer.

"Now, we need to make our way back out of the castle without being caught," said Mrs. Tinkermeyer.

"Oh, I do think it's a little late for that," said Lilibeth, who was standing behind the army and had entered the hallway too quietly for the friends to have noticed.

The Wicked Witch snapped her fingers and an iron cage immediately appeared, entrapping the Army of South Grace.

Chapter Twenty

"Tell me ... how did you manage to escape from my dungeon?" said Lilibeth.

"We're just smarter than you are," said Mr. Tinkermeyer.

"Perhaps your dungeon isn't as effective as you thought it was," said Mrs. Tinkermeyer.

"Perhaps ... perhaps not. This time I'm not going to take any chances. I doubt you'd be able to escape from my dungeon if I turned you all into ... oh ... let's say ... stink trees," said Lilibeth with a wicked grin on her face.

The Wicked Witch began to raise her hand and point towards the army; however, before she could cast her spell, the Wicked Witch began to laugh and sneeze uncontrollably. Theresa and Aiden had been very speedy with their magic rings.

Mr. Bunnymunch and Acorn quickly ate through the bars of the iron cage, while Mr. and Mrs. Tinkermeyer dug through their pockets and pulled out several, small artifacts.

"Quickly! Everyone to the stairs. Aiden and Theresa, keep her laughing and sneezing as long as you can," said Mrs. Tinkermeyer.

A flash of black light came from the Wicked Witch, who launched a fireball in the direction of the army, since she was no longer busy laughing or sneezing. The fireball narrowly missed the army.

"Our rings stopped working!" exclaimed Aiden.

Another fireball barely missed the heads of the army members as they ran towards the stairs.

Suddenly, a massive, blindingly-bright ball of light appeared in the middle of the hallway and flew directly at the Wicked Witch.

"Run!" yelled Terrance.

As the Wicked Witch screamed in terror, the army members ran out of the hallway and down the stairs as fast as they could.

"Oh my goodness me, Terrance, that was excellent thinking to use your ring like that! I'm sure she thought that ball of light was actually fire. Well done!" said Mrs. Tinkermeyer.

"We need to head back to the dungeon. She will be expecting us to leave through one of her main exits that's closer, but we can

THE CASTLE OF THE WICKED WITCH

leave through the hole munched by Mr. Bunnymunch and Acorn. She won't expect us to do that because she doesn't know it's there," said Mrs. Tinkermeyer.

The Army of South Grace quickly retraced its steps back to the cell in which the friends had awoken earlier.

Along the hall at the top of the staircase leading to the dungeon were two castle guards. Before the guards could react to seeing the Army of South Grace, the Tinkermeyers used small, gun-like artifacts to put the guards to sleep and levitate them up towards the ceiling.

"That will keep them out of our hair for a few minutes ... plenty enough time to escape," said Mrs. Tinkermeyer.

When they reached the cell, Mr. Tinkermeyer placed a very small, copper box underneath the hole leading outside that had been munched by Mr. Bunnymunch and Acorn.

"Everyone step back just a bit," said Mrs. Tinkermeyer.

The copper box rapidly transformed itself into a stairway leading up to the hole.

"That's ingenious!" exclaimed Theresa.

"Quickly everyone! Up the stairs. Mr. Pommier, please go first as our lookout," said Mr. Tinkermeyer.

When Mr. Pommier reached the outside of the castle, he quickly announced, "It's safe! Best be runnin' up here right quick before the castle guards come."

The army hurriedly ran towards the woods. Suddenly, the trees began to move and formed a barrier that prevented the army from escaping.

"It's the Wicked Witch!" cried out Theresa.

"She's up there, in the lower tower!" shouted Terrance.

"... and trees you shall now become!" screamed the Wicked Witch. She raised her hands and a large ball of black fire formed above her.

The Silverglade children attempted to use their magic rings on the Wicked Witch again, but her magic was protecting her from them.

Chapter Twenty

Mr. Bunnymunch suddenly felt inspired by his friends' use of their magic rings. "Cover your ears everyone!" he said.

The army members all covered their ears as Mr. Bunnymunch had directed.

The ring hanging from Mr. Bunnymunch's neck began to glow. Mr. Bunnymunch opened his mouth and looked to yell in the direction of the Wicked Witch. The powerful roar of a lion sounded from his mouth and resonated throughout all of the Majestic Moonlit Mountains. The Wicked Witch was knocked back on her feet. Before Lilibeth had even landed on the floor of the tower, every window and every mirror in her castle had been shattered from the force of Mr. Bunnymunch's roar. In a few places, some pieces of stone fell from the castle.

The Army of South Grace was also knocked to the ground, except for Mr. Bunnymunch. The friends quickly rose to their feet, with Aiden grabbing up the twins to make sure that they were ok.

"The trees have moved out of our way! Let's go!" yelled Aiden.

Chapter Twenty-One
The Unbinding of Lapis Lazuli

"This fuzzy tree is so comfortable!" said Theresa.

"It's just like being wrapped up in a coziest blanket you can imagine," said Terrance.

The Army of South Grace had succeeded in escaping from the Wicked Witch of the Majestic Moonlit Mountains and was again just outside of the Village of Lapis Lazuli, hiding within the branches of the same fuzzy tree where Mr. Bunnymunch and Acorn had hidden before when the rest of the army was captured.

"Oh my goodness me, Mr. Bunnymunch, that took a lot of courage and ingenuity for you to do back there. Your mighty lion roar saved us. Well done!" said Mrs. Tinkermeyer.

"Oh, it was nothing. It was Lionora's Mighty Roaring Ring that you should thank, not me. I'm just a little bunnymunch," said Mr. Bunnymunch.

"Nonsense! It was you that was smart enough and courageous enough to use it in a time of great danger and great need. You should be proud of yourself," said Mr. Tinkermeyer.

"They're right, you know. You should be very proud indeed! But now ... we need to start making our way to the Village of Poofle. I know we'll arrive there a little early, but I don't think we should stick around here any longer. We have the unbinding ring and that's what we really came for," said Aiden.

"Yes, the ring was our main reason for coming here, but we need to unbind everyone in the Village of Lapis Lazuli from Lilibeth's wicked enchantment first," said Mrs. Tinkermeyer.

"We will examine the ring and learn about its powers after we unbind the citizens of the town. It won't take long to do, and maybe that will distract the Wicked Witch and slow down her plans

Chapter Twenty-One

enough so Del will have time to work out a new enchantment to place on her ... so she can be good again," said Mr. Tinkermeyer.

"Don't we also need to find out more about her plan?" asked Mr. Pommier.

"That's quite right, Mr. Pommier. We don't know what her plans are yet, and maybe someone in the town can give us some more information once we remove this nasty, controlling charm from them," said Mrs. Tinkermeyer.

"Mrs. Tinkermeyer, do you know how to use the unbinding ring on the whole town? Won't it take a long time to use the artifact on each villager?" asked Theresa.

"Oh my goodness me, Mr. Tinkermeyer and I know how to use it to unbind an enchantment. That part's easy. It's learning how to use it to un-unbind an enchantment that's going to be difficult," replied Mrs. Tinkermeyer.

"I think the best way for us to do this is run as fast we can to the center of town and use the ring from there. Could the rest of you come with us? It would help if you formed a circle around us once we reach the center of town. Just use your magic rings or whatever else you have in case anyone tries to stop us before we can use the unbinding ring," said Mr. Tinkermeyer.

"We'll do the best we can. Theresa, Terrance, do you think you can handle using your rings again to help out just in case we encounter a few unfriendly people in town? They won't have magic like Lilibeth, so it should be really easy to do," said Aiden, trying to be as encouraging to his family as he could be.

"I think we can handle it," said Theresa and Terrance in unison.

"Is everyone else fine?" asked Aiden.

"Let's be off then!" said Mrs. Tinkermeyer.

The Army of South Grace ran into the center of town, as Lilibeth's wicked thunderstorm rumbled in the gloomy sky above. Fortunately, there was no one to be seen, so the dash to the center of town was rather easy.

"Let's form that circle around the Tinkermeyers like Mr. Tinkermeyer requested," said Aiden.

The Unbinding of Lapis Lazuli

As Aiden, Theresa, Terrance, Acorn, Mr. Bunnymunch, and Mr. Pommier formed a circle around the Tinkermeyers, Mr. and Mrs. Tinkermeyer embraced one another.

"Is everyone ready?" asked Mr. Tinkermeyer.

"Yes," said all of the members of the Army of South Grace in unison.

"Let's start, my wife," said Mr. Tinkermeyer.

A warm, copper-colored glow surrounded the Tinkermeyers and then filled the entire town of Lapis Lazuli.

"It feels so ... peaceful," said Theresa.

The glow subsided.

"That should do it," said Mrs. Tinkermeyer.

How can such a small ring be powerful enough to unbind an enchantment from a whole town?

"It's not. Be glad you have a wizard and a wizardess here with you," said Mrs. Tinkermeyer, smiling.

"Are you tired from that spell? It has to have been difficult to cast," said Theresa.

"Oh my goodness me, love is never tiring, my young friend," said Mrs. Tinkermeyer.

"Let's go find some townsfolk. Now that the enchantment is no longer on them we might be able to figure out why these citizens where charmed in the first place," said Mr. Tinkermeyer.

"Let's go to the mine. They're the most likely people to know what's happened," said Mrs. Tinkermeyer.

As the army approached the mine, the many miners who had been working deep inside appeared. They were leaving the underground passages since they were no longer being forced to work by the Wicked Witch's enchantment. They were quite tired from working so hard for so long.

"Was it you folks that stopped the wicked magic?" asked one of the miners.

"It was the Tinkermeyers," said Theresa, pointing towards the army's artificers.

Chapter Twenty-One

"We're awfully sorry to trouble you, but do you know why the Wicked Witch had enchanted you?" asked Mrs. Tinkermeyer.

"Of course we know! We were doing all of the dirty work for her. She plans to use our lapis lazuli to enchant all of Oz. She was taking our jewelry and working her wicked magic on it. She was going to charm everyone!" said the miner.

"How horrible!" exclaimed Theresa and Terrance in unison.

"What happens if the Wicked Witch comes back? Can't she just put a new enchantment on everyone? Then they'd have to start working for her again," said Mr. Bunnymunch.

"That's right! That's exactly what she'll do," said Angelique, who had witnessed from her general store the magic done by the Tinkermeyers. "We need to stop her from being able to use and abuse this town again."

"Here ... take this," said Mrs. Tinkermeyer. She took the unbinding ring from her hand and gave it to Angelique. "If the Wicked Witch comes back, all you have to do to unbind people from her enchantments is concentrate on the enchanted person, think about the charm being removed, and say the words 'weeble-weeble-bind, weeble-weeble-free' and the charm will be gone."

"Thank you so much!" said Angelique, as she looked at the gold ring now on her finger.

"But Mrs. Tinkermeyer ... won't you need that ring to be able to un-unbind the enchantment on Lilibeth?" asked Aiden with great concern.

"I suspect that our best option is Del's plan to place a new enchantment on Lilibeth. You see, it's terribly difficult to un-unbind an enchantment even if you know exactly what you're doing. It's also going to help us and all of Oz out a lot more in the long run to prevent Lilibeth from using Lapis Lazuli to create charmed jewelry. If her enchanted jewelry were to spread all over Oz, then there would be a lot more trouble for us and everyone. Anyways, these people deserve to be free from Lilibeth's hexes," said Mrs. Tinkermeyer.

"I agree with Mrs. Tinkermeyer," said Mr. Bunnymunch.

"Now that we know about Lilibeth's plans I think it best we head out to the Village of Poofle and wait for our friend, Del, there," said Mrs. Tinkermeyer.

Aiden gave out a loud whistle, and the Silverglade's carriage guided itself to him.

"On behalf of all us Lapis Lazulians, thank you for your help! Travel safe and please do come to visit. I'll keep your unbinding ring safe until you return," said Angelique.

Angelique and all of the Lapis Lazulians waved goodbye to the Army of South Grace, which left the town by way of the path leading to the top of the plateau under which the mine was located.

Chapter Twenty-Two
The Village of Poofle

The journey to the Village of Poofle took the Army of South Grace almost two weeks to accomplish. The friends could have shaved a few days of travel time off of their journey had they been in a hurry, but they knew that they would easily arrive in the Village of Poofle before the Good Warlock Del would be there to meet them, so they took some time to enjoy the scenery. The Levitating Lake of the Lapis Lazuli Plateau and the tree houses at the tops of the seven-hundred-foot fur trees of the Great Southern Plain were among the favorite panoramas of the army.

The Village of Poofle was a unique village indeed. The wicked thunderstorm of the Wicked Witch of the Majestic Moonlit Mountains was expanding far around the village but not within the village itself – something was blocking its entrance into the skies above the plateau. The village and the surrounding region were filled with Poofle Trees of various species, which created a very interesting look for the village. What made the village especially unique, though, was the Meandering Road. The road started as the path from the Village of Lapis Lazuli leading up to the top of the Lapis Lazuli Plateau and ended at the Village of Poofle; however, it was the area of the road in-between those two points that tended to meander. Sometimes the Meandering Road was very straight. Other times the Meandering Road was very long and winding. For this reason, a good witch had created signs at each end of the road that would inform any passerby of the length of time it would take to reach the other end. When the Army of South Grace passed by the sign in the Village of Lapis Lazuli, it was informed that the time for it to reach the Village of Poofle would be about two weeks at a casual pace. The road had to be followed if the army didn't want the pixies of the Lapis Lazuli Plateau to make it become lost for

The Village of Poofle

several years. Sticking to the road was the best option, considering the army's schedule to meet with Del. Although the Great Southern Plain was not situated on top of the Lapis Lazuli Plateau, as was the Village of Poofle, the Meandering Road took the Army of South Grace through the Great Southern Plain. Mr. Bunnymunch had let the army know that they were lucky, since he knew of one person who had the misfortune of traveling along the Meandering Road when it decided to meander far north of North Grace, outside of the Land of Oz.

Once the army had reached the Village of Poofle, Mr. Bunnymunch guided it to the Poofle Inn, a building that had very obviously been constructed from Poofle Trees.

"Good day, fine visitors to the Village of Poofle! My name is Mrs. Pooflewink and I am one of the innkeepers here. Would you like a room, or two, or three, or four, or five, or six, or seven, or eight for the night?" said Mrs. Pooflewink.

"No, thank you. We have a carriage with plenty of room for all of us, but thank you anyways for your kind welcome. We are here looking for the Good Warlock Del. He told us to meet him here. Have you heard from him in recent days?" said Aiden.

"So you all are our son's friends? You still have another week until he arrives, but please make yourselves at home. Even if you're staying in your carriage, my husband and I will happily be your hosts for your visit here in the Village of Poofle. Is this your first time here?" said Mrs. Pooflewink.

"Yes, this is our first time here. It's a lovely village," said Theresa.

"Why thank you ... Miss Theresa, is it? We do take pride in our lovely Poofle Trees. If you'd all care to follow me into the dining room, we will bring you some lunch. And don't be trying to pay us like so many silly folks in Oz do. Everything is free here. Just take what you need. That's how we live here. Everyone takes what they need and gives what they can. Most of our food comes from Poofle Trees, so we have plenty of food," said Mrs. Pooflewink.

Chapter Twenty-Two

"I've never had food made from Poofle Trees before. Is it tasty?" said Terrance.

"Very!" said Mr. Pooflewink, who was just bringing in a large tray full of food for the group. "Please, everyone take a seat and we'll enjoy a meal together."

"These are just some appetizers to get us started while Mr. Pooflewink whips up something extra special for you honored guests of Del," said Mrs. Pooflewink as her husband left the dining room to return to the kitchen. "Thank you for helping our son re-enchant our daughter. Lilibeth really is a good girl, but she got caught up in that nasty dark magic stuff … and … well, it just breaks a parent's heart to see her daughter go down that road. She meant well, as I know Del has explained to you, and she's going to come back to goodness forever one of these days," she said.

"Oh my goodness me, I'm sure she will. You're her mother, so you have special insight. As a parent myself, I know that you have to trust your instincts with your children … so Lilibeth will return to goodness forever, as you said," commented Mrs. Tinkermeyer.

"Thank you for saying so. I know in my heart she's good … now, let's start in on these appetizers before they get cold," said Mrs. Pooflewink. "You know … I remember when Lilibeth and Del were young children and would play out in the Poofle Trees. Those children always had a gift for making those Poofle Trees grow. Mr. Pooflewink and I could see that there was always a farmer in our Del and farmer in our Lilibeth."

"I'm sure you've always been very proud of your children," said Mr. Tinkermeyer.

"Oh yes! We've always been very proud of them both, regardless of … well, regardless," said Mrs. Pooflewink.

The Pooflewinks shared many childhood stories of Lilibeth and Del with the Army of South Grace during their meal. For the next week, the Pooflewinks shared more stories while they showed the army around the village. They also gave the army some advice on how to talk with Lilibeth, although the army was rather sure that the advice would only work if the Pooflewinks were to confront

The Village of Poofle

Lilibeth themselves; however, the friends were happy for the attempt that the Pooflewinks were making at helping the army.

***

Del arrived at the precise instant that he said he would. The Army of South Grace was waiting inside the Poofle Inn for the Pooflewinks when Del made his appearance. His parents were preparing a picnic for all of them to enjoy in the Poofle Tree Park.

"Your timing is perfect! We are about to leave for a meal with your parents in Poofle Tree Park," said Terrance.

"I know. My parents always have the best picnic meals," said Del.

The Pooflewinks laid out the picnic for the army underneath one of the green Poofle Trees. The army had learned earlier during its visit that the green poofles on the green Poofle Trees were the leaves and the orange poofles were the flowers. Different Poofle Trees had various color combinations, so it was very difficult to determine what was a flower and what was a leaf on a Poofle Tree if someone was not familiar with them.

"Army of South Grace, were you able to retrieve the unbinding ring from Lilibeth and find out some information on her plans?" asked Del.

"Yes to both questions," said Mrs. Tinkermeyer.

"The Tinkermeyers used the unbinding ring to free the citizens of the Village of Lapis Lazuli from the charm the Wicked ... I mean, your sister placed on them," said Theresa.

"We decided the Lapis Lazulians should keep the ring for now so they can't be re-enchanted by Lilibeth. She was using the Lapis Lazulians to make charmed jewelry out of their lapis lazuli. She was going to charm everyone in Oz using the jewelry," said Aiden.

"I think you made the right decision to leave the ring with them. That would be very bad if she used their stones to enchant Oz. She knows how good lapis lazuli jewelry would be in charming the masses ...," said Del.

Chapter Twenty-Two

"How has your enchantment been coming along?" asked Mr. Bunnymunch.

"I have finished creating it and we can depart tomorrow for her castle," said Del.

"Are ya thinkin' it will work on her for sure?" asked Mr. Pommier.

"I don't know, but let's hope for the best," said Del.

"I'm sure it will work. You've always been very good with enchantments," said Mr. Pooflewink.

"Anyways, that dark magic stuff can't keep a hold of our precious Lilibeth forever ... this is just a phase, so I know it will work ... it will definitely work," said Mrs. Pooflewink.

In order to get everyone's mind off of the wickedness of his sister so they could relax for a little while, Del took a few poofles off of the tree and began to juggle them, which the children found especially amusing. After the army and the Pooflewinks had had their fill of food, Del led them all in a fun game of poofle tag.

***

The next morning, the Army of South Grace left for Lilibeth's castle.

"Let's all get on the carriage and head out. It would be wise for all of us to remain outside of the hidden part of the carriage so we can have as many eyes as possible on the lookout for Lilibeth and anyone she has managed to recruit," said Del.

"I hope that Meandering Road has decided to become short today. We can't take two weeks, or longer, to make our way back to Lilibeth," said Mr. Bunnymunch.

"Oh my goodness me, she could easily take over the Majestic Moonlit Mountains in that time if we aren't careful," said Mrs. Tinkermeyer.

"Don't worry. We have ways around that. Do you remember how I said you'd all be safe here because of the local good warlocks and good witches?" said Del.

"Now that you mention it, I do. Are they going to be helping us somehow?" said Mr. Tinkermeyer.

"My parents are two of those witches," said Del, and he nodded to his parents, waving goodbye to them.

Mr. and Mrs. Pooflewink held hands, smiled, and the world turned bright white to the Army of South Grace.

Chapter Twenty-Three
The Return to the Castle of the Wicked Witch

The bright, white light became weeping willow trees, blanket trees, and fuzzy trees. The carriage was now just east of the Village of Lapis Lazuli.

"Where are we?" asked Aiden.

"We are on the road between the Village of Lapis Lazuli and my sister's castle. My parents couldn't transport us any nearer for fear of her noticing the use of their magic so close to her," said Del.

"Shouldn't we find it much easier to enter her castle this time?" asked Theresa.

"Right, didn't we take away all of her guards? I mean, weren't all of them Lapis Lazulians?" asked Terrance.

"I hadn't thought of that. Good thinking, children," said Mr. Tinkermeyer. "If she does have any guards left they'd be very few in numbers, since we left that unbinding ring with Angelique. If the Wicked Witch charmed anyone then Angelique would hopefully have undone those charms."

"We also have a good warlock, a good wizardess, and a good wizard … and good friends. That has to give us an advantage over Lilibeth," said Aiden.

"It sure does! She's certain to have some tricks up her sleeves, but so do we," said Mrs. Tinkermeyer.

"I think I may be seein' one of her tricks right now through those trees," said Mr. Pommier.

"What is it? What do you see, Mr. Pommier?" asked Aiden.

"Look closely. Ya'll can see a smidgen of her castle when the wind blows the leaves. There's somethin' around it … glowin'," said Mr. Pommier.

"Oh my goodness me, I see it, too …," said Mrs. Tinkermeyer.

"It's probably just more lightning from this wicked thunderstorm," said Mr. Bunnymunch.

"No, I don't think it is. The glow stays there when there's no lightning anywhere to be seen," said Theresa.

"It also looks like it's made of lapis lazuli," said Terrance.

Aiden stopped the carriage and parked it before they reached the edge of the forest where the trees were still lively and providing good coverage. Del cast a spell around the carriage to dim its lights some so that the Wicked Witch wouldn't be able to see it as easily. With the dark clouds of the wicked thunderstorm overhead, a carriage made of Lantern Trees could be seen from quite a way off.

The army walked the remaining distance to Lilibeth's castle.

"It seems to me as though we are going to have more difficulty than we all had suspected," said Mrs. Tinkermeyer.

"Del, we could use your help for a moment," said Mr. Tinkermeyer, as he pulled a baobab wood pyramid out from his pocket.

Mr. Tinkermeyer placed the baobab wood pyramid into his wife's hand. As she held up the pyramid and pointed it towards the castle, Mr. Tinkermeyer and Del both placed their hands onto the device. The three of them began to hum. An emerald-green light surrounded the artifact and their hands. Suddenly a bolt of emerald-green energy shot out from the pyramid and collided with the glowing light around Lilibeth's castle. After a few seconds, the bolt disappeared and the artifact was no longer surrounded by the emerald-green light.

Mrs. Tinkermeyer, Mr. Tinkermeyer, and Del all let out a simultaneous sigh.

"Well, it was worth a try," said Mrs. Tinkermeyer.

"What just happened? What is that pyramid?" asked Aiden.

"The pyramid is an artifact that Mrs. Tinkermeyer and I designed. It's to help open doors and other impenetrable objects. This glowing, lapis lazuli light around the castle is a magical barrier … and I don't see how we're going to get past it," said Mr. Tinkermeyer.

Chapter Twenty-Three

"I, personally, don't see how my sister could create a barrier as powerful as this. This sorcery is beyond her skills," said Del.

"What are we going to do? We have to get back into the castle so you can re-enchant the Wicked ... I mean so you can re-enchant your sister," said Aiden.

"We're going back to the Village of Lapis Lazuli. They'll know what to do," said Terrance, rather nonchalantly.

"How will they know what to do? There aren't any sorcerers or witches there," said Aiden.

"Yes, but the barrier is made of lapis lazuli light, so the Lapis Lazulians must know what Lilibeth did to erect the barrier," said Theresa.

"Ingenious!" said Mr. Tinkermeyer.

"Oh my goodness me! What bright children you are. The Lapis Lazulians are the experts on lapis lazuli, so let's head back to the village and find Angelique. I'm sure she will either know what's going on or at least be able take us to someone who does," said Mrs. Tinkermeyer.

While the army was walking back to the carriage, a thought came to Mrs. Tinkermeyer about what had just happened. "There is something that isn't sitting well with me about our visit to the castle just now," she said.

"What's that, my wife?" said Mr. Tinkermeyer.

"Why didn't she make an appearance when we tried to break through her lapis lazuli barrier?" said Mrs. Tinkermeyer.

"I hadn't thought of that ... why didn't she come out of her castle to fight back?" said Aiden.

"She prob'ly has some other more *important* work to be doin' and she knew we wouldn't be about to do anythin' to her because of her powerful barrier," said Mr. Pommier.

"I didn't see any guards around her castle ... so maybe Mr. Pommier is right. Perhaps she is busy with some other part of her plan and didn't want to bother with us since we can't get to her anyways," said Del.

The Return
to the Castle of the Wicked Witch

Back in the Village of Lapis Lazuli, the army immediately went to the general store to talk with Angelique.

"A barrier made of lapis lazuli, you say? Well, I think I know what you're talking about. Soon after everyone was freed from the Wicked Witch's wicked charm, Lilibeth paid another visit to our village. Her brief time here was very scary ... not because of her spell casting ... but because she didn't even try to enchant anyone. She just walked right past everyone and rushed directly into the old museum. The only thing she took was our Lapis Lazuli Barrier Stone," said Angelique.

"Barrier Stone ... it's the Barrier Stone she used on her castle," said Mr. Tinkermeyer.

"She was able to make it work? Well, no one here has ever seen it been used. It's been too many years since anyone had use for it, so when the Wicked Witch came around no one was left who knew how to use it to protect us from her," said Angelique.

"Del, you said your parents were powerful enough to keep Lilibeth out of the Village of Poofle ... and they are obviously powerful enough to keep out her wicked thunderstorm. Do you think they might be willing to help us break through the barrier your sister created with the Lapis Lazuli Barrier Stone?" asked Aiden.

"I know they would be happy to help ... but it wouldn't matter. I now remember some of the history behind the stone ... and even with several more good witches and good warlocks there's no way we'd be able to get through sorcery of that power," said Del.

"I suggest you get planning on something else then, because one of her former *guards* let us know the Wicked Witch intends to use the Lapis Lazuli Barrier Stone to steal the Silver Goblet. She's going to use the goblet to flood Oz!" said Angelique.

"How can a little goblet flood Oz?" asked Terrance.

"It can flood Oz because it can produce water ... lots and lots of water," said Mr. Bunnymunch.

"That artifact was created to be helpful and provide everyone in Oz with water to drink. It wasn't meant to be used in such a

Chapter Twenty-Three

wicked manner ... but I suppose a wicked person can turn just about any artifact into something wicked," said Mrs. Tinkermeyer.

"She wants to rule the whole of the Land of Oz ... I'm sure of it. Even the threat of flooding everything could produce enough fear in the land that everyone will accept her as queen, which she has no right to be," said Del.

"Maybe it's time to return to the Silver Tower. Maybe it's time for me to deal with my pride ...," said Aiden.

"Oh my goodness me, I've been hoping you'd say that, Aiden. You know, I'm sure the Ladies Thorn and Thistle will be most happy to assist ... and I do hope they are as powerful as the rumors say they are," said Mrs. Tinkermeyer.

"We should head to the Silver Tower ... but we should go by way of my home," said Del.

"Shouldn't we find the Silver Goblet first, or should we ask for the Ladies' help in finding it?" said Terrance.

"Isn't the Silver Goblet kept guarded in the Northern Stronghold?" asked Mr. Bunnymunch.

"It used to be stored there ... but after Lilibeth's last attempt to steal it ... I may have borrowed it without anyone's knowledge. I wanted to make sure she wasn't able to find it. The Silver Goblet is hidden in my home. Since it's so close, I think it may be best for us to take the carriage there first and then head on to the Silver Tower," said Del.

Chapter Twenty-Four
The Silver Goblet

The return to Del's home was very quick. When the Army of South Grace entered the foggy area of the fog trees and fog shrubs of Lapis Lazuli Lane, the friends were immediately greeted by the fog sprites. Since the fog sprites were already aware of the unsuccessfulness that the army had had with the lapis lazuli barrier that surrounded the castle of the Wicked Witch, the tiny friends were ready to help the army travel through the foggy area as far as the sprites could go. It only took two minutes to reach Del's home, thanks to their flying help. Although everyone in the carriage enjoyed the rapid pace of the ride, the Silverglade children were able to appreciate the fog sprite ride the most. The three Silverglades were able to take their minds completely away from their troubles for those two minutes and enjoy life as much as they did before they had encountered the Wicked Witch … or before their parents had become lost.

"Thank you again for your kindness, friends!" shouted Mrs. Tinkermeyer as the fog sprites hurriedly fluttered back to the deepness of the fog, now that the army had reached its destination.

The army followed Del into his home, where he led his friends to a bookcase in his library. Del tilted one of the books forward and the bookcase vanished. A door then appeared where the bookcase had been.

"You can never be too careful when guarding artifacts as precious as this one," said Del.

"Quite right! I suspect you have various other magical protections, correct?" said Mr. Tinkermeyer.

"Of course, but they won't pose us any threat since I'm leading the way," said Del.

On the other side of the door was a long stair case, leading down what must have been at least five-hundred feet. At the

Chapter Twenty-Four

bottom of the stairs was another door, which Del opened for them. This door led to a long hallway with various entranceways along both sides. Del took them to the first door on the left.

"This looks like a broom closet door. Do you keep the Silver Goblet in your broom closet?" asked Aiden.

"Of course I keep the Silver Goblet in my broom closet! Why would anyone think to look in here for such a powerful artifact?" said Del.

Del then opened the door to his broom closet. Inside were several brooms, a mop, a bucket … and lots of cobwebs.

"Oh my goodness me, where's the Silver Goblet? I don't see it anywhere," said Mrs. Tinkermeyer.

"It's in the bucket. The bucket is designed to prevent the goblet from leaking water. No matter how you hold the bucket, the goblet will think its upright and won't release its unlimited supply of water," said Del.

"How do you get it out of the bucket?" asked Terrance.

"Please don't take offense by this, but I think that is a secret I should keep to myself … just in case someone were to overhear us talking … or cast a charm on you to force you to reveal the secret," said Del.

"Can the Silver Goblet really flood the whole Land of Oz? It's difficult to believe that a little goblet could have the power to do that," said Theresa.

"Are you familiar with the North Ocean?" asked Del.

"Yes, I've always wanted to visit it so I can see the pale gale snail whales," said Theresa.

"Before this goblet was created, that ocean used to be a desert. The artificer that created the goblet fell asleep in his cart one day due to heat exhaustion … and when he woke up he was surrounded by ocean. His Silver Goblet was floating next to his cart and it was upside-down. Had he not woken up when he did, then Oz would now be one, large ocean … although Lilibeth wouldn't have anything to flood," said Del.

THE SILVER GOBLET

"How did the goblet tip over while the artificer was asleep?" asked Mr. Bunnymunch.

"The desert was prone to wind from the pale gale snail whales, and I tend to think it was one of them that blew it over," said Del.

"How can a snail whale live in a desert" asked Aiden.

"Pale gale snail whales can swim in the air … or at least they used to swim there. I guess they don't need to, now that they have a whole ocean to live in," said Del.

"I don't think I'd ever wanna see a snail whale swimmin' in the air. That's just not somethin' I'd feel comfortable havin' fly by me … especially with all that slime. They don't eat trees, do they?" said Mr. Pommier.

"Don't worry, Mr. Pommier. Pale gale snail whales only eat pale gales," said Mrs. Tinkermeyer.

Del led the army back to the stairs, which had magically become much shorter.

"What happened to the tall staircase?" asked Theresa.

"That's the down staircase. The up staircase is only two steps. I thought that might make it easier. If someone has broken into my home and has already bothered to walk all the way down here and steal something then there's no use making them go up so many stairs … and it would slow me down unnecessarily, too," said Del.

"That's kind of funny," said Terrance, starting to laugh a little.

"You think it's funny?" asked Aiden. Aiden then grabbed Terrance, tossed him up on his shoulder, and carried him up the two stairs while tickling him.

***

Back in the carriage, the army prepared to make its way to the Silver Tower.

"We're going to have to take the South Grace Road again, because that's the only way to reach the Silver Tower … or at least it's the only way I know of to reach the Silver Tower," said Mr. Bunnymunch.

Chapter Twenty-Four

"That's going to be dangerous, since it passes so close to Lilibeth's castle," said Del.

"Could you use your magic to hide us from your sister while we pass by her castle?" asked Theresa.

"She would notice my magic immediately; however, I think Terrance has an artifact we could use to help make us less noticeable. Terrance, could you try using your ring to make the carriage lights go out?" asked Del.

"I don't know ... I thought it could only make light ... I guess I could try," said Terrance. He closed his eyes and a moment later the carriage stopped glowing.

"The lights are out!" exclaimed Theresa.

"Well done, Terrance," said Mrs. Tinkermeyer.

"I did it?!" shouted Terrance, surprised at what he had done. As he shouted and lost concentration, the lights came back on.

"Oh my goodness me ... you'll have to keep up your concentration when we pass by the castle, or else the light might go back on and Lilibeth could see us," said Mr. Tinkermeyer.

"I'll do my best," said Terrance, sounding a little nervous.

***

The Army of South Grace left the home of the Good Warlock Del and returned to South Grace Road by way of Weeping Willow Way. Mrs. Tinkermeyer, Mr. Tinkermeyer, Del, and Mr. Pommier were all inside of the carriage using some of the table space to prepare certain artifacts that the Tinkermeyers had packed just in case they were noticed by the Wicked Witch as they traveled by her castle.

The Silverglades, including Acorn, and Mr. Bunnymunch were all riding on the carriage. Everyone but Acorn was wearing a raincoat due to the wicked thunderstorm. Acorn naturally had no need for a raincoat, since he was rustproof. Mr. Bunnymunch was fast asleep in Theresa's lap, who was enjoying petting his soft, bunnymunch fur, although it was covered by his raincoat.

Occasionally, Mr. Bunnymunch let out a quiet bunnymunch snore, which would make Theresa giggle a little.

"Aiden ...," said Theresa in a rather somber voice.

"What can I do for you, favorite little sister of mine?" said Aiden.

"Do you think mother and father would be disappointed in us for being so slow with the Wicked Witch? I mean ... do you think they'd be upset with us since she's still causing so much trouble and we haven't stopped her yet?" asked Theresa.

"I've been thinking about that, too," said Terrance.

"So have I ... and I think I know what they'd say to us if they were unlost and here with us right now," said Aiden.

"What do you think they'd say to us?" asked Theresa.

"They'd say, 'Theresa, Terrance, and Aiden ... we're so proud of you for taking the time to fix your own mistakes. You aren't trying to place the blame on anyone else and you're doing your best to stop this nasty Wicked Witch.' That's what they'd say," said Aiden, placing his arm around both his sister and brother.

"Are you sure they'd say that?" asked Terrance.

"I'm positive they'd say that. They love us and they'd realize we didn't mean to release a wicked witch," said Aiden.

"That makes me feel a lot better knowing they'd say that," said Theresa.

"What else would they say?" asked Terrance.

"What else would they say? Well, I supposed they'd say, 'How good of you three for all getting along so well ... and how good of you for making such wonderful new friends ... and how good of you for thinking about us so much while we were lost,'" said Aiden.

"I hope we aren't interrupting anything important, but I think we should be getting pretty close to Lilibeth's castle about now," said Mr. Tinkermeyer as he and the rest of the army climbed up from the inside of the carriage.

"We have prepared a few artifacts just in case Lilibeth sees us ... although I'm certain she won't since we have Terrance and his

Chapter Twenty-Four

magic ring with us," said Mrs. Tinkermeyer, trying to make sure to be uplifting to the children so they wouldn't be afraid.

"Speaking of Terrance and his magic ring, I think it would be beneficial to us if we were to lose some of our lighting soon. Is that ok with you, Terrance? Are you ready to use your ring?" said Del.

"I'm as ready as I'll ever be," said Terrance.

"I think we'll need it for about twenty minutes. That way we can be sure not to attract Lilibeth's attention. Do you think you can manage to give us twenty minutes of unlightedness, Terrance?" asked Del, giving Terrance a friendly squeeze on the shoulder, which also included a friendly calming spell just as a precaution.

"Sure thing, Del," said Terrance.

"Terrance, why don't you come back here and sit next to me? I'll make sure nothing diverts your attention from using your ring," said Mrs. Tinkermeyer. She also wanted to make sure that Terrance wasn't sitting beside Aiden while his older brother was trying to steer the carriage. Any sudden movements by Aiden to try to avoid an obstacle could have distracted Terrance and caused him to lose concentration, making them all very well lighted and visible again. Mrs. Tinkermeyer didn't want to say this out loud, though.

Terrance crawled back into the coach of the carriage and sat down next to Mrs. Tinkermeyer, who gently placed her arm around him for protection and comforting. Mrs. Tinkermeyer knew that the three Silverglades would be afraid of the darkness. Although it was plenty bright enough for the rest of the army, since there was lightning, the Silverglades were used to the very bright lights of their farm and the Village of Illume being around them constantly at all hours of the day and night.

Terrance closed his eyes. After a moment, all of the light coming from the carriage disappeared. Although the carriage maintained a strong air of elegance, there was something special missing to its look.

The Army of South Grace remained very quiet while it traveled unilluminated by the castle of the Wicked Witch. The friends spoke only in whispers and only when necessary, just in case some of the trees or other plants had decided to spy on them for the Wicked Witch – although any such spying they presumed would be caused by a wicked enchantment placed on the offending plant by the Wicked Witch.

When the carriage passed by the small road leading from South Grace Road to Lilibeth's castle, Mr. Bunnymunch noticed something that disturbed him.

"Look at the Spectral Pandanus Tree!" exclaimed Mr. Bunnymunch, although still in a quiet whisper. "It's the only plant around that looks to be alive, but it's glowing a very eerie black color. It looks very wicked to me."

"That's due to a wicked charm from my sister. Once she's made good again she'll remove the enchantment and make it look all pretty again … but for now, that's not a very pleasant sight to see … not a pleasant sight at all," said Del.

"Mrs. Tinkermeyer, how's my little brother doing?" whispered Aiden.

"He's doing magnificently, Aiden. I'm very proud of him for keeping such good concentration for so long. He's really doing his parents proud right now," said Mrs. Tinkermeyer, knowing that it would be beneficial for Terrance to hear that he was doing a good job with preventing the Wicked Witch from spotting the carriage.

"Mrs. Tinkermeyer … Del … do you see something different about the castle?" asked Theresa.

"Something different? What? What? What? What do you … oh … I see. The lapis lazuli barrier is gone. That can only mean one thing," said Mrs. Tinkermeyer.

"She's leaving to find the Silver Goblet," said Del.

"Aiden, please take us into the trees and hide us as best you can," said Mr. Tinkermeyer.

Just as Aiden stopped the carriage among some partially living trees and shrubs, Lilibeth appeared from the small road that led to her castle. She was riding on an enchanted, black carriage that resembled a sort of dark dragon. The dark dragon carriage was encompassed by the lapis lazuli barrier. The Wicked Witch rode at

Chapter Twenty-Four

top speed north along South Grace Road and soon vanished in the distance.

"She must be on her way to the stronghold in the north for the Silver Goblet. That's the only reason she'd dare leave the safety of her wicked thunderstorm at this time," said Del.

"We should keep moving south to the Silver Tower, but let's keep our lights off a little longer. We probably don't need that precaution anymore ... but I know I'd still feel safer," said Aiden.

"I agree. Is Terrance good with giving us a few more minutes of unlightedness?" asked Mr. Bunnymunch.

"Terrance is fine," said Terrance with a smile and referring to himself in the third person to try to lighten the mood.

"My sister will not be pleased when she discovers the Silver Goblet missing from the Northern Stronghold," said Del.

"That's ok, we'll be at the Silver Tower long before she can return from the Northern Stronghold. We'll have everything worked out by then," said Mrs. Tinkermeyer.

"I hope the Lady Thorn and the Lady Thistle won't be mad at us," said Theresa.

"Oh my goodness me! What nonsense! I've told you before they won't be mad. They're nice people and they're your friends. They'll just be happy to see you again ... and they'll also be happy to have a chance to help their friends. So stop worrying and start looking forward to seeing your friends, the Ladies Thorn and Thistle, again," said Mrs. Tinkermeyer.

Chapter Twenty-Five
The Ladies

The voyage to the Silver Tower took significantly less time than it had for the Silverglade's first visit there. Aiden did not drive the carriage in the casual manner that he had during their previous trip, because time was of the essence. The other members of the Army of South Grace who had not traveled through this area were fascinated by the strange plants and animals. Acorn and Mrs. Tinkermeyer both had their interests piqued by the Kitten Kudzu Mountain, although for rather different reasons. Acorn thought that it would be a fun place to play, whereas Mrs. Tinkermeyer could tell that there was some interesting magic surrounding the mountain.

The Lady Thorn and the Lady Thistle were waiting right beside South Grace Road for the Army of South Grace at the edge of the Great Garden.

"Oh my goodness me, I think the Ladies may have had some inkling that we were on our way," said Mrs. Tinkermeyer with a smile. Even though they were very concerned about the matter of the Wicked Witch of the Majestic Moonlit Mountains, Mrs. Tinkermeyer and her husband were excited to finally meet the Lady Thorn and the Lady Thistle.

"Of course we knew!" said Lady Thorn.

"How could we possibly not know that our good friends were about to arrive?" said Lady Thistle.

"Lady Thorn, Lady Thistle … we've done something bad … with your unbinding ring … please forgive us," said Theresa, trying to hold back her tears.

"You should listen better to Mrs. Tinkermeyer. We're not upset with you at all and there's nothing to forgive. You were trying to be helpful, and that's what's important," said Lady Thorn.

CHAPTER TWENTY-FIVE

"You did the right thing, as far as we're concerned. We just hope you have learned from this experience that sometimes there are people who seem to be trustworthy who are not," said Lady Thistle.

"Lady Thorn and Lady Thistle, it is indeed an honor to meet two sorceresses of your caliber. I just wish we weren't meeting in such dire circumstances," said Del.

"My husband and I are also very honored to make your acquaintances," said Mrs. Tinkermeyer.

"Oh don't be silly, we're just two, funny, old ladies who enjoy our gardening," said Lady Thorn.

"We're always happy to make new friends," said Lady Thistle.

"Ladies, since you already seem to know what has happened ... could you please help us with the Lapis Lazuli Barrier Stone? We need to find a way to break though the lapis lazuli barrier around Lilibeth so Del can try to re-enchant her," said Aiden.

"Yes, that is a particularly powerful barrier," said Lady Thorn.

"But we can manage it quite easily. We have better tricks up our green sleeves than Lilibeth has up her wicked black sleeves," said Lady Thistle.

"We'd normally offer to have you spend some time in the Silver Tower and rest, but you need to start back to Lilibeth's castle straight away," said Lady Thorn.

"If you leave right now you'll return just before she does to her castle," said Lady Thistle.

"But what about the barrier? Can you come with us or give us an artifact to help us with it?" said Terrance.

"We'll meet you there. We have a few things to do here about the Great Garden before we can go to Lilibeth's castle," said Lady Thorn.

"Don't you worry one bit, though. We'll be there in plenty of time and everything will turn out just fine," said Lady Thistle.

● The Ladies ●

***

The Army of South Grace turned back again towards the north. They all sat on top of the carriage in order to enjoy the pleasant weather, which wouldn't be so pleasant once they returned to the castle of the Wicked Witch.

"The Ladies seemed a little calmer than I had expected them to be. I have to wonder if they fully understand what's going on here ... we let a wicked witch free and she's doing wicked things," said Aiden with great concern showing on his face.

"Well of course they seemed calm. Artificers of their caliber are always calm ... or at least I would expect them to be. The Ladies are very close with nature and understand a lot more things about the world than any one of us does. They also would never be afraid of a wicked witch. Two powerful sorceresses aren't going to be afraid of a little wicked witch," said Mrs. Tinkermeyer.

"Let's just hope they're as powerful as you claim they are ... but ... we do have three farmers, two artificers, a clockwork squirrel, a bunnymunch, a tree guard, and a good warlock in our mighty army, so we really don't have any reason to be afraid of a silly wicked witch, now do we?" said Aiden, trying to cheer up both his twins and himself.

"Quite so, young man! Quite so! We are more than a match for the Wicked Witch of the Majestic Moonlit Mountains. Even without the help of the Ladies Thorn and Thistle we would have eventually stopped Lilibeth's wicked plan and found a way to bring her back to goodness," said Mr. Tinkermeyer.

"Now don't you go forgettin' that we have a wanderin' wollemi pine tree in the Army of South Grace. Even though Wilma can't be here she's still a part of the effort!" said Mr. Pommier.

"That's right, we can't forget Wilma! She gave us a lot of wonderful food to eat. I've enjoyed it every day," said Mr. Bunnymunch as he munched away on an apple that Wilma the wandering wollemi pine tree had provided to them.

Chapter Twenty-Five

"Aiden, what are we going to do when we get back to Lilibeth's castle? I mean ... what if the Ladies haven't arrived yet? What do we do?" asked Terrance.

"Honestly, I don't know. I don't even know what we do if the Ladies *are* there. We have some time until we arrive so maybe it would be to our advantage to come up with a plan of attack. Mrs. Tinkermeyer, you're very good at planning. Do you have any suggestions?" said Aiden.

"Oh my goodness me, I will have to give that some thought. Lilibeth's Lapis Lazuli Barrier Stone is a very tricky artifact to deal with," said Mrs. Tinkermeyer.

"Isn't the lapis lazuli barrier gone now?" asked Theresa.

"No, she still has that blasted stone. She took it with her," said Mr. Pommier.

"Wait, Mr. Pommier, I think she may have made an excellent point. Theresa, what a brilliant thought! The Lapis Lazuli Barrier Stone is in the far parts of North Grace. We will reach her castle a day or so before she's able to return. That gives us a huge advantage. Why didn't I think of that before ...?" said Mrs. Tinkermeyer.

"I don't understand; can't she just use the Lapis Lazuli Barrier Stone when she returns to her castle?" asked Mr. Bunnymunch.

"Yes, she can; however, we'll be inside her castle long before she can raise the barrier around it. Since Lilibeth has the stone with her in the north, there isn't anything protecting her castle right now. We can sneak inside and hide there until she returns. Once she has restored the lapis lazuli barrier around her castle we can sneak up to her and Del can place his enchantment on her. We really should have thought about this more thoroughly before we came to find the Ladies," said Theresa.

"Nonsense! Nonsense! Nonsense! Of course we should have come to ask the Ladies for their help. They are your friends and they should know if you're in any danger. Besides, it's good to have two good sorceresses as backup when there's a wicked witch involved," said Mrs. Tinkermeyer.

"Theresa, although your plan is quite brilliant, there is one thing you're forgetting. Lilibeth is a Wicked Witch, and even though she has a Lapis Lazuli Barrier Stone she's bound to have other enchantments of her own making protecting her castle. The good news is that with the Tinkermeyers and myself here we should be able to handle any of her wicked enchantments," said Del.

"I hadn't thought of that …," said Theresa.

"It's ok, my sweet Theresa. That's one of the many reasons we have an army of friends. No matter how well one of us may think out something, there's always room for friendly advice for improvement," said Aiden.

"Exactly, and it's especially good to have the Tinkermeyers here with their artifacts that tell us when one of Lilibeth's enchantments is gonna cause us any problems," said Mr. Pommier.

"We're forgetting something else," said Mr. Bunnymunch.

"What else are we forgetting, my tiny friend?" asked Aiden.

"We're forgetting that there could be more guards inside of the castle. We don't know if Angelique was able to free all of the Lapis Lazulians from the charm Lilibeth placed on them to make them do her will," said Mr. Bunnymunch.

Acorn appeared to whisper something into Aiden's ear in response to what his friend, Mr. Bunnymunch, had just said.

"Acorn says that since we have plenty of time to reach the castle before Lilibeth returns we should pay a quick visit to Lapis Lazuli and ask Angelique if she's disenchanted everyone. That way we'll know if there are any guards in the castle or not," said Aiden.

"Even if there are some guards, they won't be a match for us. I think we can handle a few guards on our own very easily. Lilibeth's guards are no match for the Army of South Grace!" said Terrance.

"Then we have a plan, and a darn good one at that," said Mr. Tinkermeyer.

Chapter Twenty-Six
Theresa's Plan

After a quick visit with Angelique in the Village of Lapis Lazuli, the Army of South Grace learned that Lilibeth indeed had no more guards in her castle. Angelique had been able to remove the enchantments from the last remaining guards once the Wicked Witch had departed for North Grace and the Northern Stronghold.

The army walked from a secret hiding spot in the woods where Aiden had hidden his family's carriage to the castle of Lilibeth. Although there were no guards in sight when the friends arrived, the Army of South Grace did encounter another obstacle.

"I guess this explains why it's not raining here. The rain would put out this fire," said Aiden.

The castle was surrounded by a magical fire of glowing, black flames that resembled a moat of sorts. The fire was twice as tall as Aiden, so jumping over it was not an option. They all stood for a moment in front of the castle to figure out a way to manage the black flames.

"Del, do you think you could handle this magical fire? I'm not sure if we have any artifacts appropriate to the occasion," said Mrs. Tinkermeyer.

"I know I can handle it ... at least with the Silver Goblet I know I can handle it. I'm just afraid to remove the goblet from its hiding place ... so let's see what I can do on my own first," said Del.

Del walked closer to the black fire and raised his arms, with his palms facing the sky. A sparkling, blue mist began to form in a ring shape around the castle. The flames were engulfed by the mist, which quickly extinguished the fire.

"Hmm ... that wasn't as difficult as I expected it to be," said Del, allowing a small grin to show on his face.

Theresa's Plan

"We knew you could do it!" said Theresa and Terrance in unison.

"She probably won't be expecting us to enter using the front door ... so let's try that," said Mrs. Tinkermeyer.

"There don't seem to be any enchantments on the door so let's go on in," said Mr. Tinkermeyer, holding several artifacts, including the Artifacts-and-Magics Compass, in hand to examine the castle.

Aiden pushed open one of the large doors and poked his head inside.

"All seems clear," said Aiden.

"Let's get ourselves inside quickly. Quickly! Quickly! Quickly!" said Mrs. Tinkermeyer.

The army entered the castle, with Mr. Bunnymunch and Acorn in back making sure that no one from the outside was watching them enter.

"If I hadn't already visited the Silver Tower I'd be amazed at the size of this room," said Aiden.

The army was in a gloomy, stone room filled with pillars and strange contraptions that looked to be wicked beasts. In front of the army were two staircases made of onyx that curved, forming an almost-semicircle leading to the upstairs.

"What are all of these artifacts doing here?" asked Theresa.

"Those aren't artifacts. They are my sister's attempts at artwork," said Del.

"This is art?" asked Aiden.

"Yes ... well, at least to my sister it is. These are beasts that she has imagined as being her minions. I suspect that one day she plans to make an army of created beasts, but we're not going to let her realize that particular plan," said Del.

"They look very scary. I don't see how anyone could, or would want to, create such horrible beasts," said Terrance.

"Oh my goodness me, that's how wicked people are ... now let's get ourselves upstairs. I think that setting up camp here right by the front door might make us look a little too conspicuous," said Mrs. Tinkermeyer.

Chapter Twenty-Six

"How long will it take for Lilibeth to come back to her home?" asked Terrance.

"It could be at any moment now, or another week. It just depends on how long she takes at the Northern Stronghold searching for the Silver Goblet, which she isn't going to find there," said Mrs. Tinkermeyer, who was taking the lead in escorting the army up the stairs.

"She'll prob'ly be right quick in makin' her way back here once she's done. I'm sure she won't wanna be away from her wicked thunderstorm for very long at all," said Mr. Pommier.

"What should we do in the meanwhile?" asked Theresa.

"Wait quietly. That's all we really can do. We don't want to do anything that will draw her attention to us when she arrives," said Aiden.

"Look over there," said Mr. Pommier, pointing to an alcove just to the side of the top of the stairs behind them. "That's a perfect place to hide. When she comes up the stairs she won't be able to see us hidin' in that dark hole. We can give her quite the surprise!"

"Very good, Mr. Pommier! That's the perfect place. She wouldn't expect us to be there at all," said Mrs. Tinkermeyer.

"I doubt she'll expect us to be inside any part of her castle," said Aiden.

Aiden sat down in one of the corners of the alcove. He opened his arms, motioning for Terrance and Theresa to come join him and Acorn, who was already curled up on Aiden's feet. The twins sat down next to their older brother and rested their heads on his shoulders.

"That looks like a good idea to me. I'm sure Lilibeth won't be returning immediately, so why don't you three go ahead and take a nap just like little Acorn is doing. We all need to be well-rested when Lilibeth makes her entrance," said Mrs. Tinkermeyer.

The Silverglades were happy to do as Mrs. Tinkermeyer had suggested, because they were all very tired from doing so much traveling. Aiden, Theresa, and Terrance spent their rest period dreaming about being back on the farm with their parents returned

Theresa's Plan

from being lost and all watching together one of the Lightning Bug and Lightning Grass lightning storms that helped to make Silverglade Mountain one of the most magnificent sights in all of Oz.

While the Silverglades slept, the rest of the group made plans for watch-keeping and sleeping shifts. Mr. and Mrs. Tinkermeyer also prepared some of their artifacts while the army discussed its plans.

"I think it would be prudent to make sure we have at least two members of the army on watch at all times. We must be prepared for Lilibeth," said Mr. Tinkermeyer.

"I fully agree. My sister is a very powerful witch and we can't take any chances," said Del.

"Del, do ya think your sister is gonna be makin' her appearance durin' the day, or durin' the night? That'll make a world of difference in bein' prepared for her," noted Mr. Pommier.

"She's a wicked witch, so she'd be traveling at night, right?" said Mr. Bunnymunch.

"With her wicked thunderstorm I'd expect her to return during the daytime. You see, she'll want to witness firsthand how everyone is afraid of her wicked thunderstorm during the day … and she'll enjoy seeing its dark gloom during the daytime when it's supposed to be bright out," said Del.

"That makes sense to me, Del. Let's plan to have everyone awake during the day and we'll sleep in shifts at night," said Mrs. Tinkermeyer.

"I hope she isn't too angry when she returns. An angry wicked witch will be even scarier than a happy wicked witch," said Mr. Bunnymunch.

"Why would she be angry when she arrives? She won't know we're here," said Mr. Pommier.

"She won't have the Silver Goblet. She'll be very upset that she went all the way to the Northern Stronghold for nothing," said Mr. Bunnymunch.

Chapter Twenty-Six

"That's why we need to be extra careful to keep quiet and be ready for her when she arrives," said Mrs. Tinkermeyer.

***

The plans that the Army of South Grace had made for sleeping in shifts were unnecessary, because the Wicked Witch of the Majestic Mountains had not required very much time at all to determine that the Silver Goblet was no longer being stored in the Northern Stronghold.

The Silverglades, including Acorn, were awakened from their rest by the roaring thunder of the wicked thunderstorm, which had suddenly become intensely awful.

"What's happening? Why did the storm worsen so much and so abruptly?" asked Aiden as he held on to his brother and sister to make sure that they were ok.

"It sounds to me like my sister is very close by … and not in a very pleasant mood," said Del.

The wicked thunderstorm continued to increase in its booming rage. All of a sudden, a thunderous roar shook the entire castle with such great force that it almost knocked Mrs. Tinkermeyer off of her feet.

"Oh I wish this storm would stop!" said Theresa, hiding her head in Aiden's chest.

"I don't think that was thunder," said Mr. Tinkermeyer, who had a hold of his wife's arm to make sure that she didn't fall.

"Oh my goodness me, that was the front door. Lilibeth has arrived. Everyone be very quiet. We don't want her to hear us. She could be coming up these stairs any moment now," said Mrs. Tinkermeyer.

The sound of the clicking heels of the Wicked Witch on the onyx stairs filled the castle.

Del reached into his pocket and pulled out the brilliant-white ribbon that he had been twirling in his fingers when the army had first visited him at his home. No one else moved, for fear of alerting the Wicked Witch to their presence.

Theresa's Plan

The clicking sound was coming very close ... and then a dark figure appeared at the top of the stairs just a few feet from the alcove where the Army of South Grace was hiding. It was Lilibeth, and she appeared to be in an intensely stormy mood. She quickly walked down the hall and then stopped, as though she had a sudden epiphany.

"You!" yelled Lilibeth. She spun herself around and pointed her finger directly at the alcove. "Get out of my home!" she shrieked.

The Army of South Grace immediately found itself in the wet yard in front of Lilibeth's castle. The friends were all rapidly drenched with the rain water from the wicked thunderstorm.

"I guess she was angry," said Aiden, who was sitting on the ground with the twins cuddled up to him and Acorn sitting at attention on Aiden's feet. He then whistled to call the carriage to pick them up.

"She took that a lot better than I thought she would," said Mrs. Tinkermeyer.

The lapis lazuli barrier then reappeared, surrounding the castle.

"What do we do now?" asked Theresa, in a scared voice.

"We wait for the Ladies," said Aiden.

"Del, why didn't your sister put us in her dungeon or enchant us ... or do some other wicked thing to us?" asked Mr. Tinkermeyer.

"She looked very frustrated to me ... so she probably just didn't want to take the time to deal with us. Maybe she doesn't see us as a threat to her anymore ...," said Del.

"Not a threat to her? She can just wait and see what our next plan is. We most certainly are a threat to her! I'm sure the Lady Thorn and Lady Thistle will arrive soon, but let's get back into that castle if we can. Mr. Bunnymunch, it's common knowledge that your people live underground," said Mrs. Tinkermeyer.

"That's correct. It's very safe there and quite cozy. We also enjoy munching through the ground to make our homes," said Mr. Bunnymunch.

Chapter Twenty-Six

"Would you be up to munching your way through the ground and under the castle? It's possible that this lapis lazuli barrier stops at the surface of the ground," said Mrs. Tinkermeyer.

"That will not be necessary," said a voice coming from the dead woods around Lilibeth's castle. The voice came from atop the Silverglade's carriage that was arriving thanks to Aiden's whistle. The voice belonged to Lady Thistle.

"There's no need to dig into the castle now that we're here," said Lady Thorn.

The carriage stopped next to the army. The Silverglades stood up and looked excited to see their friends, the Ladies Thorn and Thistle.

"What's your plan? How do we stop Lilibeth? And ... is it true? Are you really sorceresses?" asked Aiden.

"It's true. Now I believe Del has an enchanted ribbon for us?" said Lady Thistle, smiling.

"It's right here," said Del, who handed the brilliant-white ribbon to the Lady Thistle.

"Why do you need a hair ribbon? How can it stop the Wicked Witch?" asked Theresa.

"This is the artifact Del enchanted to be used on his sister. We're going to borrow it for a moment" said Lady Thorn.

"How dare you come to my home!" screamed the Wicked Witch, as she made an appearance from the front doors of her castle. "You must all leave right now!"

The Wicked Witch pointed at the army and the Ladies just as she had done to remove the army from her castle shortly before. When nothing happened, the Wicked Witch screamed in anger.

"Your magic isn't quite as powerful as you thought it was, is it, Lilibeth?" said Lady Thistle.

"It doesn't matter! You'll never be able to touch me. This barrier is impenetrable. I am safe from anyone who tries to meddle in my affairs. Go home!" yelled the Wicked Witch.

The Ladies Thorn and Thistle turned and faced one another. They reached out and held hands using their ring hands, with the rings directly touching one another. The Lady Thistle then placed the brilliant-white ribbon that Del had enchanted across their hands. The Ladies smiled at one another.

The rings on the Ladies' hands began to glow and a bright, green aura surrounded the Ladies as they continued to gaze into one another's eyes. The lapis lazuli barrier shattered. Lady Thorn winked at Lady Thistle.

Suddenly, the aura around the Ladies became blindingly bright and filled the whole area surrounding Lilibeth's castle. A wave of green energy spread throughout the Majestic Moonlit Mountains, dissipating the clouds of the wicked thunderstorm as the energy wave stretched outwards.

The green aura gently subsided. The castle was gone and the cottage the Silverglades had first encountered in that spot had returned.

Chapter Twenty-Seven
Lilibeth the Good Witch

Lying gently on the ground among some white roses was Lilibeth. She was wearing her original white, silk gown from the day that the Silverglades and Mr. Bunnymunch had first met her. Instead of the white hat that she had worn before, Lilibeth wore in her hair the brilliant-white ribbon that had been on the Ladies' hands.

"What happened?" asked Terrance.

"Where did the castle go?" asked Theresa.

"I ... I think the Lady Thorn and Lady Thistle managed to re-enchant Lilibeth," said Aiden.

"Not quite. Re-enchanting her and un-unbinding the old enchantment would have been too messy," said Lady Thorn.

"We did something that will be a little more permanent," said Lady Thistle.

Del walked over to where his sister was silently lying among the white roses. He kneeled down beside her and took her hand. With a smile he said, "Wake up, sister. It's time for you to open your eyes and enjoy the sunshine with me."

Lilibeth's eyes opened. She looked at Del for a moment, then reached up and hugged him as if she hadn't seen him in a very long while.

"I haven't felt this good for ages. Thank you, brother," said Lilibeth.

"Ladies, if you didn't put an enchantment on her or un-unbind the enchantment that we accidentally removed ... then what exactly did you do? Is she ... good again?" asked Aiden.

"She is indeed good again. We took away all of the damage that the black magic had done to her soul. Lilibeth has spent a long time being a wicked witch, so we had to use a particularly powerful spell on her, but it's one that will definitely last and can't be unbound," said Lady Thorn.

"We used Del's ribbon as a foundation for our spell. When he enchanted the ribbon, he poured his love for his sister into it. That love helped us to remove all of those nasty black magic stains from her so she could be good again, like she used to be before she started using all of her black magic spells," said Lady Thistle.

"We're so sorry that we caused all of this trouble," said Theresa.

"Oh my goodness me, everything is all fine now, Theresa. Wickedness never lasts forever," said Mrs. Tinkermeyer.

"What's going to happen to Lilibeth?" asked Mr. Bunnymunch.

"Is she gonna pay for her crimes now?" asked Mr. Pommier.

"I'll be happy to accept any punishment that I'm given. I've done a lot of very wicked things and I deserve to be punished for them. I'm just so very sorry for all of the harm I've caused," said Lilibeth.

"You've suffered enough. I'm taking you home to spend some time with the family. We've all missed the Good Witch Lilibeth and we'd like to get to know her again," said Del.

"That sounds like a good idea to me," said Glinda, who suddenly appeared amidst a soft, white glow. "Punishment is given to people by people who do not have a solid understanding of discipline or compassion. After Lilibeth has spent some time with her family, which I'm sure we all agree she and her family deserve, I think that she would best be disciplined by being made the guardian over the Silver Goblet that she intended to use for wicked purposes," she said.

"That sounds like a very suitable disciplinary action to me, and I think my sister will end up enjoying doing this good thing," said Del.

"Glinda, it's an honor to meet you," said Mrs. Tinkermeyer, giving a little curtsy. "Do you think that being guardian of the Silver Goblet will help teach Lilibeth to never touch the wicked magics again?"

Chapter Twenty-Seven

"I have a gift for her that should help with that part of the discipline," said Glinda. She held out her hand and a small necklace appeared. The chain was made of fine silver, and from it hung a pendant made of moonstone. Glinda then placed the necklace around Lilibeth's neck.

"Thank you, Glinda. How will this help me?" asked Lilibeth.

"This is the Moonstone Amulet. It will help you to understand hope a little better so that you don't turn to dark magic when there is always a solution to any matter through goodness," said Glinda.

"What a beautiful pendant that is," said Theresa. She walked over to Lilibeth and examined her Moonstone Amulet for a moment, after which she gave Lilibeth a big hug. "I'm glad that you're good again," she said.

"Thank you, friend Theresa. I'm glad, too," said Lilibeth.

"We have something for you Silverglade children and young man that's from all three of us," said Lady Thorn, indicating herself, Lady Thistle, and Glinda.

"Young man? ... I like the sound of that," said Aiden.

"Well you should get used to it. You're not a child, and I think you've proven that quite well during your recent adventure. You've acted as a very responsible adult," said Lady Thistle.

"Oh my goodness me, she's quite right. You've been an amazing older brother to Theresa and Terrance here. You've stood up to a wicked witch and led your family to do many good things. And don't think that just because you accidentally freed a wicked witch that you're not a responsible adult! You did the right thing," said Mrs. Tinkermeyer.

"If it weren't for all of you I'd still be a wicked witch, so freeing me from that enchantment ended up being a very good thing after all. You brought me back to goodness," said Lilibeth.

The Ladies took the hands of Aiden, Theresa, and Terrance and placed on their fingers new rosewood rings.

"These were made especially for you. They will help you to grow Silver Lilies, but more importantly they will help to protect the family ties of their wearers," said Lady Thistle.

"Will they help us to find our parents?" asked Terrance.

"Exactly," said the Ladies in unison.

"That's just splendid. Now you three can return to finding your parents and helping them become unlost," said Mr. Tinkermeyer.

"I'm sorry to be changin' the topic here, but Lilibeth … do ya … do ya mind if I ask ya somethin'?" said Mr. Pommier.

"Not at all. What would you like to ask me?" replied Lilibeth, who knew that he would be asking about his tree friend.

"Why did ya come after Wilma and attack her with fire? I mean … she's just a wanderin' wollemi pine tree and hasn't done nothin' to no one …," said Mr. Pommier.

"She's the rightful ruler of the Majestic Moonlit Mountains, so I wanted her out of the way so I could have my wicked rule. I'm so very sorry for the wicked things I did to her and to you … and to everybody," said Lilibeth.

"Rightful ruler? She never told me a thing about that," said Mr. Pommier.

"Maybe she thought you knew. Maybe that's why you were assigned to guard her and she just presumed that you knew since you were her royal guard. That's exactly what you are! You're a royal guard!" said Theresa.

"Makes sense. With my memory I prob'ly did know and plum forgot. A royal guard … I guess that means I should be gettin' back to her soon since there's no more Wicked Witch of the Majestic Moonlit Mountains to be worryin' about around these parts," said Mr. Pommier.

"Glinda, do you think that perhaps I could also, in addition to my job as keeper of the Silver Goblet, spend some of my time working for the Lady Thorn and the Lady Thistle in the Great Garden? I've done so much harm to many of the plant friends in the Majestic Moonlit Mountains that maybe I should do some penance for that, too," said Lilibeth.

"That sounds like an excellent idea to me, and the Silver Tower is where you'll have to reside anyways for the time being in order to best protect the Silver Goblet," replied Glinda.

Chapter Twenty-Seven

"We always have room for extra workers in our garden," said Lady Thorn.

"Your family has a background in farming, so you'd be a great asset to us," said Lady Thistle.

"Lady Thorn, Lady Thistle, we don't have your unbinding ring to give to you just at the moment, but we will have it soon. We lent it to Angelique, a new friend of ours in the Village of Lapis Lazuli, so she could use to protect the Lapis Lazulians from Lilibeth's enchantments. Thank you again for allowing us to borrow it," said Aiden.

"We've already had the opportunity to visit with Angelique and she kindly returned the ring to us. She was happy to return it once she knew that the wicked witch would no longer be causing her any trouble. Now, Lilibeth, I think you have something that needs to be returned to the Village of Lapis Lazuli," said Lady Thorn.

"Perhaps you, your brother, and the rest of the Army of South Grace could go together to return it," said Lady Thistle.

The Army of South Grace said its goodbyes to Lady Thorn, Lady Thistle, and Glinda. The army then traveled with Lilibeth to the Village of Lapis Lazuli, where they together returned the Lapis Lazuli Barrier Stone to the Lapis Lazulians. The residents were all so happy to be done with the Wicked Witch that they welcomed the Good Witch Lilibeth to their town with open arms and made her an honorary Lapis Lazulian.

Chapter Twenty-Eight
The Next Adventure

Three months had passed since the Silverglades had returned home to their farm to spend some time thinking about how to use their new rosewood rings to help their parents become unlost. Aiden, Theresa, Terrance, and Acorn were sitting among the Silver Lantern Trees on their family's mountain, which seemed a lot smaller now that they had spent time in the Majestic Moonlit Mountains. There were no Silver Lilies in sight, since it was long past harvest time. In place of the Silver Lilies was more Lightning Grass, because it helped ready the soil for the next season of Silver Lily growing. The Silver Lilies were hibernating just under the surface of the ground. Since their return home, the Silverglades had made it their daily routine to sit on the mountain and simply take pleasure in being home and with family.

"I do hope that Lilibeth and Del are enjoying themselves at the Silver Tower," said Theresa.

"With the Lady Thorn and the Lady Thistle there to be their friends, I'm sure they're having an absolutely marvelous time," said Aiden.

"Can we go visit them sometime, Aiden? We need to thank them in person for all of the magnificent books that Glinda and the Ladies sent to us," said Terrance.

"Of course we can. We'll go right after the next Silver Lily harvest. We can surprise them with the gift of more Silver Lilies," said Aiden.

"They'll be so happy to see us! And I'm sure they could use more Silver Lilies," said Theresa.

"What's that small cloud over there? It looks like dust flying up along the road," said Terrance.

Chapter Twenty-Eight

"It looks like something very small moving very quickly ... and it's coming in this direction," said Aiden.

The dust cloud was moving faster than any vehicle that any of the Silverglades had ever seen; however, Acorn was very quick to recognize what the source of the dust cloud was.

Acorn jumped up onto Aiden's shoulder and gave a little chirp into his ear.

"Well is that so? Terrance, Theresa, I think we're about to get a visit from a very dear friend of ours," said Aiden.

The dust cloud quickly ascended Silverglade Mountain. Rather than spiraling up the mountain, following alongside the stream of Silver Water, the dust cloud hopped over the segments of the stream. The strange phenomenon stopped directly in front of the Silverglades.

"Mr. Bunnymunch!" shouted the twins, who immediately jumped up and went to hug and pet their friend.

Mr. Bunnymunch dropped a letter that he had been holding in his mouth into the Lightning Grass. His fur was very puffy, thanks to all of the electrical current.

"It's good to see you again, my Silverglade friends. Mr. and Mrs. Tinkermeyer were going to send you this letter through normal means, but we decided it would be more fun, and faster, if I were to deliver it to you myself," said Mr. Bunnymunch.

"That's just wonderful of you to do!" said Aiden with a slight laugh.

Aiden reached down and picked up the letter.

"Open it! I bet they say they miss us. I sure do miss them!" said Theresa.

"I'm sure they miss us as much as we miss them. Now let's see what they have to say ...," said Aiden.

Our Dearest Silverglade Friends,

It's been three months since our adventure with the Wicked Witch of the Majestic Moonlit Mountains and we must tell you that we miss you terribly. Please come visit us soon! Our monkey bread baobab tree is always open to you.

Was Botania the Good Witch happy when you gave her the letter from Lady Thorn and Lady Thistle? I'm sure she was excited to receive a response from Senior Artificers of the Silver Tower!

Since we have not yet heard from you that your parents have become unlost, we have decided to discuss the matter with the Army of South Grace. We feel that it's time for the army to regroup and start a new adventure together. As such, we are planning to meet you on the farm in one week to help you find your parents. Del and Lilibeth will be joining us, as will Mr. Pommier and Mr. Bunnymunch. Wilma, the Queen Tree of the Majestic Moonlit Mountains, says that she will also be helping, but she will not be traveling with us, although she did insist that Mr. Pommier join us again in our travels. She is very thankful to you for helping protect her from the Wicked Witch.

If you have any questions, just ask Mr. Bunnymunch. He will fill you in on all the details.

With Much Love,
The Tinkermeyers

"What wonderful friends we have. Our parents are definitely going to become unlost now!" said Aiden.

"We have to start preparing! What should we do first, Mr. Bunnymunch?" said Theresa.

"You should pack and get your carriage ready. The Tinkermeyers, the Good Witch, and the Good Warlock want to examine your farm first, since it's where your parents became lost.

Chapter Twenty-Eight

After that we will be going wherever they think we should go ... which could be just about anywhere," said Mr. Bunnymunch.

"To tell you the truth, Mr. Bunnymunch, we've all been a little restless since we returned from our last adventure, so I think we're more than ready to start a new one. What do you two think?" asked Aiden of his brother and sister.

"Let's start packing!" the twins shouted in unison.

"Our next adventure begins!" shouted Aiden.

Aiden, Theresa, Terrance, Acorn, and Mr. Bunnymunch all ran down the spiraling path of the mountain towards the cottage where the Silverglades could start packing and begin their next adventure to find their parents ... but that's a tale for another time.

Made in the USA
Columbia, SC
04 July 2024